LEGEND OF THE GALACTIC HEROES

VOLUME 4

STRATAGEM

YOSHIKI TANAKA

HAIKA SORU

SAN FRANCISCO

LEGEND OF THE GALACTIC HEROES

VOLUME 4
STRATAGEM

WRITTEN BY
YOSHIKI TANAKA

Translated by Tyran Grillo

Legend of the Galactic Heroes, Vol. 4: Stratagem
GINGA EIYU DENSETSU Vol.4
© 1984 by Yoshiki TANAKA
Cover Illustration © 2007 Yukinobu Hoshino

Cover and interior design by Fawn Lau and Alice Lewis

HAIKASORU
Published by VIZ Media, LLC
P.O. Box 77010
San Francisco, CA 94107

www.haikasoru.com

Library of Congress Cataloging-in-Publication Data

Names: Tanaka, Yoshiki, 1952- author. I Huddleston, Daniel, translator.
Title: Legend of the galactic heroes / written by Yoshiki Tanaka ; translated
   by Daniel Huddleston and Tyran Grillo
Other titles: Ginga eiyu densetsu
Description: San Francisco : Haikasoru, [2016]
Identifiers: LCCN 2015044444I ISBN 9781421584942 (v. 1 : paperback) I ISBN
   9781421584959 (v. 2 : paperback) I ISBN 9781421584966(v. 3 paperback) I ISBN
9781421584973 (v.4: paperback)
Subjects: LCSH: Science fiction. I War stories. I BISAC: FICTION / Science
   Fiction / Space Opera. I FICTION / Science Fiction / Military. I FICTION /
   Science Fiction / Adventure.
Classification: LCC PL862.A5343 G5513 2016 I DDC 895.63/5--dc23
LC record available at http://lccn.loc.gov/2015044444

Printed in the U.S.A.
First Printing, June 2017

MAJOR CHARACTERS

GALACTIC EMPIRE

REINHARD VON LOHENGRAMM
Commander in chief of the imperial military. Imperial prime minister. Duke.

PAUL VON OBERSTEIN
Chief of staff of the Imperial Space Armada. Acting secretary-general of Imperial Military Command Headquarters. Senior admiral.

WOLFGANG MITTERMEIER
Fleet commander. Senior admiral. Known as the "Gale Wolf."

OSKAR VON REUENTAHL
Fleet commander. Senior admiral. Has heterochromatic eyes.

FRITZ JOSEF WITTENFELD
Commander of the Schwarz Lanzenreiter fleet. Admiral.

ERNEST MECKLINGER
Deputy manager of Imperial Armed Forces Supreme Command Headquarters. Admiral. Known as the "Artist-Admiral."

ULRICH KESSLER
Commissioner of military police and commander of capital defenses. Admiral.

AUGUST SAMUEL WAHLEN
Fleet commander. Admiral.

KORNELIAS LUTZ
Fleet commander. Admiral.

NEIDHART MÜLLER
Fleet commander. Admiral.

ADALBERT FAHRENHEIT
Fleet commander. Admiral.

ARTHUR VON STREIT
Reinhard's chief aide. Rear admiral.

HILDEGARD VON MARIENDORF
Chief secretary to the imperial prime minister. Often called "Hilda."

HEINRICH VON KÜMMEL
Hilda's cousin. Baron.

ANNEROSE VON GRÜNEWALD
Reinhard's elder sister. Countess von Grünewald. Lives in seclusion at her mountain villa.

ERWIN JOSEF II
37th emperor of the Galactic Empire.

RUDOLF VON GOLDENBAUM
Founder of the Galactic Empire's Goldenbaum Dynasty.

DECEASED

SIEGFRIED KIRCHEIS
Died living up to the faith Annerose placed in him.

KARL GUSTAV KEMPF
Died in battle at Iserlohn.

FREE PLANETS ALLIANCE

YANG WEN-LI
Commander of Iserlohn Fortress. Commander of Iserlohn Patrol Fleet. Admiral.

JULIAN MINTZ
Yang's ward. Ensign.

FREDERICA GREENHILL
Yang's aide. Lieutenant.

ALEX CASELNES
Administrative director of Iserlohn
Fortress. Rear admiral.

WALTER VON SCHÖNKOPF
Commander of fortress defenses at
Iserlohn Fortress. Rear admiral.

EDWIN FISCHER
Vice commander of Iserlohn Patrol Fleet.
Master of fleet operations.

MURAI
Chief of staff. Rear admiral.

FYODOR PATRICHEV
Deputy chief of staff. Commodore.

DUSTY ATTENBOROUGH
Division commander within the Iserlohn
Patrol Fleet. Yang's underclassman. Rear
admiral.

OLIVIER POPLIN
Captain of the First Fortress Spaceborne
Division at Iserlohn Fortress. Lieutenant
commander.

WILIABARD JOACHIM MERKATZ
Imperial Navy veteran who defected to
Iserlohn. A "guest admiral" who is treated
as a vice admiral.

BERNHARD VON SCHNEIDER
Merkatz's aide.

ALEXANDOR BUCOCK
Commander in chief of the Alliance Armed
Forces Space Armada. Admiral.

LOUIS MACHUNGO
Yang's security guard. Warrant officer.

JOB TRÜNICHT
Head of state. Chairman of the High
Council.

DECEASED

NGUYEN VAN THIEU
A fierce commander of Yang's Iserlohn
Patrol Fleet. Died in pursuit after the Battle
of Iserlohn.

PHEZZAN DOMINION

ADRIAN RUBINSKY
The fifth landesherr. Known as the "Black
Fox of Phezzan."

RUPERT KESSELRING
Rubinsky's son and chief aide.

NICOLAS BOLTEC
Imperial resident commissioner. Former
aide to Rubinsky.

ALFRED VON LANSBERG
Count who defected to Phezzan.

LEOPOLD SCHUMACHER
Former captain in the Imperial Navy.
Defected to Phezzan.

BORIS KONEV
Independent merchant. Old acquaintance of
Yang's. Working in the office of the Phezzan
commissioner on Heinessen.

MARINESK
Administrative officer on board the
Beryozka.

DEGSBY
Bishop dispatched from Earth to keep an
eye on Rubinsky.

GRAND BISHOP
Ruler in Rubinsky's shadow.

TABLE OF CONTENTS

CHAPTER 1:

Mutations of history and consequences of victory are determined in an instant. Most of us live idly on as echoes of such instants, as they retreat into the past. Those cognizant of them are few, and those who willfully set them in motion fewer still. Unfortunately, the latter always win the day, bolstered by armies of malice.
—D. Sinclair

Knowing the future, directly experiencing the present, and indirectly experiencing the past: each offers its respective thrill of happiness, fear, and anger. Those who live in the past are destined to be slaves of regret.
—E. J. Mackenzie

I

THE YEAR WAS 489 of the imperial calendar. Spring arrived late but with a vengeance against winter's tenacious purchase, decorating the streets of the imperial capital of Odin in an abundance of flowers. The season changed and those flowers withered, giving way to thick, fresh verdure as winds ushered in the first invigorating blush of summer.

It was the middle of June, a time of year when temperatures across the midlatitudinal zones of Odin's northern hemisphere were at their most pleasant. Today, however, was unusually hot and humid. Clouds drifted far above the children weaving through fields on their way home from school.

The building which housed the office of the imperial prime minister was made of light-gray stone and boasted an air of intimidation that exceeded its purpose. Naturally, it hadn't been built for its current figurehead, Reinhard von Lohengramm. Many imperial family members and noblemen before him had taken its high seat, exercising authority as imperial deputies over thousands of fixed-star worlds. Reinhard was the youngest and mightiest to ever hold office in its confines. Whereas his predecessors had been appointed by the emperor, he had been the first to make the emperor appoint *him*.

A solemn, melancholy young woman walked through this building's hallowed corridors. Although the cadence of her step, muted garb, and pale-blond crop presented a man's appearance, her light makeup and the orange scarf peeking out from her collar betrayed this impression.

As the prime minister's chief secretary, Hildegard von Mariendorf, or Hilda, had earned the reverent salute she received from Reinhard's guards, who granted her entrance into his office.

Hilda thanked them warmly and sought out the handsome young Reinhard inside. The imperial military's commander in chief had been gazing out the window but swung his luxurious golden hair in Hilda's direction as she entered the spacious room. He cut a striking figure, decked out in his magnificent black uniform trimmed in silver.

"Am I disturbing you, Your Excellency?"

"Not at all. I would hear your business, fräulein."

"I come bearing a message requesting a personal meeting from Admiral Kessler. He says it's urgent."

"I see. Kessler's in that much of a hurry, is he?"

Ulrich Kessler, who held concurrent posts as commissioner of military police and commander of capital defenses, was not without fault, but neither was he one to let impatience or confusion get the better of him, as both the prime minister and chief secretary were aware. Kessler's urgency was therefore not to be taken lightly.

"I'll see him. Bring him in," said the empire's de facto dictator, brushing away golden locks from his forehead with slender fingers. He'd never once shirked any duty of his station—a fact not even his enemies could deny.

As Hilda turned on a heel, a faint light spread its rays through the window. Thick clouds descended on the horizon, giving way to a scattering of sickly white.

"Thunder."

"The Weather Bureau is predicting thunderstorms. An atmospheric disturbance, they say."

The faint crack of an electrical discharge in the distance approached their eardrums. The sound intensified until a hammer of light crashed down into the frame, sending legions of reinforcements in the form of raindrops across the windowpanes.

Ulrich Kessler was shorter and broader shouldered than his young lord. A handsome, virile man in his midthirties, his countenance nonetheless told a seemingly longer story of military service. His eyebrows were flecked with white, and his temples had prematurely grayed, surrounded by waves of solid brown.

"Thank you for agreeing to see me on such short notice, Duke von Lohengramm. I have it on good word that two extremist supporters of the old aristocratic regime have infiltrated the capital. I came here as soon as I was notified."

The young lord, stationed by the window, looked over a shoulder at his subordinate.

"And how is it that you came by this information?"

"Actually, Your Excellency, it was an anonymous report."

"An anonymous report?" said the prime minister, displeased. Those two words were like noxious insects corrupting the flower garden of his soul. He'd always been wary of anonymous intel, despite knowing its worth.

A silver flash snaked its way through the sky amid baying thunder, breaking the silence like smashed porcelain. Its ominous reverberations lingered in their ear canals. Before these faded, Reinhard steeled himself and urged the chief of military police to go on with the details of his report.

Kessler manipulated a small box, bringing up a holographic image before the young prime minister's eyes. Although not handsome per se, the face belonged to a man of obvious character and pedigree, one whose features betrayed nothing of the darkness behind his smile.

"Count Alfred von Lansberg. Age 26. As one of the nobles who took part in the Lippstadt Agreement, he defected to Phezzan following the defeat."

Reinhard nodded in silence. He recalled the name and face. An active participant in numerous ceremonies, von Lansberg had never shown a sliver of animosity toward Reinhard. More harmless than not, having been born in the peacetime of the Goldenbaum Dynasty, von Lansberg was a cultured man of scholarly disposition who poured his energy into mediocre poetry and novels. *The type who's never worked a day in his life*, thought Reinhard. *A man ill-equipped for these turbulent times*. To be sure, his acquiescence to the faction opposing Reinhard was less an act of hatred than the simple result of being a victim of his own high pedigree and the traditional values of which he deemed himself gatekeeper.

The hologram of von Lansberg's face gave way to a slightly younger man's that had all the qualities of a capable businessman. It was, explained the chief of military police, that of Captain Schumacher.

Leopold Schumacher had graduated from IAF Academy at age twenty, ascending the ranks to captain a decade later. Being of ignoble birth, he'd played second fiddle to the front lines for much of his career and, unlike Wolfgang Mittermeier, had gained few opportunities to distinguish himself through military service. Considering this, he'd gotten surprisingly far. Fortified by keen powers of reasoning and exemplary performance during missions, he was more than capable of mobilizing a large force to action. He was destined to go far.

Reinhard noted with regret that greed had left its fair share of kinks in his network. But whatever he might have lacked in human resources, he made up for in material resources. Since losing his redheaded comrade Siegfried Kircheis last year, he'd been reluctant to bury his grief.

Which raised the question: why had Count Alfred von Lansberg and Schumacher abandoned their haven of Phezzan to infiltrate enemy-controlled Odin?

"I take it they forged identification to gain entry," said Reinhard, "and under false names?"

Kessler's answer was a categorical no. They hadn't so much as raised an eyebrow at passport inspection. Had it not been for the anonymous tip, their true identities might never have been discovered. Given that IDs were issued by the autonomous government of Phezzan, Phezzan had clearly been complicit in this matter, prompting Kessler to seek His Excellency's political judgment.

After seeing Kessler out with a promise of further instructions, Reinhard returned his gaze to the sky, now clamoring with thunder and lightning.

"I suppose you know an imperial historian once compared Rudolf the Great's angry bellows to thunder, Fräulein von Mariendorf."

"Yes, I do."

"Quite the simile."

Hilda avoided an immediate reply, instead studying the elegant figure of the young prime minister, whose solemn attention extended well beyond the window. Hilda heard malice in Reinhard's voice.

"As for this phenomenon we call thunder…"

Reinhard's regal features glowed in a flash of lightning, resembling a statue made of salt.

"…its energy is wasted the moment it's used. It gives off a tremendous amount of heat, light, and sound but rages madly just for the sake of it. That's Rudolf to a T."

Hilda opened her shapely lips but closed them without a word, guessing her answer was furthest from Reinhard's mind.

"But not me. I'll never be like him."

Hilda felt those words being directed partly to Reinhard himself, partly to someone who wasn't in the room.

Reinhard turned back to the room and to the youthful aristocrat standing in it.

"Fräulein von Mariendorf, what do you think? I'd like to hear your opinion."

"Regarding Count von Lansberg's motivation for returning to Odin?"

"Yes. He could just as easily live out his days quietly on Phezzan, banging out that doggerel he has the audacity to call poetry, yet he returns to face certain danger. Why do you think that is?"

"Von Lansberg always was a romantic."

Not exactly rich in humor, Reinhard seemed tickled by her retort all the same, and his mouth rippled into a broad smile.

"I respect your insight but find it hard to believe that good-for-nothing poet returned to his old home in search of romance. I'd be inclined to agree with you if he was an older man, but not one year has passed since the civil war."

"As you say. Count von Lansberg's reason for coming back would have to be much more significant to be worth the risk."

"What could it be, then?"

Reinhard enjoyed his dialogues with the wise noble. Not merely for allowing him the company of a woman, but because he appreciated the informal debates between intellectual equals and he valued the stimulation and vitality she brought to his thinking.

"As history has shown, terrorism against the powers that be is enough to prompt any romantic into action. Could it be that, in hopes of satisfying his unflagging loyalty and sense of duty, Count von Lansberg has made a decisive, infiltrative move?"

Hilda had answered well. Last year, she'd taken over something of the late Siegfried Kircheis's irreplaceable value to society.

"By *terrorism*, do you mean to say he plans on assassinating me?"

"No, I think it's something else."

"Why?"

To Reinhard's pregnant question, Hilda provided a push. Assassination was more likely a means for redeeming one's past rather than for building a future. Were Reinhard to be assassinated, someone else would take his place and all the power that came along with it. One reason why the noblemen regimented under the Lippstadt Agreement had been defeated was that Duke von Braunschweig and Marquis von Littenheim had been ultimately in disagreement over who should rule in Reinhard's place after he was overthrown. As Admiral Kessler had surmised, there was reason to suspect Phezzan's involvement in Count von Lansberg's infiltration. The collapse of a unified power resulting from Reinhard's death would bring about social and economic mayhem, and that was the last thing Phezzan wanted, at least for now.

"That's where my mind is at. If Phezzan is intent on committing any act of terrorism, it won't be an assassination, but the abduction of someone important."

"In that case, who's the target?"

"I can think of three people."

"Myself being one of them, of course. And the other two?"

Hilda stared directly into his ice-blue eyes.

"One would be Your Excellency's sister, the Countess von Grünewald."

Even as these words escaped Hilda's lips, color spread through Reinhard's complexion, prelude to a surge of violent emotion.

"If any harm should come to my sister, I'll make that blasted good-for-nothing poet wish he'd never been born with a capacity to feel pain. I'll kill him in the cruelest way imaginable."

Hilda saw no reason to believe that Reinhard wouldn't carry out every word of that vow. If indeed Count Alfred von Lansberg had yielded to the temptation of insubordination, then he had unleashed the next wayward avenger.

"Duke von Lohengramm, I've exceeded my brief. Please forgive me. There's hardly any reason to suspect that your sister would be abducted in this case."

"How can you be so sure?"

"Because abducting women as hostages goes against everything Count von Lansberg stands for. As I was just saying, he's a romantic at heart. Rather than bear the ridicule of abducting some helpless maiden, I think he'll go another route, one not so easily realized."

"You're right. Maybe Count von Lansberg is just a foolish poet, after all. Still, if Phezzan is involved in this plot as you suggest, it could be an expedient means to an end. The Phezzanese are realists in the worst possible sense. They'll probably force Count von Lansberg's hand by whatever methods will yield maximum effect with the least amount of effort."

Reinhard's feelings for Annerose, the Countess von Grünewald, held constant sway over his reason. This psychological fortress he'd built around her, as far as its weak spots were concerned, was nothing like the stalwart sociopathy of Rudolf the Great, who was sometimes referred to as the "Steel Giant."

"Duke von Lohengramm, I've narrowed it down to three possible targets of abduction. I've already crossed Your Excellency's name off that mental list. And even if you were Count von Lansberg's intended target, he seems oblivious to the fact that Phezzan is pulling the strings. I would also rule out the Countess von Grünewald, because I doubt Count von Lansberg is even aware of her. This leaves us with the third candidate. The only one, it seems to me, who meets all the criteria."

"And who might that be?"

"He wears the emperor's crown, even as we speak."

Reinhard betrayed no surprise. He'd come to the same conclusion as Hilda, although his tone underscored its unexpectedness.

"You mean to say that our romantic intends to abduct the emperor?"

"I doubt Count von Lansberg would see it as an abduction, but rather the duty of a loyal retainer delivering his juvenile lord from enemy hands. He would do it in a heartbeat."

"A poet I can handle. But what about the other parties involved? What could Phezzan possibly stand to gain by abducting the emperor?"

"That remains unclear. Unless, of course, Phezzan's involvement was never discovered."

"Now we're getting somewhere." Reinhard nodded, concluding that the possibility of Hilda's inferences was more than likely. Not that he could blame Phezzan, considering its utilitarian way of thinking and Count von Lansberg's character.

"So the Black Fox of Phezzan rears his ugly head once more. He never dances alone, but plays his flute in the shadowy recesses of the curtains. Serves that good-for-nothing poet right for being their lapdog," muttered Reinhard, his voice tinged with loathing.

Although Reinhard felt no sympathy for the "good-for-nothing poet," neither could he bring himself to celebrate the victory of Phezzan's landesherr, Adrian Rubinsky.

"Fräulein von Mariendorf, I suspect it was one of Phezzan's spies who anonymously reported the infiltration of von Lansberg and his crew. What do you think?"

"Yes, I believe Your Excellency speaks correctly."

For a moment, Hilda expected Reinhard to smile. Instead, the young prime minister returned his ice-blue eyes one last time to the window, his face stern as rock, tracing the pathways of his thoughts.

II

The unseasonable weather carried over into the next day, shrouding the central imperial graveyard in sheets of water droplets that were neither mist nor rain. Even the rows of spruce trees, which on clear days parsed sunlight into shafts of crystal, stood solemn in the haze.

Leaving her landcar behind to wait, Hilda walked along a stone path, holding a bouquet of fragrant, golden-rayed lilies. Three minutes later, she reached the grave that had brought her there.

The grave was far from magnificent. Even the inscription carved into the immaculate white gravestone was rudimentary:

HERE LIES MY FRIEND

SIEGFRIED KIRCHEIS

BORN IC 14 JANUARY 467

DIED IC 9 SEPTEMBER 488

Hilda stood before the gravestone, her white cheeks wet with tears. MY FRIEND. For how long would people rightly and fully comprehend the weight of those words? Reinhard had repaid the redheaded comrade who'd saved his life many times over: as imperial marshal, minister of military affairs, and, lastly, commander in chief of imperial forces, he'd devoted himself to the important task of being third imperial commander, as so many admirals before him had dreamed of becoming themselves. Reinhard was still in mourning over his redheaded friend, and for him the gravestone's inscription carried a deeper hidden meaning than what was written there.

Hilda left her bouquet of lilies on the cold, wet, flat gravestone, wondering if the temperature would enhance or weaken their fragrance. Even as a girl she'd never been one for flowers and dolls, and her gentle, ordinary father had been too occupied with concerns of heredity and environment to care.

Hilda had never met Siegfried Kircheis. But had it not been for Kircheis's victory in the Kastropf uprising two years prior, Hilda's father, Franz von Mariendorf, might not have lived. She felt she owed him something, at least. Immediately before the Lippstadt War, Hilda had persuaded her father to negotiate with Reinhard, bringing peace to the Mariendorf earldom and delivering the house of Mariendorf from the clutches of death. Hilda had never overestimated her own meritorious service, either.

Siegfried Kircheis had been unequaled in his abilities, insights, and loyalty. He had assisted Reinhard as advisor and earned the highest accolades in such campaigns as the Kastropf Rebellion, the Battle of Amritsar, and the Lippstadt War. Had he lived on, who knew how, and by what monumental deeds, he might have altered the course of history through his antialliance operations.

Still, as a man, he hadn't been perfect, and would certainly have made a few mistakes along the way, resulting not least of all from possible conflicts of emotion and clashes of ideals with Reinhard himself. They had, in fact, butted heads often. When Kircheis had saved Reinhard by his own person, he had been unarmed. Until then, only Kircheis had been permitted to carry the handheld weapons prohibited to others. When Reinhard revoked that privilege, treating his redheaded friend as he would have any other subordinate, the tragedy of it all tore at the blond dictator with talons of remorse. The Westerland massacre had also driven a wedge between them, leaving a sense of immeasurable, unresolved regret.

Hilda shook her head. Tiny droplets of water stuck to her short blond hair. An unpleasant heaviness weighed on her shoulders. She looked at the epitaph once more. Despite being a gift from the heart, maybe the lilies weren't so appropriate for Siegfried Kircheis. Maybe they were an omen. Maybe she needed to learn more about flowers.

Hilda turned and left. She'd come here at great pains and left unable to find any words with which to honor the dead.

Located in the western portion of the imperial capital's center, the Freuden mountainous zone spanned six hours by landcar. Mountain ridges met at a single point from three directions, colliding in gnarled waves of rock. Deep ravines and chains of lakes had formed where the ranges and waterways intersected. At such high elevations, mixed flora gave way to conifers and to stubborn clusters of alpine vegetation that seemed to kiss the sky, glossed by the rainbow brilliance of perpetual snow hit just so by sunlight.

Pastures and natural flower beds dotted the land between the forests and promontories, unassumingly asserting themselves as ideal cradles for the mountain villas that adorned them. These villas, almost without exception, belonged to royalty, although most of their owners had perished in the Lippstadt War. Eventually they would be handed over to lay citizens, but for now they just stood there, abandoned and untended.

The villa of Annerose, the Countess von Grünewald, was situated on a Y-shaped peninsula jutting out into the middle of a lake.

A gate of evergreen oak stood at the peninsula's base, its door left open. It was here where Hilda disembarked from her landcar. The petty officer serving as her driver stressed the late afternoon hour and the distance she had yet to walk. He encouraged her to use the car, but she refused.

"That's okay—it'll give me a chance to stretch my legs."

To Hilda it seemed a crime not to luxuriate in this atmosphere, so cool and refreshing as to be sweet.

The unpaved path inclined slightly into thickets of hazelnut trees, through which percolated the babble of a stream running alongside.

Accompanied by her driver, and with a gallant step—a characteristic her future biographer would surely stress—Hilda walked for some time before stopping at a curve in the path. The trees ended, revealing a fragrant meadow, and standing in it a trim, two-story wooden villa. Hilda walked slowly toward the beautiful, slender young woman standing before it, being careful not to startle her.

"The Countess von Grünewald, I presume."

"And you are?"

"Hildegard von Mariendorf, His Excellency Duke von Lohengramm's private secretary, at your service. I would be ever so grateful for your time."

Those deep-blue eyes quietly regarded Hilda, who met their gaze despite a vague tension taking root within. *Here is someone*, thought Hilda, *who doesn't have a combative bone in her body, and against whom deception and strategy would be futile.*

"Konrad!"

A young boy emerged from the villa at once. The golden hair of Annerose's servant, in all its subtle variations, glowed in the waning sunlight. He looked no older than fourteen.

"You called, Lady Annerose?"

"We have a guest, whom I am obliged to entertain. Escort the driver to the dining room, would you, and fix him some supper."

"Right away, Lady Annerose."

As the driver took his leave with the boy, his expression a blend of gratitude and anticipation, Annerose led her unexpected visitor to a cozy, old-fashioned salon with a fireplace.

"Countess, isn't that Viscount von Moder's boy?"

"Yes, he's all that's left of the von Moder family."

Hilda knew that name as one of the royal families against which Reinhard had fought. By some twist of fate, Annerose had become his guardian.

Looking out the window, she saw the sun setting, that much closer to summer solstice. A ray of light fell from the sky, weaving a band of gold around a distant beech forest until it disappeared. The sky went from deep to dark, and before long the silhouettes of trees were indistinguishable against its expanse. Stars filled the night with their hard light, making it seem that all one had to do was peel away a layer of atmosphere to touch the cosmos. *In the day, the sky belongs to the earth; at night, it belongs to the universe*—Hilda remembered hearing that once. Annerose's younger brother had waged battle in that same sea of stars, had indeed conquered some of them, and was readying himself for another round.

Flames danced vigorously in the fireplace. Spring and summer came to these mountains two months later than at the capital's center, while autumn and winter came two months earlier. The twilight air grew by the second from cool to cold, against which the glowing fire seemed like a thick coat sewn from human spirit and flesh. Hilda sat on the sofa and, not wanting to be impolite, stifled a sigh of satisfaction. Relaxation was a luxury she couldn't afford. After Hilda divulged the reason for her visit, the beautiful countess gracefully looked away.

"So Reinhard insists on guarding me, does he?"

"Yes, Duke von Lohengramm has reason to fear you will become a terrorist target. He was hoping you might come back and live with him but said you'd probably never agree to it. At the very least, he hopes you will allow him to place armored guards around the Freuden perimeter."

Hilda waited for Annerose to speak. Hilda did not expect an immediate reply and knew better than to force one from her.

Reinhard had told her what to expect in a manner less becoming of a dictator than of a little boy genuinely worried about his elder sister's safety. He might have called upon her himself, but knew she wouldn't have seen him, and so had entrusted the matter to Hilda.

It's because of her that we live in the world we do, thought Hilda, unable to restrain a certain wonderment. The enchanting Annerose, whose gentle modesty gave an impression of early spring sunlight, was the keystone of her generation. Twelve years ago, while she was housed in the late Emperor Friedrich IV's rear palace, was when the dam burst. Future historians would say as much—that the downfall of the Goldenbaum Dynasty had been set into motion by this single elegant creature. Were it not for his sister, Reinhard von Lohengramm's precipitous rise to power would have been impossible. No one altered history, and the world, at a whim. Like pollen carried to a barren landscape in anticipation of new flowers, their flourishing was up to the wind.

At last, Hilda had her timid answer.

"I've neither the need nor worthiness to be guarded, fräulein."

Hilda and Reinhard had anticipated this answer. As the one entrusted with the prime minister's request, Hilda was prepared to change her mind.

"With all due respect, Countess, you both need and are worthy of it. At least Duke von Lohengramm thinks so. We'll make sure your quiet life goes unchanged. Won't you, at the very least, agree to some extra protection around the villa?"

A prudent shadow of a smile revealed itself on Annerose's lips.

"Let us speak no longer of the present. Our father, after spending his modest fortune, ended up forfeiting his estate and moving into a small house downtown. That was twelve years ago. It felt like we'd lost everything, but we also gained new things to replace it. Reinhard's very first friend was a tall boy with fiery red hair and a pleasant smile. I told that boy, 'Sieg, you be nice to my little brother, okay?' "

The logs shifted in the fireplace with a loud pop. Orange flames danced, casting shadows of speaker and listener in turn. Listening to the beautiful countess speak, Hilda saw that humble downtown corner of the capital reconstructed before her very eyes. There stood a girl in her teens, smiling that same transparent smile, and a redheaded boy whose face burned as brightly as his hair. And there was the other boy, watching them like some angel that had lost his wings, grabbing the hand of his redheaded friend and saying, with a conviction beyond his tender years, "It's settled, then. We'll always be together."

"The redheaded boy made true on that promise. No, he did more than I ever could've hoped for—something no one else could've done for me. I've robbed Siegfried Kircheis of his life, of his entire existence and everything beyond it. He is gone from this world, even as I continue to live in it."

Hilda said nothing.

"I'm a woman full of sin."

In all her experience with eloquent diplomats, scheming tacticians, and even stern public prosecutors, this was the first time Hilda had ever found herself at a loss for words. Knowing there was little use in arguing, she held firm, calm and unashamed.

"Countess von Grünewald, please forgive me for speaking this way, but I would speak nonetheless. If anything were to happen to you because of terrorism from the old royalists, would Admiral Kircheis rejoice in Valhalla?"

Under any other circumstance, Hilda would have barred herself from such tactless reasoning. She'd never been one to let emotions get the better of her. In this case, however, it seemed like the only way.

"Besides, I would implore you to think not only of the dead, but also of the living. Duke von Lohengramm can't be saved, Countess, if you forsake him. Admiral Kircheis was too young to die. Don't you think that Duke von Lohengramm is, too?"

Something other than the firelight trembled on the mistress's porcelain-white face.

"Are you saying I've abandoned my little brother?"

"I believe Duke von Lohengramm wants to fulfill his duty toward you. If only you would accept his wishes, then he might come to think that his existence still means something to his sister. And that's incredibly important not only to Duke von Lohengramm, but to everyone."

Annerose turned unconcernedly toward the fireplace, but her attention seemed far from the writhing flames.

"When you say everyone, are you including yourself, fräulein?"

"Yes, I won't deny that. More importantly, there's an even larger sphere of people out there. I doubt the tens of billions of citizens of the Galactic Empire wish to see their sovereign fall into ruin."

Annerose was speechless.

"He has repeatedly assured me your life won't be interrupted in any way. And so, I ask that you please grant Duke von Lohengramm—no, Lord Reinhard—this one wish. After all, everything he's willed in his life has been for your sake."

For a few moments, time flowed silently around them.

"I'm most grateful for your concern, fräulein, and for being so considerate of my younger brother."

Annerose looked at Hilda and smiled.

"Fräulein von Mariendorf, I leave everything to your discretion. I've no intention of ever leaving my mountain villa, so please do whatever you feel is best."

"I'm eternally grateful, Countess von Grünewald," said Hilda, with heart.

Maybe Annerose just didn't want any trouble, but she'd accepted nonetheless.

"And please, from now on, call me Annerose."

"I will, and please call me Hilda."

Hilda and her driver lodged that night in Annerose's villa. When Hilda entered the lavish upstairs bedroom, Konrad brought her a pitcher of water.

"May I ask you a question?"

"By all means, go ahead."

"Why won't you leave Lady Annerose be, when all she wants is to live in peace? I'm the only one she needs to protect her. Anyone else would just get in the way."

Hilda met the boy's eyes—brimming as they were with anger, doubt, and a certain air of valor—with kindness. His heart, as yet untainted by self-interest, had not yet experienced the ravages of time.

"Then let this be my promise to you as well: Lady Annerose will not be disturbed in the slightest. The guards will never step foot inside this villa, nor will they ever compromise your duties. Understand that you're not the only one who wishes to protect Lady Annerose."

Konrad bowed in silence and left, leaving Hilda scratching her head of short blond hair and scanning the room's interior. Like the downstairs salon, it was confining but had a modest charm all its own. The cushions and the tablecloth were handmade, clearly the work of this house's mistress. Hilda opened the window, taking in a view of the night sky, which to her was so narrow that all the stars seemed to touch one another.

See how the light of the stronger stars overpowers the weaker, thought Hilda. *Such are the ways of this world and the histories of those living in it.* She couldn't help but smile bitterly at her own foolish desire for peace. At least here, in this room, warmth and comfort were givens. Heeding the call of Hypnos, Hilda yawned and closed the window.

III

In contrast to Hilda's sojourn in the Freuden Mountains, Reinhard's work was decidedly prosaic. Business-related matters were practical by nature, and when they concerned a diplomatic battle with Landesherr Adrian Rubinsky, known widely as the formidable "Black Fox of Phezzan," and his agents, sentiment was not an option. Since Reinhard put little stock in the politico-moral standards of Phezzan's leaders, he anticipated that their negotiations would be nothing more than an exercise in self-interest on their part. Once a military man, always a military man; once a merchant, always a merchant; once a villain, always a villain; and he'd learned to treat each accordingly. The Phezzanese, in all their craftiness, were not to be underestimated, but feared for taking down anything that stood in their way.

Commissioner Boltec received summons from Reinhard on the afternoon of June 20. Boltec had been grumbling over the spices in his Phezzanese Wiener schnitzel and was glad when Reinhard's message interrupted his lunch by way of the military police. The neckline of the two-piece worn by his female secretary didn't hurt his mood, either.

As he approached the prime minister's office, the muscles in his face redistributed themselves into the mask of a scrupulous man. As an aspiring actor, it pained Boltec to think that his talents in this exquisite art would go unrecognized.

"First off, I'd like you to confirm something for me," said Reinhard, offering Boltec a chair and taking a seat in his own, his tone intimidating yet refined.

"Of course, Your Excellency. What is it?"

"Are you here under Landesherr Rubinsky's full authority, or are you just his lackey?"

Boltec regarded the elegant prime minister with humility, only to be met with keen scrutiny.

"Well?"

"The latter, as a matter of course, Your Excellency."

"A matter of course, is it? I've never known the Phezzanese to value form over substance."

"May I take that as a compliment?"

"Take it however you like."

"Okay."

Boltec shifted in his seat. Reinhard spread the corners of his mouth into a faint smile, casually lobbing his first shot.

"What exactly does Phezzan want?"

Boltec strained to maintain his discreet performance, watching through wide-open eyes.

"With all due respect, Your Excellency, I have no idea what you're talking about."

"Oh, you don't?"

"I don't. Whatever it is, I'm not in any sort of position to—"

"That's upsetting to hear. For a first-rate play to become a first-rate drama, a first-rate actor is required. But your performance is so transparent it takes out all the fun, don't you think?"

"That's a bit harsh." Boltec smiled ashamedly, but Reinhard knew he wasn't about to take off his mask, or his gloves, anytime soon.

"Then let me ask it this way: what does Phezzan stand to gain by abducting the emperor?"

Boltec was speechless.

"Or do you think Count von Lansberg is ill-suited for the task, I wonder?"

"I'm impressed. Was it that obvious?"

Although it was unclear if he was speaking from his heart or from a script, Boltec looked at Reinhard with admiration all the same, knowing when he was defeated.

"Then, naturally, Your Excellency is aware it was a Phezzanese agent who tipped you off."

Seeing no reason to respond to this, Reinhard focused his ice-blue eyes on the commissioner with indifference. Boltec's blood ran cold.

"In that case, Your Excellency, you can be assured I've told you everything I know." Boltec leaned forward. "On behalf of the Phezzanese government, I humbly offer our cooperation in Your Excellency's designs on total rule."

"So that's Rubinsky's intention?"

"Yes."

"And yet your overture to this professed cooperation is to aid relics of the high nobility in abducting the emperor. Care to explain?"

Boltec hesitated but decided to play the card he'd been saving for the right moment. He lowered his shields and spoke frankly.

"Here's what I'm thinking. Count Alfred von Lansberg is rescuing his emperor, Erwin Josef II, from the hands of a traitorous retainer. At least that's what he tells himself, while to all other eyes the emperor is defecting to the Free Planets Alliance by way of Phezzan to set up a government-in-exile. Of course, it'll all be a sham, but I know that you, Duke von Lohengramm, would never tolerate such a state of affairs."

"Go on."

"Your Excellency, do I really need to spell out how this would give you irrefutably just cause to suppress the Free Planets Alliance?" Boltec smiled. He seemed to be pandering to his listener, but such was not the case.

The seven-year-old emperor, Erwin Josef II, was beyond Reinhard's control; that much was true. That this boy, a temporary steward of the throne Reinhard would one day usurp, had been crowned emperor there was no doubt, but his age presented a major problem. Should his usurpation come with bloodshed, accusations of infanticide would inevitably spill from this age's cup into the next.

The emperor card was moot so long as Reinhard was the one holding it. Dealt into the alliance's hand, however, it could be played like a malicious joker, destroying the alliance from within.

If, as Boltec had suggested, the emperor submitted to the alliance's guardianship, Reinhard would have conclusive and just cause to invade the alliance. He didn't mind being accused of the emperor's abduction, or, for that matter, of abetting the high nobility's reactionary plot to staunch social revolution in the empire. Either way, the circumstances were in his favor. Public opinion was guaranteed to be divided over the emperor. Even this would be to Reinhard's superlative advantage. Not only militarily, but also politically. Phezzan's offer, assuming it was genuine, was a most welcome favor.

"What, then, do you recommend? Am I expected to just bow my head in deference to Phezzan's good will?"

"I'm detecting some cynicism," Boltec said.

"Then tell me, in no uncertain terms, what you would have me do. Poking each other is all fun and games until we're perforated with holes."

Even Boltec, crafty as he was, couldn't parry Reinhard's thrust.

"I'll get right to the point. Duke von Lohengramm, you must take secular authority, and all the political and military hegemony that goes with it, into your hands. Phezzan has every intention of monopolizing universal economic interests, inclusive of interstellar distribution channels and transport, so long as those interests are under Your Excellency's control. Would this suit you?"

"It's not a bad plan, but you've left out one thing. What's to become of Phezzan's political status?"

"We're hoping Your Excellency might consider self-governance under suzerainty. The sets and props stay the same—only the director changes."

"I'll give it some thought. Then again, if the alliance doesn't accept the emperor's defection, then no matter how superlative the drama, the plot will never advance," Reinhard said. "What's your sense on that front?"

Boltec responded with a self-confidence bordering on insubordination.

"On that point, rest assured that Phezzan will take care of things. We'll do whatever it takes."

If only there were a single coolheaded diplomat in the alliance, they could use the emperor as their trump card of anti-imperial diplomacy. In defiance of all humane or sentimental criticism, the emperor would be delivered straight into Reinhard's hands. Not only did Reinhard have no reason to refuse, but a useless joker would be forced on him if he wasn't careful. Phezzan could protect him. The absurdity of not spreading the very fire he'd started wasn't lost on Reinhard. It was time they upped their ante.

"Commissioner, if Phezzan wishes to make a pact with me, there's something else you must grant me."

"And what might that be?"

"It should be obvious. You must grant the Imperial Navy free passage through the Phezzan Corridor."

Phezzan's commissioner failed to conceal his surprise, having never expected the future to be so resolutely decided at that instant. He looked away, faltering momentarily for all the calculations and decisions running through his synapses. An unforeseen attack had revealed a weak spot in the commissioner's protective barrier.

"What else did you expect? Cat got your tongue?" Reinhard's cold, magnificent laughter rained down on Boltec.

The commissioner barely got ahold of himself. "I-I'm not at liberty to answer right away, Your Excellency."

"Didn't you say you'd aid me in my quest for hegemony? You should be more than willing to comply with my demands. Seeing as I have any number of justifications to invade, it would be futile to close off that avenue."

"But…"

"You're sweating, Commissioner. Is it possible your true intention is to mark a trail along the Iserlohn Corridor with imperial corpses, leaving Phezzan to reap the benefits while the rest of us are busy duking it out? I wouldn't put it past you."

"Now you're overthinking the matter, Your Excellency."

The commissioner's feeble protest registered nowhere on Lohengramm's radar. Reinhard's laughter struck Boltec's eardrum like a plucked harp string, sharper than a needle.

"Very well, then. Phezzan has its own interests and opinions. But so do the empire and the alliance. If two of these three powers were to combine forces, it would only be in Phezzan's best interest to be one of them, would it not?"

With those words, Reinhard had won Boltec over. The young blond dictator held the empire and the alliance in the palm of his hand and had hinted at the possibility of annihilating Phezzan. Boltec knew, with every fiber of his being, that Reinhard would surrender his leadership to no one.

CHAPTER 2:

I

AFTER ENTERING the prime minister's office in good spirits, Boltec returned to his own in poor spirits. His legs felt like they were knee-deep in mud.

Among his subordinates, those predisposed to optimism anticipated the change of season, bracing themselves for another winter. Although one might think even the most adamant pessimists were aware of this, they couldn't afford to boast of their foresight, and like turtles retracted their necks instead, to guage their surroundings from within their shells.

As a leader of men, Boltec had never been one for despotism, but like any diplomat, he wore different masks inside and outside the office.

"That golden brat has dealt us an outrageous hand," said his secretary.

"Which is?"

"He threatens to join the alliance and overtake Phezzan militarily. We can't think for a moment that Phezzan is the only one that stands to gain."

The commissioner didn't need to look at the man's face to know he was holding back his anger.

"But how could he do such a thing? Duke von Lohengramm would never join forces with the alliance. That's a groundless hypothesis if I've ever heard one."

The commissioner laughed at his subordinate's logic. If such thinking was what passed for probable truth these days, not only would the present leaders of the alliance be ignorant when the curtains rose on the empire and Phezzan's collaborative production, *The Emperor's Flight*, but the possibility wouldn't even cross their minds. Reinhard had somehow been made aware of this by the alliance. Assuming he played his cards right, his combined military forces would be enough to annihilate Phezzan, and then some. Had not that golden brat brought about a coup d'état between alliance diehards last year?

The alliance was much in debt to Phezzan, as it continued to strengthen Phezzan's semicolonial states. But if Phezzan were destroyed, so too would be that debt along with it. There was no guarantee the alliance's unprincipled leaders wouldn't let greed get the better of them.

They might also deal a fatal blow. Boltec gnashed his teeth over the new developments brought about by his conversation with Reinhard. By the time he became aware of where and how his calculations had gone awry, his king had been driven into a corner of the chessboard, helpless and alone. To avoid unilateral defeat, he would concede to the opponent who had him in check. He sneered at the arrogance of this joint alliance.

It wasn't supposed to have gone this way. At all. Perhaps Phezzan had taken the initiative, more than happy to join the alliance. Using an agent to secretly inform on Count von Lansberg's infiltration, they'd courted Reinhard's anxiety and suspicion as a double doorway to negotiation. It seemed like a good idea, but he couldn't take his opponent seriously. It was a childish mistake for someone who had always acknowledged the expertise of Phezzan diplomats and political strategists.

"What's your plan, Commissioner?" the secretary asked, mustering a sense of duty and bravery as best he could.

Boltec turned to his subordinate, wearing his most authoritative mask. "What do you mean?"

"Regarding Count von Lansberg and Captain Schumacher. Would you rather we destroy our plans, get rid of those two, and feign ignorance?"

Boltec had no answer.

"Far from ideal, I know, but there's always the future."

The secretary ducked his head, expecting an angry rebuttal, but Boltec remained deep in thought.

He had his own status to think about. He'd gone from landesherr's aide to imperial commissioner—a perfectly respectable position by Phezzan's political standards. Among the Phezzanese, obligations to duty ran weak. Petty officials were treated as nobodies lacking in mettle and were considered to have little aptitude for business. A position as high as Boltec's warranted suitable respect, but if he failed in a major imperial diplomacy effort and betrayed the landesherr's trust, he would be scorned as unworthy of his position and banished as a common official.

And if he yielded to Reinhard von Lohengramm's intimidation and opened the Phezzan corridor to the Imperial Navy? Regardless of their military preparedness, monopolization of trade routes would extinguish Phezzan's independence and prosperity in one stroke.

Phezzan was no totalitarian state. The trade routes were an efficient cooperative system they'd voluntarily created to shield their own freedom and profit from conflict. At least, that was how they would be remembered.

Then there were the proud independent traders, who would never hand over their precious Phezzan Corridor to the Imperial Navy. A violent rebellion was inevitable, one that would harm Phezzan's independence and neutrality as a trading nation. Dominion was nominally permanent, but an elder council sixty members strong would be convened in response to demands from more than 20 percent of the electorate. If a two-thirds majority approved, they could oust the landesherr from his political seat.

Since the time of founder Leopold Raap, this system had never been used. In the event Adrian Rubinsky granted the Imperial Navy passage through the Phezzan Corridor, resistance would rage. Assuming this became a reality, Rubinsky would become the first landesherr in history to be impeached from the throne. To Boltec, this was inconceivable. Irrespective of how it was represented in the official records, Rubinsky's ascent to landesherr was the design of the Church of Terra's Grand Bishop. Any announcements of candidacy, speeches, voting, and counting of ballots constituted an epic performance for the public audience at large.

Boltec cocked a half smile. Those merchants holding fast to their liberty and independence—who thought themselves so shrewd, pragmatic, and clever—were easy targets. For a moment, he was jealous of those simpleminded idealists who, by the efforts they'd expended to amass their great fortunes, believed themselves to be of the highest rank in the universal pecking order.

If Rubinsky was overthrown, Boltec's status and security as his confidant would be unsustainable. Until now, as the landesherr's foremost advisor, he hadn't so much as heard the footsteps of a potential rival. But Rupert Kesselring, who after Boltec's transfer had taken over his position as aide, had, with the perspicacity of someone twice his age, quickly consolidated his power of influence within the autonomous government. Were Rubinsky and Boltec to be ousted, that greenhorn would take the seat of highest authority with all his nonchalance, although without endorsement of the Grand Bishop—a figure who 99.9 percent of Phezzan's citizens didn't know was their true ruler—this would never happen.

Although Rupert Kesselring had aimed for the seat of highest authority, so long as that old stagehand turned his stale face away, his ambition would end in an unfinished dream too big for him to contain.

At this point in his thinking, Boltec's heart rate spiked. When it came to guaranteeing absolute authority over Phezzan, that old stagehand's support was crucial. So was it not better to do the opposite? Even with the Grand Bishop's endorsement, he—that is, Nicolas Boltec—would meet the requirements for becoming Grand Bishop himself. Was that such an arrogant wish? Not even Adrian Rubinsky was born to be Grand Bishop, his seat on the council of elders nothing more than a token position. Maybe it was time Nicolas Boltec joined forces with Reinhard von Lohengramm in ruling the universe.

Today had been a succession of failures. They'd been placed in check by that golden brat, although it seemed easy enough to overturn the game board. That didn't mean they were going to grant passage through the Phezzan Corridor, but it could serve them in future negotiations. And they still had their trump card. Because that clever golden brat didn't know of the existence of a mysterious old man who had spread his black wings into every corner of the cosmos. He was a strong enough weapon, one whose position would be strengthened by any circumstance, violent or not.

Boltec knew they had to proceed as originally planned. Aborting the mission was not an option. Doubts over their ability to carry out that mission had incurred Rubinsky's displeasure. They would need to turn their losses into gains, and if anyone could do it, it was Nicolas Boltec.

The commissioner pulled himself together. He put the secretary, who'd been eyeing Boltec with caution, at ease with a confident smile. They would proceed as planned with the emperor's abduction. He had champagne brought out in anticipation of their victory.

II

The rain drew a veil across the imperial capital. Staring at the droplets creeping down his window, Leopold Schumacher thought to himself how unseasonable this year's weather had been. Normally the streets of Odin would be filled with sunshine and greenery, its commoners rejoicing in the abundance of nature to placate their dissatisfactions.

"Captain, aren't you going to eat?"

The table was decked with wine and food, and Count Alfred von Lansberg was speaking from behind the captain, lustfully eyeing every dish. Without waiting for an answer, he poured himself a tall glass of dark beer and downed it in a gulp.

Its full-bodied flavor was just as he'd remembered, unrivaled by anything in Phezzan. Alfred was certainly not lacking in naive patriotism. Schumacher looked over his shoulder in silence. Despite knowing the beer was brewed in a factory funded by Phezzan, he saw no need to spoil the young count's mood. Even the hotel they were staying in was Phezzan funded and Phezzan managed, and he almost wondered, rather cynically, whether the very air they breathed might not soon bear Phezzan's trademark.

What the hell was he doing here anyway? A cloud of self-deprecation cleared from his head.

Schumacher couldn't help but notice how the behavior of officials at the spaceport had changed for the better. Whereas before they trifled with their power and authority, bowing to those of higher status while oppressing common citizens and blatantly demanding bribes from all comers, now they attended to their duties with courtesy and diligence. The regulation of law and order proved that Duke von Lohengramm's reform had taken root in at least one section of the social system. He'd emerged from exile to lay the foundation of reform and regulation.

The young Count Alfred von Lansberg, for his part, was intoxicated with the sweet heroism of rescuing the emperor. Count Jochen von Remscheid, popularly called "Leader of the Loyalists," had encouraged him with promises of a high position in the government-in-exile and a piece of the territory the government would one day claim.

"The reward is trivial. It's the actions that count," affirmed Alfred.

It was a sound argument. Schumacher had also been promised the rank of commodore, but that was the least of his concerns. Alfred still believed in the righteousness of his own actions; Schumacher, not so much. The Galactic Empire had fallen into ruin—a bare shadow of the mighty Goldenbaum Dynasty. Reinhard von Lohengramm's rise to power had been decided with the demise of Lippstadt's noble coalition. The establishment of a government-in-exile went against the grain of history. Behind the tenaciously chivalrous Count von Lansberg and the reactionary dreamer Count von Remscheid, it was the Phezzan party realists who'd written their script, while the true scenario had been invisibly annotated between the lines.

Left to his own devices, Schumacher would never have participated in something so futile as reversing the planet's rotation. He'd given in to coercion not only to save his own skin, but also because to oppose the plan would have jeopardized the new lifestyle of his defector subordinates. Nevertheless, Schumacher's heart was ill at ease. Once this matter was settled, he vowed to put a sizable dent in Phezzan's profits. More than revenge, this time it was not wanting to be forced by similar mechanisms to go against Phezzan's wishes that drove him to act.

Something else troubled Schumacher. Despite never being much of an optimist, that single drop of pessimism that had been added to a large, brimming glass was enough to ruin the delicate equilibrium of its surface tension, and all the wine might come spilling out at any moment. It was wholly connected to his pride as a military campaigner. Supposedly, Schumacher would simply be able to snatch the young emperor right out from beneath Duke von Lohengramm's nose and set up a government-in-exile within the Free Planets Alliance. In the future, he would overthrow von Lohengramm and make his triumphal return to the imperial capital of Odin. Schumacher was shocked to hear of this plan from the landesherr's aide, Rupert Kesselring. It had seemed little more than a reckless pipe dream at the time. But as the idea grew on him, and despite his reservations, Schumacher came to see the words and deeds of Commissioner Boltec, stationed in the imperial residence, as nothing more than evasive maneuvers. He couldn't abide Boltec being tasked with general management of this place.

Schumacher imagined the worst-case scenario: Phezzan investigating the abduction of the emperor or, on the other hand, spoon-feeding that information to Lohengramm in order to make them his scapegoats for something in return. Either that, or…

There wasn't enough information to determine whether his hunch was correct. Schumacher detected an unpleasant bitterness in the dark beer flowing down his throat. He didn't enjoy being manipulated by others—even in service of a lofty goal, to say nothing of a far less obvious one.

III

Once everything was in place, Schumacher and Alfred went over their plans for invading Neue Sans Souci.

Neue Sans Souci's blueprints weren't publicly available, and even with Phezzan's organizational assistance, they were hard to come by. An effective authoritarian political system was one that kept its citizens in the dark, which meant that preventative measures against terrorism were a must.

The magnificent palace was divided into quadrants. The East Garden was the nucleus of the administration, a place where royal audiences and meetings were held. The South Garden was the official residence of the imperial family. The West Garden, also called the "Rear Palace," was home to the many beautiful ladies of the court. And the North Garden was a hunting ground of vast fields and forests, where deer and foxes were released to be hunted for sport. There were many other buildings and gardens of uncertain affiliation, totaling sixty-six square kilometers. The water fountains numbered two thousand, the total length of marble corridors was four hundred kilometers, and the gazebos totaled 752. An absurd number of extravagances besides spoke of the palace's sheer scale. Reinhard's sister Annerose had once set up a mansion in the northern section of the West Garden.

"Security at Neue Sans Souci is surprisingly minimal."

As an aristocrat, Alfred von Lansberg had passed through the palace gate on many occasions. It had always been customary within the empire to employ flesh-and-blood human beings instead of machines. Although this practice did not date back as far as Rudolf the Great in his prime, in the past imperial guards were placed at twenty-step intervals in the gardens and corridors. In the last of Friedrich III's six so-called Crimson Years of reign, conspiracy, assassination, and terrorism were rampant, while the establishment of the North Garden Dragoon Brigade and the West Garden Infantry Brigade incited rebellion among the guards.

Although Friedrich III's successor, Maximilian Josef II, put an end to what were essentially imperial private armies in the North and West Gardens, this time there was a danger of them uniting to overthrow the new emperor in competition for inheritance of the throne. Empress and former maidservant Sieglinde started carrying a gun for her husband's protection. One couldn't anticipate every eventuality, however, and the emperor was poisoned. He survived but was left half-blind by the attempt. Although Josef II had all the qualities of a benevolent ruler, without the cooperation of the morally upright Chief Justice Münzer, Empress Sieglinde's devoted counselor, who had regulated national politics as prime minister, he probably would have been taken out by other means. Though afflicted by his damaged eyes, Maximilian Josef defended against internal dissolution of the empire and laid fresh cornerstones, earning him the title of "Great Rebuilder." Looking at the big picture a century and a half later, the same one who'd rebuilt the empire had also set in motion an interminable war with the alliance.

Following this incident, sentiments leaned heavily toward automation, but even with high turnover, the presence of soldiers in the palace never dwindled.

Reinhard von Lohengramm had made huge cuts in palace expenses, completely shuttering the West and North Gardens, along with half of the buildings in the East and South. All political duties, save the occasional constitutional function, were planned and approved through the prime minister's office. The number of vanity parties and garden functions had also plummeted, and the once-sleepless palace lost its splendor and looked more like a ghost town with each passing day.

"I'll guide us through Neue Sans Souci once we're inside. It may be closed off, but it's not like it's been rebuilt, only abandoned," said Alfred.

He guaranteed that nearly every door, corridor, and gate would be usable. Furthermore, he said in a hushed tone, the grand palace was filled with hidden rooms and passageways—so many, in fact, that Lohengramm couldn't possibly be aware of all of them—of which they could make effective use.

This information wasn't new to Schumacher, who had thought it to be nothing more than a rumor. Generations of emperors, fearing assassination and revolt, had built small rooms fortified with double-reinforced walls for refuge or escape, dug underground tunnels, and turned Neue Sans Souci into a labyrinth with access points concealed in bushes of the garden.

Many of these passages had been used, each time spawning a comedy and a tragedy apiece. When Emperor Wilhelm II's second son, Archduke Albert, was fifteen years old, he had gone exploring in the underground maze accompanied by the emperor's aide-de-camp. Even now, a century later, his body had yet to be found. It was said that Wilhelm II's favorite mistress, Dorothea, had planned the whole thing. Having given birth to Albert by the emperor who loved her, she became the target of Empress Konstanze's violent hatred. And so, when the empress fell ill and was confined to her sickbed, Dorothea, fearing that her son would be harmed by the empress, entrusted him to the care of a young officer, who smuggled the boy through the underground passageways to the Free Planets Alliance, where he lived out his life in peaceful exile. Another theory had it that Empress Konstanze was behind it all, and that she'd somehow lured Albert underground, where he was left to die.

Generally known to be true was that, immediately after Archduke Albert disappeared in the depths along with his aide-de-camp, Wilhelm II died of natural causes, and that the day after the empress's own son took the throne as Cornelius II, Dorothea died from apparent poisoning. An inexplicable fever caused Empress Konstanze to die insane just one month later. It was more than enough to arouse people's curiosity and suspicion. From these two apocrypha, a pair of sequels had arisen, as some aristocrats claimed to have seen a mature Albert aboard a Phezzanese passenger boat, while certain military personnel said they heard the voice of the accursed boy while investigating the underground labyrinth some ten years later.

This was, of course, the tragedy. Comic relief came two decades later. Cornelius II became gravely ill without having produced an heir, and the aristocrats were running around frantically, wondering if anyone would succeed him. To that end, a man appeared who was said to be the spitting likeness of a mature Archduke Albert. Everything about him led much of the aristocracy to believe him. Cornelius II, who all these years had suspected his mother of criminal acts, summoned his "little brother" to his deathbed for a tearful meeting. The aristocracy expected him to become the new emperor Albert I, and the nobles vied to be the first to lick his boots.

When Albert, as this man was known, was offered a grand aristocrat's summer villa free of charge, he thanked them for their favor and generously arranged for his future position and territory. His popularity was all the greater, until catastrophe struck. His Highness Prince Albert, first in line to succeed the emperor, absconded with imperial jewelry worth fifty million reichsmark and, taking an innocent young maid with him, fled the imperial capital of Odin. In his wake, he left a throng of dumbfounded nobles, along with a dozen young women with shattered dreams of one day becoming empress as bearer of his son. Half of those young women bore his shameful illegitimate children, and several nobles named Albert went so far as to change their names so as not to be associated with the conniving impostor. Among the general populace, the aristocracy became the butt of ridicule.

Some had wondered whether this man wasn't the real Albert after all. But because the audacious impostor had disappeared without a trace, the truth would never be known.

Whether poetic and prosaic, in the five centuries that had transpired since the reign of Rudolf the Great, the rafters of Neue Sans Souci had come to be hung with all manner of legends. Alfred von Lansberg said as much to Schumacher.

A helpless "poet of action," thought Schumacher, but Alfred didn't have a malicious bone in his body, so there was no reason to harbor any ill will toward him. He used to think he was incapable of feeling contempt toward others. Unlike Alfred, Schumacher wasn't willing to wager his life for something he didn't believe in. Or maybe he was just reading too much into things.

Eying Alfred, Schumacher felt inclined to aim for success, if only to please him. Besides, far more intriguing was the prospect of pulling one over on that golden brat, once and for all.

I∪

Meanwhile, the golden brat himself, targeted as the emperor's "cruel captor," had summoned his own staff officer to discuss countermeasures.

If secretary-general Paul von Oberstein, the Imperial Space Armada's chief of staff, was surprised to hear talk from Reinhard of a conspiracy between Phezzan and the remaining high nobles to abduct the emperor, he didn't look it. He had never been one to display his emotions to begin with. With the optical computer built into his artificial eyes, he regarded the young lord seriously and nodded.

"That's typical of the Black Fox of Phezzan. They're responsible for the script and production, pulling all the strings from behind the scenes."

"If he should appear onstage, he'll be picked off from the orchestra pit. This would put others at risk."

"So what will you do? Do you plan on accepting Phezzan's offer and allowing them to abduct the emperor?"

A cold smile came to the elegant imperial marshal's lips. "Yes, I think it'll be fun to let them try."

"Shall we relax the palace's defenses? To make it easier for them."

"No need," responded Reinhard bluntly. "It's not that well fortified to begin with. There exists a man who could occupy Iserlohn Fortress without bloodshed, so why would I cooperate with someone who can't even manage to abduct one emperor?"

Abduction of the emperor—to the performers it was a rescue operation, which, if successful, would lead to an implicit pact with Phezzan, moving toward the endgame of a military showdown with the alliance. If they failed, Reinhard would have just cause in subjugating Phezzan as the true culprit behind the emperor's abduction. Reinhard had free choice no matter how the cards were shuffled.

Phezzan's overconfident commissioner Boltec, for his part, had too many tricks up his sleeve. There was no room for error. So long as they feigned ignorance as innocent bystanders and negotiated off the record, a compromise on the Phezzan end was inevitable. That idiot had failed. And the reason he'd failed was because he'd misjudged Reinhard von Lohengramm as a possible puppet, on par with that good-for-nothing poet. Boltec would surely make up for his ignorance and impropriety.

"That reminds me, von Oberstein. I'd like you to keep an eye on that fiercely loyal good-for-nothing poet and his gang. I doubt you'll need to do more than that, but Phezzan might just try to kill them. In which case, you'll want to save them before that happens."

"As you wish. Saving them might work in our favor."

The empire could use them as living proof of a Phezzanese plot, thus lending leverage to their negotiations with Phezzan. And if Schumacher proved himself capable enough, he might provide suitable entertainment for Reinhard.

"Incidentally, I trust your subordinates have been keeping an eye on former vice prime minister Gerlach?"

Both of von Oberstein's artificial eyes gleamed strangely as he answered in the affirmative.

"And have you made necessary preparations for his capture?"

"I have. If he is judged to be a conspirator in the emperor's abduction—no, his *rescue*—I'll be the most satisfied courtier of all time. Perhaps the truth of the conspiracy will come to light when we least expect it."

Reinhard studied his chief of staff's face but saw nothing to indicate he was joking.

"I doubt that."

First, Gerlach had neither the courage nor wherewithal to rebel against Reinhard. Second, even if the remnants of the aristocratic faction pulled Gerlach into their schemes, not only would they have to smuggle him out of the imperial capital, they'd also have to promise him a high position in the exile government in which case a power struggle between them was unavoidable. And while that good-for-nothing poet may have been a backstabber, he wasn't likely to get in anyone's way.

Without perfect mutual understanding of intentions between the planners and the executors, Count von Lansberg might just pay Gerlach a visit for want of more allies or to share in the pleasure of his great enterprise.

Logic and too many variable factors limited them. Since Reinhard was obligated to respond to Phezzan's plans to the bitter end, there was no need for him to overthink the issue.

"We can only keep an eye on things, but I'm okay with that. Let's have that good-for-nothing poet and his friends' patriotic activities monitored."

"That goes without saying, but"—here the artificial-eyed chief of staff cleared his throat a little—"if the emperor is abducted, the person in charge of security will, of course, fall under suspicion. Admiral Mort will pay for it with his life."

"You mean they'll kill him?"

Reinhard drew a picture in his mind of the honest, indispensable mature warrior.

"Admiral Mort is an old-fashioned man. In the event of the emperor's abduction, even if Your Excellency were to pardon him, his pride would prevent him from accepting it."

Von Oberstein's expression was grim, as if reprimanding the young lord's momentary weakness. Reinhard, who knew nothing of the leniency expected to be granted to the high nobility, wasn't always so thorough when it came to his allies. However deep his indignation, if a guiltless subordinate were to be put to death as a result of his own machinations, it would not sit well with him.

It's a bloody road we're on, Reinhard muttered internally. Had Siegfried Kircheis been alive, he would never have stood by and watched Mort be made a scapegoat. When Reinhard had used the Westerland Atrocity as a political maneuver, Kircheis had warned him against acting out of remorse more than anger. But Reinhard had no regrets when he lost Admiral Kempf thereafter.

"Understood. It's a sacrifice we'll have to make. When the time comes, we'll pin it all on Mort, and Mort alone. No one else."

"Mort's direct superior officer is Kessler."

"Kessler is a rare man. If the military police commissioner becomes a criminal, the troops will lose heart. Slap him with a warning and cut his pay, and leave it at that."

The chief of staff sighed to himself. "I would say just one thing, Your Excellency, although it may offend your ears. You can't clear a path through a thick forest without uprooting a few trees or overturning a few rocks."

Reinhard turned his ice-blue eyes toward von Oberstein. Their discernment lacked severity. They were oddly inviting. "You speak as if you were giving a lecture on Machiavellianism to a bunch of middle schoolers. Do you think I don't already know that?"

"So you say, but sometimes, Your Excellency, to this humble servant, it would seem you forget elementary things. Since the dawn of human history, all heroes have built their thrones atop not only the corpses of their enemies, but also those of their allies. No monarch's hands are without blemish, and their subordinates are well aware of this fact. I would remind you that granting death is one way of repaying loyalty."

"Does that mean you would gladly spill your own blood for my sake, if it came to that?"

"If it were necessary."

"Remember you said that…I'm through with you. Dismissed."

The irritation in Reinhard's voice hit von Oberstein in a delicate wave.

For a moment, he thought to say something, and without closing his mouth, he gave a bow and took his leave.

The first to welcome von Oberstein when he returned home was an old dalmatian, who wagged his tail proudly and made way for his master to enter the foyer. The butler who greeted von Oberstein extended his arms to take his master's clothes and inquired as to what vintage of wine he would like with that evening's meal.

"None. Any moment now, I expect to be summoned by Duke von Lohengramm. No alcohol for tonight. A light meal will be fine."

Just as he was finishing his meal, the visiphone rang, and Reinhard's chief aide Arthur von Streit appeared on-screen.

"Mr. Chief of Staff, Duke von Lohengramm urgently summons you. The duke is still at the prime minister's office. Please meet him there," said Rear Admiral von Streit politely and formally, although he thought it curious that von Oberstein wore his uniform even while eating at home. The artificial-eyed chief of staff saw no need to explain himself.

After briefly welcoming the chief of staff a second time, the elegant prime minister dispensed with pleasantries and got down to business.

"I forgot one thing."

"And what might that be?"

"Don't tell me you didn't already anticipate this. If not, you wouldn't have responded to my summons so quickly."

"Much obliged. I merely assumed you had thought about a new emperor to replace Erwin Joseph on the throne."

"And what do *you* think? Do you have your heart set on any candidates?"

This conversation, which would have given outsiders much to gasp over, was between them as detached as talking about the weather.

"There's a grandchild born of former emperor Ludwig III's third princess. The father is Count Pegnitz, who abstained from last year's civil war. He's a man who has no interests other than his collection of fine ivory figurines. The mother is Count Bodendorf's niece. A girl, obviously, but maybe it's high time we had an empress."

"How old is she?"

"Five months."

Again, nothing in von Oberstein's expression or voice suggested humor. That Reinhard laughed at all was due to his zealous nature.

A seven-year-old child was vacating the throne, only to be replaced by a five-month-old baby. Someone not even old enough to talk was going to be the sovereign of the universe, leader of all peoples, defender of galactic law.

There was probably no *tableau vivant* in existence worthy of this folly. Adults would bow and scrape for an infant still in diapers, to whom their ranks as high officials and admirals would mean nothing, and whose babbling they would be forced to accept as imperial gospel.

"So what do you intend to do? Will you seek out other candidates?"

Von Oberstein's tone of voice was more of a command than a question. Reinhard's smile faded, and he nodded gravely.

"Fine. Let's give that suckling babe the throne. Not the most entertaining toy for a child, to be sure, but one that anyone would be happy to have, even if she were alone in space. Two would be one too many."

"Very well. By the way, it seems some of the payments for Count Pegnitz's ivory figurines are in arrears. This has landed him in hot legal water with merchants. How do you propose we settle those?"

"What are the plaintiff's terms?"

"Seventy-five thousand reichsmark."

"Have it taken care of. It wouldn't look too good for the father of the new empress to be imprisoned for unpaid debts. Withdraw the necessary funds from the Imperial Household Ministry budget."

"As you wish."

Von Oberstein bowed, rose, and took his leave to retire for the night.

Had Reinhard been blessed with the authority to take the imperial throne himself, how much more the panorama would be enhanced, thought the blond youth. But while he exercised that authority as his own, for now his heart was waiting with folded wings. The Goldenbaum family, which had monopolized authority for a span of five centuries, reigning at the apex of a class society, and becoming the source of all social ills—above all, wealth and the inequality of political privilege—was about to tumble down from its golden palace straight into the gutter. The excitement of revenge began to well up from his stomach, coiling an unpleasant sourness around a thought that Reinhard would rather have spat out. After hesitating for a few seconds, he did just that.

∨

Leopold Schumacher's plan of action hinged on one essential thing: a diversionary tactic. As Alfred von Lansberg and Schumacher were planning their infiltration of Neue Sans Souci, in another sector of the imperial city, large-scale subversive activities were, as they had hoped, being fomented in institutions ranging from military circles to the police.

Alfred appeared skeptical about this.

"It's not a bad idea, but Duke von Lohengramm is no dolt. He'll see right through it."

Unlike the other high nobles, he refrained from denouncing Reinhard as the "golden brat." It was the same courtesy Schumacher extended toward Alfred.

"Still, it's worth a shot. I intend to get Phezzanese agents to do it."

"That's just not right. They're already supporting our noble cause from the sidelines. Isn't that enough, Captain?"

Schumacher saw it differently. Their actions were anything but noble, and the only reason they'd been roped into Alfred's cause was because he knew they—not Phezzan—were the ones behind this. He kept this to himself.

"True, we shouldn't hope for too much."

"What's more, Captain, we'd stand out for exploiting a Goldenbaum family retainer."

"I see. You're right, of course," said Schumacher, meaning not a word of it.

Putting Phezzan in direct charge of subversive activities made them more than complicit—it made them primary actors. No matter how acrimonious their countermeasures toward Phezzan, they would never be enough. If something went wrong, not even Phezzan could guarantee that Alfred and Schumacher wouldn't be sold to Duke von Lohengramm. So why not attach an appropriate value to Phezzan's secret?

Schumacher again grew annoyed. As a military man who'd fought against the brightest on the battlefield, he felt coerced into an unproductive scheme.

"You're not someone to live out his career covered in manure," said Rupert Kesselring, the landesherr's aide.

Although there was no need to single out someone like him from the rest of humanity, maybe he wasn't *qualified* to live his life covered in manure. Paradoxically, the young, careless aide had spoken true.

"More important, Captain, is how we get inside," said Alfred with due emphasis. "I intend to use this route. It traverses the North Garden and comes out at the base of the statue of Sigismund I in the South Garden. Seeing as it passes through a closed area, there's little chance of being discovered."

Alfred's finger moved vigorously across the map. As the Phezzan commissioner had so patronizingly declared when handing it over to him, possession of this map meant an end to all his troubles.

The corridor started in an underground storage facility beneath the Imperial Natural History Society building. It was 12.7 kilometers long and had been built five generations ago by Alfred's ancestor at the command of Emperor Georg II. That same ancestor had been granted the emperor's prized mistress in return for his meritorious service. Ever since then, his bloodline had been entrusted with a gracious motto: *Should any danger near the throne, safety lies in paths unknown.*

"My fate in carrying out this important mission was decided five generations ago. The only problem now is figuring out how to break into the Natural History Society, although it beats having to break into the palace itself."

Count von Lansberg's fateful mission was outside the realm of Schumacher's concern. He was anticipating the many variables required to see his own plans to fruition. As he scrutinized the map, questions piled up inside him.

VI

On the evening of July 6, Count Alfred von Lansberg and Leopold Schumacher plumbed the depths of Neue Sans Souci.

That night, outside the imperial capital's southern suburbs, droves of military police were mobilized to expose a secret armory run by radical republicans. Despite correctly identifying the location and seizing the weapons stored there, they apprehended no one. Commissioner Boltec had arranged this under strict orders from Schumacher, renovating the basement of an abandoned house, filling it with arms and equipment, and transforming it into a warehouse in a matter of three days. It was enough to cover their tracks on the night in question, but Schumacher ordered them to demolish the warehouse to add to the confusion. To conceal this incident from civil authorities and news organizations, they'd prepared a landcar in front of the Imperial Natural History Society building where the tunnel began, ensuring that Schumacher and the others would be immediately escorted to the safety of the commissioner's office once they returned.

It was almost absurd to think it took a tunnel dug deep into the planet to save the emperor of a Galactic Empire, ruler of the entire universe, from fear of assassination or treason. Even Schumacher couldn't shake the feeling of looking like idiots as they made their way through that very tunnel.

At least they wouldn't be walking every kilometer of it, and travel aboveground would take longer than under. Schumacher was driving a lightweight, four-person landcar outfitted with solar cells. It was made with a special organic resin that melted when exposed to a certain acid. Schumacher planned on leaving no traces.

Having been built for the utmost practical use, the tunnel was devoid of the rococo decorations clogging every other building the Goldenbaum Dynasty put its name on. The inner wall, a half circle with a 2.5-meter radius, was coated in reinforced concrete. To facilitate an emperor's escape, five generations ago the head of Count von Lansberg's family had apparently installed all sorts of devices to deter potential pursuers. These, too, were all but forgotten.

Once they reached a gray wall, the two of them got out of the landcar. A fluorescent circle glowed faintly in the ceiling. Alfred pushed the ring on his left index finger into its center. After ten seconds of an extremely low-frequency hum, the ceiling opened without a sound.

Five minutes later, they came out into the South Garden and were inside the target building. Had this been during former Emperor Friedrich IV's reign, they'd have been accosted multiple times for identification by guards. All the more ironic, then, that the times were on their side.

The imperial bedchamber was located on a wide balcony on the second floor. There, a lone boy sat in his canopied bed. Having not yet shed the skin of his childhood, and wearing his luxurious silk pajamas, he clutched a teddy bear that was half his size. His blond hair, brown eyes, tapered jaw, and smooth, pale skin caught the eyes of the intruders. And then they were caught by the boy's eyes when he unexpectedly looked up to see two adults entering his room.

"Your Majesty."

The young count's voice quivered with reverence.

This boy, object of Alfred's unconditional piety, was none other than the leader of the Galactic Empire, Emperor Erwin Josef II.

The child emperor looked at this young nobleman, who'd taken a knee to pay him reverence, with a strangely abstruse expression. Not because he'd been woken up in the middle of the night, for he was already awake when they entered, but because he was utterly lacking in youthful sensitivity. As Alfred made to open his mouth again, the child emperor cut him off, pointing an accusatory finger at Leopold Schumacher.

"Why doesn't this one kneel?" he asked, his voice shrill.

"Captain, here before you sits His Majesty the Emperor, ruler of the entire universe."

Schumacher, cool yet cynical, was in no mood for ceremony. Seeing that Alfred was insistent on it, however, he kneeled. Not out of any respect for the emperor, but out of compassion for his partner in crime. Schumacher gave his best mock obeisance. It was all he could do to combat the incongruity of it all. He would be glad if this was the last time.

"I am Your Majesty's subject, Count Alfred von Lansberg. I have come to rescue Your Majesty from the hands of a traitor. As this is a most unusual situation—please pardon any discourtesy on my part. Risking our lives in Your Majesty's esteemed service will be our reward as your humble servants."

Blatantly ignoring his loyal servant's impassioned speech, the seven-year-old emperor fiddled roughly with his bear, not as if Alfred's words were meaningless but as if he didn't understand them to begin with. At such an age, it would have been natural for him not to grasp Alfred's solemn diction, but Alfred—knight, patriot, and romanticist to the core—had expected the young lord to be a shining prodigy. A flicker of despair beset Alfred's eyes, but he persuaded himself that it was beyond his place as a retainer to question, and that being entrusted with this task was honor enough. From now on, he would refrain from lofty speeches.

The child emperor indifferently pulled and twisted an ear on his bear and, when he finally tore it off, threw the one-eared bear to the floor. He sluggishly got off the bed and turned his back to the two dumbfounded men. Clearly, there was something wrong with this child.

"Your...Your Majesty."

Alfred's voice belied his confusion, just as the child emperor's behavior had belied any impressions of his grace. Alfred hadn't exactly counted on praise and gratitude, but at the very least he had thought to be met with a response befitting the ruler of a great empire, even if a childlike version of the same. Erwin Josef's speech, conduct, and appearance sadly lacked a certain angelic quality expected of someone in his position.

"What shall we do, Count?" asked Schumacher.

Alfred shrugged, then sprang into action. He leapt toward the sacred and inviolable emperor, grabbing him from behind.

The emperor let out a piercing scream. Schumacher shot a hand to the boy's mouth. Alfred apologized for taking drastic measures, worried even now about being unable to observe decorum as his servant.

They heard a woman's voice from beyond the door.

"Your Majesty, what's the matter?"

For a moment, the two men froze. As Schumacher restrained the struggling child, Alfred pulled out his particle gun and swiftly concealed himself in the shadow of the door. The thin figure of a woman in her late twenties or early thirties appeared in her nightgown. The emperor's nanny and private tutor, no doubt. Under any other circumstance, Schumacher would have grilled her on Erwin Josef's discipline and education.

The woman approached the extravagant canopied bed, stumbling over the teddy bear on the floor. She picked it up and, noticing the missing ear, let out a dispirited sigh, as if this were a routine matter.

"Your Majesty," she was calling out again, when she made out the figures of the intruders.

Her mouth dropped open, but her scream was over before it began when she became aware of Alfred's gun. Fortunately for both parties, she fainted and fell to the floor like a cheap doll. The two intruders heard a flurry of footsteps. They exchanged glances and made their escape.

Far from a rescue, this was outright abduction, Schumacher chided himself shamefully. He sympathized with Count von Lansberg, but this whole thing was turning into an unimaginable farce involving the world's most ungrateful child and two adults with a pipe dream. If this changed the course of history, then wasn't history itself a farce?

Surely the maidservants had immediately informed the palace guard of the situation, but whether due to the confusion or because animosity toward Reinhard's sect from an old retainer of the imperial court had delayed things, the soldiers didn't respond until more than five minutes had passed.

The head of the imperial guard, Admiral Mort, was sleeping in a lodging house attached to the main guard office but came running as soon as he received a report of unusual activity, naturally anxious to confirm the emperor's well-being above all else. But the aging chamberlain was too flustered to give even a basic summary of events.

"Where is His Majesty the Emperor? That's all I want to know." Admiral Mort's tone was neither sharp nor furious, but nonetheless had an intimidating air the weak courtiers were ill equipped to resist. The aging chamberlain barely regained his composure and, mustering as much dignity as he could, gave an indirect account of two intruders who'd broken in and abducted the child emperor.

"Why didn't you say so sooner?!"

Mort scolded the chamberlain but, not wanting to waste time on investigating his culpability, called his aide-de-camp and calmly ordered a sweep of the palace. The aide-de-camp's face went stern as he consented to the order, rushing out of the room to mobilize his men.

"I don't think I need to tell you to keep this matter to yourself, Chamberlain."

The chamberlain only nodded in response to Mort, who, judging from his expression, was more worried about being accused of negligence than for the emperor's safety.

The petty soldiers knew nothing of the emperor's abduction. Neither did they need to know. Only aware that something serious had happened, they grabbed their infrared sensors and starlight scopes and canvassed the palace's expansive grounds, with its more than one hundred thousand private homes, like packs of nocturnal animals.

At last, the aide-de-camp hurried back and gave his assessment. Infrared had picked up residuals of some unusual activity, which disappeared somewhere near His Majesty Sigismund I's statue.

"There appears to be an underground passage that leads to the outside, but it's beyond my station to lay a hand on the emperor's statue. With your permission, I'll investigate it at once."

Mort stood stock-still, not saying a word. Only now did he remember hearing of a vast labyrinth beneath Neue Sans Souci. A feeling of crushing defeat invaded the chest of the veteran military man, just as the intruders had invaded the palace. He'd always prided himself on doing his utmost to fulfill the duties allotted to him to the letter, and until tonight had done just that. From now on, that accomplishment would be spoken of in the past tense, if at all.

Ulrich Kessler had overcome countless dangers on the battlefield, courageously working his way up the ladder to become general. But when he heard news of the emperor's abduction, he couldn't stop shaking. Changing into his military uniform, he ordered the closing of all spaceports, called for roadblocks at all major roads leading out into the suburbs from the imperial capital, and mobilized a regiment of military police. He wondered who could have pulled off such a heinous crime. His brain cells scrambled and settled on two names: Count Alfred von Lansberg and Leopold Schumacher. But hadn't Duke von Lohengramm just the other day relaxed the monitoring of their activities? And why now?

Kessler's expression changed from shock to worry before going momentarily blank, as if he were staring into an abyss. Only after much conscious effort did he manage to slip on yet another mask as he carried himself, clad in his impeccable black-and-silver uniform, outside his official residence.

CHAPTER 3:

I

AT 3:30 ON THE MORNING of July 7, the prime minister of the Galactic Empire, Duke Reinhard von Lohengramm, was forced out of bed by an urgent message from military police commissioner Admiral Kessler. As Kessler bowed his head in gratitude on the screen of his visiphone, Reinhard thought, *So they went through with it after all.* He rather welcomed this turn of events. His relaxation of monitoring Count von Lansberg had had its intended effect.

When Reinhard arrived at his office, Hilda came running. The imperial prime minister's chief secretary, a constant fixture alongside a public figure like Reinhard, received constant communications from the officer on duty. Likewise, Reinhard's chief aide Rear Admiral von Streit, secondary aide and now lieutenant von Rücke, and Captain Kissling, head of the imperial guard, came at once.

Captain Günter Kissling was a young officer of twenty-eight with stiff, coppery hair and topaz eyes. Those eyes, along with his peculiar way of making hardly a sound even when walking in his military shoes, earned him comparison to a panther among those to liked him and to a cat among those who didn't. Naturally, Reinhard hadn't given him the responsibility of being his personal bodyguard because he cared about these characteristics, but because he saw in him that special combination of bravery and composure that went above and beyond the norm. His distinguished military record across multiple wars didn't hurt, either.

Before long, Admiral Kessler, accompanied by Admiral Mort, appeared before Reinhard. Under the careful watch of Reinhard's closest aides, the two of them knelt before their lord and apologized for letting the intruders get away.

"Instead of apologizing for your indiscretion, Kessler, I would rather you'd carried out your assigned duties. Just make sure His Majesty doesn't leave the capital."

Kessler took his leave to mobilize a military police squadron. He wondered if anyone noticed he'd been doing all he could to avoid looking directly at the young lord's face. This left Mort. Still kneeling, his head hung heavy with guilt.

Reinhard's ice-blue gaze fell expressionless onto the back of Mort's head, but for reasons contrary to what everyone suspected. He was in no position to be angry, but he wasn't about to let anyone know that. He had no choice but to let his arrow fly from its bowstring.

"Vice Admiral Mort, tomorrow—no, it's already tomorrow, isn't it?—I will notify you of your punishment at high noon today. Until then, you are to be sequestered in your office. Make whatever arrangements you need to ensure you have no regrets."

Mort bowed his head even more deeply. Fully taking the young lord's hint, he left quietly, thankful to be alive. Reinhard watched him until he was gone, feeling Countess Hildegard von Mariendorf's fearless, discerning blue-green eyes burning a hole into him.

"Is there something you wish to say to me, fräulein?"

"Only what I told you the other day. Namely, the likelihood of Phezzan sending their agents here to abduct a certain someone."

"Yes, I remember."

Reinhard's response was cold and transparent.

"Duke von Lohengramm, you fortified your sister's villa with guards. That was understandable under the circumstances. And yet I find it strange you didn't extend the same level of protection to the emperor's own person, and that you let him fall into the hands of intruders on your watch."

Hilda took care to keep her voice neutral, but the gist of her words hit Reinhard where it hurt, and so the imperial prime minister couldn't very well abandon his good humor.

"And your conclusion is, fräulein?"

"Here's what I think. You, Duke von Lohengramm, joined forces with Phezzan and deliberately allowed them to abduct the emperor. Am I wrong?"

Hilda was never one to entertain lies, and Reinhard had no intention of telling any.

"You're not wrong."

Hilda shook her head in disappointment. The elegant imperial prime minister felt the necessity of the assertion, on top of everything else.

"But I'll tell you one thing: I'm not joining up with that lot—those Phezzanese. I'm just using them. I've promised them nothing."

"Do you think you can just lead Phezzan around by the nose?"

"As if they haven't tried to do the same to me?"

Reinhard spat with blunt disdain at the very notion. Only then did he reveal to Hilda his conversation with Commissioner Boltec. Hilda listened, her narrow shoulders drooping as every word aligned more closely with her assumptions.

"Does this mean you intend to launch a full-scale assault on the Free Planets Alliance?"

"I do. But that was decided long ago. Only the timing has accelerated. Either way, one couldn't ask for a more splendid justification."

"And was scapegoating Vice Admiral Mort also part of your brilliant strategy?"

"No harm will come to his family."

Knowing this wasn't an excuse, Reinhard ended the conversation with a wave of his hand.

One hour later, secondary aide Lieutenant von Rücke announced that Vice Admiral Mort had committed suicide. Reinhard nodded in silence. He ordered a shaken von Rücke to make all the necessary arrangements and to ensure that neither Mort's reputation nor his family would be harmed. Reinhard was beginning to see what an epic hypocrisy this all was. But it was better to have done it than not. If it was something for which he should be punished and reprimanded, then he would get his comeuppance sooner or later, although by whose hand he couldn't say.

He called for Hilda.

"Assemble all admirals and senior admirals."

"As you wish, Duke von Lohengramm."

Reinhard wasn't sure whether to take her curt smile as a sign of their reconciliation or an ill omen against it.

II

At that time, the Galactic Imperial Navy had three senior admirals (Paul von Oberstein, Wolfgang Mittermeier, and Oskar von Reuentahl) and ten admirals (August Samuel Wahlen, Fritz Josef Wittenfeld, Kornelias Lutz, Neidhart Müller, Ulrich Kessler, Adalbert Fahrenheit, Ernest Mecklinger, Karl Robert Steinmetz, Helmut Lennenkamp, and Ernst von Eisenach). Müller was still bedridden after injuries sustained in the Battle of Iserlohn, and Kessler was leading an investigation into the emperor's abduction under strict secrecy. The remaining eleven answered Reinhard's summons.

One would think that everyone's pleasant dreams had been interrupted, as the invisible hand of daybreak was just brushing away the darkness, but none seemed to have gotten much sleep. Despite losing Siegfried Kircheis and Karl Gustav Kempf the previous year, Reinhard's admirals were as vibrant as ever. A pair of ice-blue eyes scanned the council room.

"There was a minor incident tonight at Neue Sans Souci," said Reinhard by way of understatement. "A seven-year-old boy was abducted."

There was no wind, yet the air in the room stirred as these brave, long-serving soldiers held their collective breath and let it out at once. Any man unable to extrapolate the identity of the abductee wouldn't have been sitting there anyway. Only von Oberstein appeared unfazed, but the other admirals surmised he was just being his usual expressionless self.

"I've put Kessler on a manhunt, but the criminals are still at large. I'd like to hear your opinions before dealing with tonight's developments. You may speak freely."

"It goes without saying the criminals are remnants of the high nobles' faction rallying together to restore their influence. I see no reason to suspect anyone else," said Mittermeier, receiving grunts of agreement from his comrades.

"Still, to abduct His Majesty the Emperor? We cannot underestimate the organizational power and ability of the high nobles. But who might their ringleader be?" said Wahlen.

Von Reuentahl's mismatched eyes glistened.

"Whatever happens, it'll all be clear soon enough. Once the criminals are apprehended, Kessler will make them squeal. And on the off chance they should get away, you can be sure they'll boast of their achievement. What would be the purpose of the abduction if they weren't going to broadcast it far and wide?"

"I think you're right, in which case we'll have to retaliate. I wonder if they're ready for that."

Wittenfeld addressed Lutz's doubts.

"More than ready, I would say. Maybe they'll even use the emperor to shield themselves against our attack. As pointless as that would be."

"Yes. For now, at least, they're confident enough to stave off our pursuit."

"Since when did they grow such nerve? They can't evade us forever, so long as they're in the empire."

"Or could it be they're setting up a secret base in the frontier?"

"You mean a *second* Free Planets Alliance?"

At this point, the calm voice of Paul von Oberstein cut through the tension.

"I think we should set aside the possibility of a second Free Planets Alliance for now and focus on the existing one. The remnants of the high nobles and the republicans may seem like oil and water, but who's to say they wouldn't make an illicit union if it meant keeping von Lohengramm from establishing hegemony? If our criminals take refuge in the Free Planets Alliance, you can be sure we won't be able to strike so easily."

"The Free Planets Alliance?!" said several admirals in unison.

Although it was a known fact that von Lohengramm had enemies left and right, they had never expected remnants of the high nobles to join forces with the Free Planets Alliance. Had a fundamentally impossible oath been sworn between the reactionary conservative and republican factions?

"As von Reuentahl has said, His Majesty's whereabouts will become clear soon enough. For now, I'd like us to refrain from jumping to premature conclusions. If those insurgents calling themselves the Free Planets Alliance are complicit in this treacherous plot, rest assured we'll make them pay for it. Greed has blinded them to the bigger picture, and their regret will bury them if we don't first."

Reinhard's spirited words had an equally inspiring effect on his admirals, who straightened themselves with fresh resolve.

"During the emperor's absence, we'll bide our time by saying he's sick. The seal of state is in the safe custody of the prime minister's office, so the government will be unaffected. I demand only two things from all of you. First, you are to breathe not a word of the abduction to anyone on the outside. Second, you will assemble all fleets under your direct command and be ready to launch at a moment's notice. As for other matters, I'll give you instructions as needed. We've been at this since before daybreak, so let's adjourn."

The admirals stood to attention and watched as Reinhard took his leave, after which they dispersed home to resume their usual duties. Mittermeier clasped von Reuentahl on the shoulder as he was leaving.

"How would you like to come to my place for breakfast?" he offered.

His wife, Evangeline, was a gourmet cook, or so he was always saying, and Mittermeier had yet to partake of her specialty—a dish she called "Gale Wolf."

"Sure. I guess I could let you talk me into it."

"There's nothing wrong with following orders."

"On occasion, no."

The two of them walked shoulder to shoulder down the corridor, bowing to a few soldiers who passed them by.

"All things considered, it's just like Duke von Lohengramm to keep his cool under such dire circumstances," said Mittermeier, his voice full of admiration.

He was just trying to make conversation, but those words lodged themselves in von Reuentahl's brain. Rescuing an emperor from a power-ful retainer was the stuff of fairy tales, and he couldn't believe the act had been committed so recklessly. Someone out there stood to gain from it.

Duke von Lohengramm not least of all.

If Reinhard had the seven-year-old emperor killed, he would be attacked outright for his cruelty, but an abduction put him at a far enough remove to keep his hands clean. Duke von Lohengramm could then use the apparent involvement of the Free Planets Alliance as an excuse to launch an all-out offensive against the Alliance Armed Forces on an unprecedented scale. This whole drama was about to shake humanity to its core as nothing less than a prelude to a political and military sea change. The heterochromatic admiral could hear his own blood raging inside him. Or was it just the excitement of diversifying his choices for the future?

"I suppose we can expect deployment on an unprecedented scale at any given moment," muttered Mittermeier.

Von Reuentahl couldn't tell whether Mittermeier had reached this con-clusion on his own or by influence of suggestion. Either way, the noses of men in high positions of power worked better than most in times of war, picking up on the subtlest pheromones of change.

These two young admirals, the "Twin Ramparts" of the Imperial Navy, had shared the same thought. Invading alliance territory without penetrating the Iserlohn Corridor meant coming face-to-face with Iserlohn Fortress Commander Yang Wen-li. The man who in May had reduced their comrade Karl Gustav Kempf to space dust. Even if they could defeat him, the road to getting there wouldn't be won without a long, hard fight. Von Reuentahl and Mittermeier respected their enemy. Little did they know that Reinhard was already considering an invasion through the Phezzan Corridor.

III

On the planet of Phezzan, separated from the imperial capital of Odin by tens of thousands of light-years of darkness, Landesherr Adrian Rubinsky was listening to chief aide Rupert Kesselring's report.

According to Count Alfred von Lansberg and Leopold Schumacher, fol-lowing his "rescue" from Neue Sans Souci, the child emperor had managed to pass undetected through the galactic military police's search network. He'd been stowed away in a secret cargo bay of *Rocinante*, a Phezzan-bound merchant ship, due to arrive in two weeks. On Phezzan, they would rendezvous with Count von Remscheid and his refugees, demanding asylum the moment they entered Free Planets Alliance territory. And when it was officially announced, all but a select few would be shaken to their cores.

After hearing this report, Rubinsky put a hand to his stern jaw.

"Even with the emperor gone, Duke von Lohengramm isn't likely to take the throne without putting some puppet in charge first."

"I agree. Claiming the throne for himself too soon would destroy the Empire, or at the very least deliver it a fatal blow. His internal administration is already in place, but he's banking on a huge military success to seal the deal."

"And I suspect that's what he'll get. In any case, Duke von Lohengramm has always been a step ahead. Boltec hasn't done so badly for himself, either."

"About that—per my own information gathering, it seems Commissioner Boltec leaves much to be desired."

Rubinsky turned to the young chief aide, his own son, and narrowed his eyes.

"And yet Duke von Lohengramm took no measures to prevent the emperor from being abducted. Boltec's negotiations were obviously effective against Duke von Lohengramm, no?"

"On the surface, yes, it looks that way, but change Commissioner Boltec from subject to object and you can see how the report works in his favor."

"You mean to say it's Boltec who's been taken advantage of?"

"Exactly."

Rupert Kesselring had knowingly fed Boltec compromising information. This man, who might one day stand in his way as a future rival, would need to be ousted from center stage as soon as possible. Rupert Kesselring was no graceful loser.

Although Boltec had been overflowing with confidence when he responded to Duke Reinhard von Lohengramm's summons, he was overcome by intense displeasure by the time he returned to the commissioner's office. Boltec could easily imagine his negotiations with Duke von Lohengramm bringing about unexpected results. Perhaps he'd made light of Duke von Lohengramm's prowess, and it hadn't been necessary to barter with him in the first place. Maybe Lohengramm had planned to facilitate the child emperor's abduction all along, flaunt Phezzan's strength, and give himself the upper hand. The moment the child emperor arrived in Phezzan, his whereabouts would be made known to Duke von Lohengramm, who would then join this performance and be made to dance. He'd played one too many tricks. It was a considerable misstep.

If Boltec, however, had been forced into promising Duke von Lohengramm right of way through the Phezzan Corridor, even Rupert couldn't help but gloat over his rival's mistakes. It was only appropriate that passage be granted through the Phezzan Corridor to extend Duke von Lohengramm's hegemonic reach, but that opportunity had to be chosen with the utmost discretion and, more importantly, at the right price. There was no point in selling himself short.

Rupert thought that Duke von Lohengramm had been dealt a serious blow by the alliance and had been baited with passage through the Phezzan Corridor. And when his opponent was in trouble, he would strengthen his position by lending a helping hand for a return favor. Even then, he wasn't likely to be welcomed, and he would rather have his derision ignored than undergo the mess of having his ulterior motives laid bare.

"Assuming Boltec is the only one in the wrong, we've nothing to worry about. But if this is to the disadvantage of all of Phezzan, then I'd say we have a huge problem on our hands. In particular, with Duke von Lohengramm as our opponent, the future looks dire."

"I haven't decided whether he has failed us. Don't proceed as such quite yet. The emperor hasn't even reached Phezzan."

Rupert started to object, but thought better of it. Even he saw the drawback of being seen to take pleasure in his rival's mistakes. The nature of Boltec's blunder would come to light sooner or later. And besides, thought Rupert cynically, if Commissioner Boltec's error meant the downfall of Landesherr Rubinsky, then Rupert should rather hope for it. When the Phezzan Corridor was surrendered to the Imperial Navy, the countless citizens who believed in Phezzan's independence and neutrality would be outraged. How would the Black Fox of Phezzan reveal himself then? Would he borrow the Imperial Navy's military power and go all out? Would be capitalize on Terra's authority and force all into acquiescence? Would he resolve things through his own popularity and political savvy? However he did it, he would bring about a dramatic transformation in the long history of Phezzan. Profound reactions were guaranteed. This was turning out to be more interesting by the moment.

After leaving the landesherr's office, Rupert Kesselring took half a day's journey from the capital to the Izmail District to pay a visit to exiled noble Count von Remscheid. News of Alfred von Lansberg's successful "rescue" of the emperor made him ecstatic.

"Clearly, Odin has had a hand in this. There's justice in this world after all."

Count von Remscheid asked him to forgive his spontaneous laughter and had a bottle of '82 white brought to him. After expressing heartfelt gratitude on that point, Rupert redirected his attention to top secret matters, including the emperor's defection to the Free Planets Alliance. The noble in exile nodded.

"I took the liberty of drawing up a list of the shadow government's cabinet ministers. Given the emergency, it still needs some fine-tuning."

"A most expedient measure."

It was indeed an emergency, for von Remscheid had had his eyes on the prime minister's seat ever since learning of plans to rescue the emperor. Even if he lacked the appropriate qualifications for the job, it was only natural for a man of his political aspirations to aim high.

"If it's all right with you, I'd very much like to see that list, Count."

In anticipation of this request, he was already putting the list in Rupert's hands. Count von Remscheid's wine-flushed cheeks relaxed into a smile.

"Well, this was supposed to be classified, but given how much we'll be indebted to Phezzan, the legitimate imperial government should know about it."

"Of course, Your Excellency will have Phezzan's full support. We'll be forced to put up a weak political front, but please know that, even as we obey him, our true loyalties will be with Your Excellency."

Rupert reverently took the sheet of paper titled "Legitimate Imperial Galactic Government Cabinet Roll" and ran his eyes down its column of surnames:

Secretary-General and Secretary of State: Count von Remscheid
Secretary of Defense: Senior Admiral Merkatz
Secretary of the Interior: Baron Radbruch
Secretary of Finance: Viscount Schaezler
Secretary of Justice: Viscount Herder
Secretary of the Imperial Household: Baron Hosinger
Chief Cabinet Secretary: Baron Carnap

Rupert looked up from the list, forcing a smile at the nobleman he despised.

"I appreciate your efforts in this selection."

"You'll note the high number of refugees in this list. I can assure you they swear undying allegiance to His Majesty. They might limit us in the long run, but they're useful for now. All I ask is that you have faith in us and in those we've chosen on your behalf."

"I trust you won't mind if I ask one question. It's only natural Your Excellency should oversee the cabinet as secretary-general, but why not assume the role of imperial prime minister?"

Count von Remscheid looked at once pleased and confused by this question.

"I considered that, of course, but it's a bit of an overreach. I would prefer the chair of imperial prime minister after I've returned to the imperial capital of Odin, by His Majesty's order."

If those were his true feelings, thought Rupert, then this was a strange matter in which to be exercising restraint.

"Granted, but you simply must take on that role at all costs. We cannot allow Duke von Lohengramm, to say nothing of the universe at large, any grounds on which to undermine the viability of the legitimate imperial government."

"I agree, but…"

Count von Remscheid was being evasive. It then dawned on Rupert that he'd given more than enough encouragement to the high nobles remaining in the imperial capital and that he likely wanted to avoid doing anything that would benefit the von Lohengramm camp.

"Let's table that discussion for another day. How are we going to deal with His Majesty's kidnappers, Count von Lansberg and Captain Schumacher?"

"Of course, we haven't forgotten about that. Count von Lansberg is prepared to take the seat of undersecretary of military affairs. Schumacher, for the time being, has been conferred the rank of commodore and has designs to make an aide of Merkatz. He did fight against that golden brat in the battlespace, after all."

Rupert reexamined the name of the man nominated for secretary of defense: Wiliabard Joachim Merkatz, supreme commander of the noble Alliance Armed Forces during last year's Lippstadt War. His tactics were sound, born of a military career spanning four decades. It seemed this veteran solider, who now had taken on the title of "guest admiral" for the alliance and was working at Iserlohn Fortress as Yang Wen-li's advisor, had been groomed to antagonize Reinhard von Lohengramm. For half a century, he'd lived the simple life of a capable military man devoted to his empire.

"It's only natural that Admiral Merkatz should be defense secretary, but what about his intentions and the leanings of the alliance?"

"I can't imagine his intentions are disingenuous. So long as the alliance recognizes the government-in-exile, they'll hand over Merkatz without question."

"I see. And how are we to deal with the troops under his command?"

Given the futility of this question, it wasn't an eventuality for which even Rupert had planned. Rupert thought, with rare emotion, that here was the type of evil noble who had embellished ambitions beyond his means with just cause, and it brought out the worst in him. Rupert detested this man. His father, Adrian Rubinsky, would have shut down this line of questioning long before it went this far.

Rupert's question was an exercise in unconscious ridicule, and the one attuned to it was not the asker but the one being asked. Count von

Remscheid was aware that his heated blood had quickly turned cold, but he kept any of this from showing on his face.

"The refugees are growing restless. They mustn't be allowed to train and organize themselves. The problem is a matter of cost."

"If it's expenses you're worried about, don't be. Just tell me how much you require, and consider it done."

"You're too kind."

Rupert hadn't said "free of charge." He kept his mouth shut regarding the official receipt and auditing of expenses. Once the legitimate imperial government's debt to Phezzan reached a certain level, they would need to be more careful. As one of its founding fathers, Rupert never thought the legitimate government would be able to repay its debt. This was only the desire of a small group of people, an unfortunate bastard child dropped into nothingness. As a mere reflection of its own misfortune, its only fate was to die a calculated death. Of course, if the child had vitality and ambition, that was a different matter—like Rupert Kesselring, for example. But that was a shot in the dark at best.

⁘

Rupert Kesselring had a lot on his plate. For someone as young and possessed of physical and mental stamina as he was, who straddled the public and private spheres, nothing was as valuable as time. After asking Count von Remscheid to copy the list of government-in-exile cabinet members, he retired for the night. All traces of the day had by then disappeared, and an evening chill had begun to weave its way through the dry air. The next morning, he would go to the landesherr's main office, and he had arranged for an overnight stay.

Rupert had been born in SE 775, Imperial Year 466, making him a year older than Reinhard von Lohengramm. This year he would be twenty-three. Kesselring was the surname of his mother, one of the many lovers to have passed through Landesherr Adrian Rubinsky's life. Or maybe she'd been his only. Rubinsky wasn't the most handsome of men, yet he held a certain magnetic attraction over women which future biographers would go to great lengths to verify.

Officially, Adrian Rubinsky had no children of any gender. *And yet here I stand*, thought Rupert, lifting a corner of his mouth. As an agent of Terra, his father was the lowest form of human filth to have ever deceived the people of Phezzan. Which made Rupert his excrement. Like father, like son, indeed.

Rupert arrived at a grand mansion in the Sheepshorn District. He opened his landcar window and placed his right hand on the gatepost. Once his palm print was confirmed, the carved bronze gate opened without a sound.

The mansion's owner was a woman of many titles. Owner of a jewelry store, her own nightclub, and several cargo ships, she was also a onetime singer, dancer, and actress. None of these occupations held much meaning. As one of Landesherr Adrian Rubinsky's mistresses, she would never be recorded in the annals of history as someone of importance, despite being a major source of influence over politicians and merchants behind the scenes. These days, Rubinsky called on her less often, so it was probably more appropriate to call her his "standby mistress." She—Dominique Saint-Pierre—had been nineteen years old when, working as a singer at a club eight years ago, she'd fallen in love with Rubinsky at first sight, before he'd assumed the landesherr title. Rubinsky had told her how entranced he was by her lively dancing, how beautifully she sang, how impressed he was by her intelligence. She was a beautiful woman with reddish-brown hair, although not as beautiful as any number of other women, and so she'd flown relatively under the radar.

The woman who greeted her guest inside spoke to him in a songlike manner.

"I take it you'll be spending the night, Rupert?"

"Even though I'm a poor substitute for my father."

"Don't be silly. Then again, it *is* just like you to say that. Want a drink?"

"Sure, I'll take a drink first. Mind if I ask you a favor while I'm sober?" said the younger of Dominique's two lovers as she brought him a bottle of scarlet-colored cider whisky and some ice cubes from the salon.

"Go ahead, what is it?"

"There's a bishop of Terra named Degsby."

"I know him. His face is unusually pale."

"I want to know what his weaknesses are."

She asked if this was to make an ally of him.

"No. To make him bow down before me."

The arrogance of his expression and tone were almost harsh, or maybe he was just getting himself riled up. The battle he would soon face would be no small ordeal, but he didn't want an ally who was his equal. What he did want was someone to make an unconditional sacrifice for him.

"He appears to be the poster boy of asceticism, but I wonder if that's true. If not, one crack in his veneer is all I'd need to break him," Dominique said. "And even if it *is* true, maybe we can change that, if we spend enough time."

"There's something else we'll need to spend: money."

"Don't worry. I'll do whatever's necessary."

Which was exactly what Count von Remscheid had said.

"Life as an aide pays that well, does it? Ah, you were saying there were certain side benefits, right? Still, between Terra and refugee nobles, things are coming to a head."

"It's pandemonium out there. At any given moment, someone in this nation is trying to take advantage of someone else. You'll never see anyone taking advantage of me, though."

Rupert's ever-graceful face appeared to fight against a momentary foreboding. He refilled his glass with more of the scarlet drink and tossed it back straight, enjoying the hot sting of it more than the taste. His stomach and throat burned. *I'll survive this*, thought Rupert. Then again, so did everyone else.

IV

Rocinante was the largest privately owned merchant ship of Phezzan to have no affiliations with any large-scale interstellar trading company. Emperor Erwin Josef II, Alfred von Lansberg, Leopold Schumacher, and Commissioner Boltec, along with the child emperor's four young maids, were its honorable guests.

It was far from the first time this ship had given safe passage to stowaways. *Rocinante* had been outfitted with ample storage rooms to harbor undocumented passengers on board. Secret doors opened by voiceprint identification, and warm water heated to the temperature of the human body circulated between the inner and outer walls to neutralize infrared detection. Asylum seekers were, in fact, *Rocinante's* largest source of income, and Captain Bomel's clandestine passengers had always slipped through imperial inspection undetected. Whether by playing dumb or through shameless bribery, Bomel always knew what method guaranteed the smoothest result. Commissioner Boltec, as imperial representative, had expressly chosen this ship to escort Erwin Josef out of Odin.

Bomel had been recommended directly by the commissioner and, because he'd been paid in advance, would do his utmost to deliver his honorable charge safely and comfortably to Phezzan. Naturally, etiquette barred him from attempting to determine the identity of his human cargo. And so, despite thinking a man in his prime, a younger lad, four women of around twenty, and a child made for an odd bunch, he knew better than to pry. He even relegated to his officers the serving of food and other amenities. Assuming this conveyance of refugees ended in success, there was a high chance he'd be given further opportunities to transport illustrious passengers.

Bomel's worries began the moment he was cleared to depart from the galactic port at Odin.

"He's an incorrigible little devil, that one," announced one of the dejected crewmen after bringing food to the new passengers. When asked why he had a blister on his left arm, the crewman said the child had hurled an entire bowl of chicken stew at him because he didn't like the way it smelled. When one of the girls tried to stop him, he made her cry by yanking her hair. Only then did the two men intervene. Even Bomel was surprised to hear this.

"His parents must've spoiled him rotten. He has no sense of right or wrong. I guess all highborn brats are the same. Anyway, you'll have to get someone else to take him his meals. I won't have any more of it."

With that, the crewman headed to the sick bay to treat his burn.

Bomel had the next meal brought by another crew member, who received a deep scratch across his cheek to show for his attempt. And when a third came back with a bruised septum, even a seasoned merchant like Bomel found himself at the end of his rope. He wasn't in the business of transporting mountain lions, he protested, and asked that he be shown some decorum. The elegant older boy prostrated himself and handed over a generous tip, and so Bomel withdrew. But just as he was about to leave, he noticed scars on the girl's hands and face.

"Forgive me for being so forward, but children require strict discipline. An undisciplined child is no different from a wild beast."

In response to this advice, the girl gave only a weak smile. Bomel had thought the girl to be an older sister or aunt, but now it seemed to him that she was a servant.

Only after he arrived on Phezzan and unloaded his cargo and stowaways did it dawn on Bomel that he'd been freighting none other than the sacred and inviolable emperor of the Galactic Empire. When, at a bar called De la Court, he heard a broadcast from the Free Planets Alliance regarding the emperor's defection, he looked down at the cup clenched in his left hand.

"I don't know if Duke von Lohengramm is an ambitious person or a usurper, but with that brat as emperor, our nation is destined to fall."

When Bomel had brought over a meal himself, Erwin Josef II had bit him hard enough on his left hand to leave a perfect crescent of teeth marks.

Blinded by the fury of his temper, the bearer of those teeth would never be able to express himself whenever his needs weren't met, except through violence.

CHAPTER 4:
THE LEGITIMATE GALACTIC IMPERIAL GOVERNMENT

I

EVEN AS THE CHILD emperor Erwin Josef II was being abducted from the galactic imperial capital of Odin, the alliance army's frontline base, Iserlohn Fortress, was indulging in a belated slumber.

Yang Wen-li, commander of Iserlohn Fortress and the Iserlohn Patrol Fleet, was thirty-one years old, making him the youngest to ever serve as full admiral in the Alliance Armed Forces. Slender and of medium build, his black hair was slightly unruly and longish for a military man, and he had a habit of brushing away the occasional bang from his forehead. He knew he should just get it cut, but after being chided at a hearing last spring for his long hair, he'd made it a point to keep it. He'd always been the type to go left when he was told, in no uncertain terms, to go right, and dutifully accepted the consequences of his contrariness. His eyes were jet-black, yet gentle, and even a little vacant. One biographer would later describe him as "intelligence wrapped in gentility, and gentility wrapped in intelligence," and those who knew him wouldn't disagree. His features were said to be "unremarkably handsome," approaching nowhere near the elegance of his rival, Reinhard von Lohengramm. He was more often depicted rather precisely as someone looking younger than his years and like anything other than a military man.

Not that Yang Wen-li wasn't self-aware. Against the wishes of those who'd hoped for him to become a historian, he'd advanced to lieutenant commander at twenty-one after successfully rescuing civilians on the planet El Facil, and at twenty-eight rose three ranks in the span of a year, making rear admiral in the Battle of Astarte, vice admiral in the Battle of Iserlohn, and full admiral thereafter in the Battle of Amritsar. His deeds of arms notwithstanding, the countless enemy soldiers he'd sent to their graves were reminder enough of his prowess. He was an artist on the battlefield, but was always the first to downplay the significance of his achievements. Being a soldier, he used to say, was a career that contributed nothing to civilization or humanity. He wanted to retire as soon as possible so that he could relax, enjoy his pension, and spend the rest of his life writing a historical magnum opus.

After fending off an invasion by an imperial fleet led by Gaiesburg Fortress in May, Yang had been laid flat with a cold for a week, and since getting out of bed, every day had chipped away at his tension.

Yang's ward was Julian Mintz, a boy who'd advanced to warrant officer. One look at Yang made Julian wonder if he wasn't just wasting his time performing high-level gymnastics inside that lonely skull of his, formulating grand tactical discourse, or pondering some deep historical philosophy. But then, Julian had nowhere near Yang's daily drive and was prone to overestimating intellectual activity.

Yang idled away doing nothing more than signing documents, pending the de facto approval of his civilian taskmaster, Rear Admiral Alex Caselnes, and aide, Lieutenant Frederica Greenhill. For the past two months he'd been whiling away the time in the central command room, reading history books and solving crossword puzzles, and breaking only for tea and naps. His demeanor was far from that of one hard at work. The field of his intelligence, overrun as it was with weeds, was in dire need of cultivation, crawling with gnats while its owner cared only about eating and sleeping.

Desperate to do something creative with his time, he began writing an essay on the theme of "Wine and Culture," but after just a few lines of the introduction, his pen stopped. The sentences he'd written were nothing short of awful.

Human culture began with wine. And so will culture end with it. Wine is the seat of intelligence and emotion, and might just be the only way to distinguish humans as such from wild animals.

Julian read this far before commenting:

"I've seen better copy in ads for dive bars."

Yang quickly abandoned this futile effort once he became aware of the degradation of his intellectual biorhythms. The commander of fortress defenses, Rear Admiral Walter von Schönkopf, later ribbed him for being a salary thief.

Not that von Schönkopf was a picture of military righteousness, either. Still a bachelor at thirty-four, since his days as captain serving as regiment commander of the Rosen Ritter he'd had a reputation for being fearless when it came to women. Although he was no match for ace pilot Olivier Poplin, lieutenant commander and captain of the First Fortress Spaceborne Division, together they taught Julian everything he knew about marksmanship and how to maneuver a single-seat spartanian fighter craft. Yang had assigned them to be Julian's instructors as top representatives of their divisions, even as he worried they might drive the boy crazy.

Episodes involving von Schönkopf and Poplin were the stuff of legend. One anecdote went as follows:

One morning, just as von Schönkopf was coming out of a certain second lieutenant lady's room, Poplin was coming out of a certain sergeant lady's adjacent room. The two exchanged glances and left, but two mornings later they encountered each other again. Only this time, von Schönkopf was coming out of the sergeant's room, and Poplin was leaving the second lieutenant's.

No evidence suggested this incident had ever taken place. It was a secondhand rumor at best. That didn't stop most from believing it. When asked about its authenticity, Poplin answered: "Why is it that only the men are identified by their real names, while the women remain anonymous? Isn't that just a little unfair?"

Von Schönkopf, on the other hand, said: "Let's just say my standards aren't quite so low as Poplin's."

It was only natural, thought Yang, that Julian should be troubled by his mentors. Julian was an attractive young man himself. While attending the Heinessen academy, he had been named flyball MVP and had turned the heads of not a few girls in his class. There were five million people on the artificial planet of Iserlohn, and as a general's adopted son who'd proved his valor destroying cruisers in his first campaign, he was naturally popular.

"Truth is, Julian can do everything you can't."

As Yang's mentor at academy, Alex Caselnes had no reservations about teasing him. Caselnes had two daughters of his own, and it was rumored he intended to marry off the elder one, Charlotte Phyllis, to Yang. When Yang found out, he responded:

"Charlotte's a nice girl. Her father, on the other hand…"

Yang Wen-li's unflagging military and political acumen compelled many to think of him as some sort of clairvoyant. Only now, he felt nothing more ominous than the vaguest sense of uneasiness. He had no idea what kinds of political, diplomatic, and strategic maneuverings were taking place in the empire, on Phezzan, or even within his own alliance, and so he continued to spend every day adding to his tally of consecutive defeats in 3-D chess, paying mind to the amount of brandy he added to his black tea.

II

On August 20, what would come to be known as the "Crooked Pact of SE 798" was publicly revealed. The Crooked Pact in question was a cooperative alliance between the old galactic imperial regime and the Free Planets Alliance against the Lohengramm dictatorship.

The Free Planets Alliance accepted the defection of Emperor Erwin Josef II and officially recognized Count Jochen von Remscheid as prime minister of the government-in-exile, otherwise known as the "legitimate galactic imperial government." In the event the government-in-exile overthrew the Lohengramm order and returned to its motherland, it would establish equal diplomatic relations with the Free Planets Alliance, enter treaties of mutual nonaggression and commerce, and encourage sociopolitical democratization through establishment of a constitution and parliament.

The Free Planets Alliance further guaranteed that the legitimate galactic imperial government would restore all rights to their original owners, cooperate fully, and establish a new and permanent peaceful order.

The alliance's High Council chairman Trünicht and the legitimate galactic imperial government's prime minister had reached an agreement in early August but had found it necessary to exercise discretion in publicizing it. The path to agreement was no by means even-keeled.

Erwin Josef II, along with Alex Caselnes, had already entered Free Planets Alliance territory in the middle of July. Under direct orders from Chairman Trünicht, both had been sheltered by Admiral Dawson in the Joint Operational Headquarters building. Although Dawson's abilities as a combatant were weak, he could be counted on in matters of utmost secrecy. Negotiations between both parties exceeded three weeks, after which time Count von Remscheid reluctantly promised to transition into a constitutional government.

That very afternoon, on August 20, Julian was talking with the black-haired admiral at Iserlohn Fortress.

"I hear Chairman Trünicht will be giving an urgent and important address."

"If it's urgent, then surely it must be important," responded Yang. His blunt attitude showed he had no interest in hearing about anything that didn't require his attention. But when orders came from Heinessen for all soldiers to watch their FTL screens, Yang said to himself, *I guess this, too, comes with the job.* He was nonetheless somewhat taken aback when the chairman's face appeared on the screen.

"To all citizens of the Free Planets Alliance: I, High Council Chairman Job Trünicht, am pleased to announce that a huge gift has been visited upon all of humanity. I am proud and overwhelmed to be the one to deliver this historic announcement."

Rejoice all you want, cursed Yang internally. Perhaps to the detriment of both sides, the alliance's youngest admiral had zero respect for its ruler and regarded him with sheer hatred.

"Recently, a defector in search of asylum became a guest of our free nation. Many people, fleeing from the cruel hands of despotism, have come here in pursuit of a free world, and we have never turned away a single refugee. But this refugee is special. You know his name: Erwin Josef von Goldenbaum."

He waited a few moments to let that sink in, enjoying the effect of his words.

Ever the demagogic politician, Trünicht was in fine form, and his announcement struck the thirteen billion citizens of the Free Planets Alliance like a giant lightning bolt devoid of light, heat, and sound. Half of the population gasped in shock, while the other half simply stared at the figure of their ruler as he puffed his chest on their screens.

The emperor of the Galactic Empire had fled, throwing away the nation he was supposed to rule, along with the people he was supposed to rule over. It was enough to make anyone question what they knew of the world.

"My dear citizens of the alliance," Chairman Trünicht went on shamelessly. "Reinhard von Lohengramm of the Galactic Empire, after purging his opposition by brute military force, now desires full dictatorial power. He abuses the emperor, who is barely seven years old, changes laws at whim, appoints cronies to key posts, and treats worlds as his personal possessions. It's not a question of the empire only, for now he has his devilish sights set on our very nation. He wants nothing less than despotic control over the entire universe, and is trying to extinguish the flame of freedom and democracy that our people have sheltered for so long. His very existence is a threat to our own. At this juncture, we have no choice but to throw away the past and work together with all unfortunate souls who have been sent running by von Lohengramm. The time has come for us to protect ourselves from the enormous threat he poses to all of humanity. By averting this threat, we can at last make lasting peace a reality."

Since the Dagon Annihilation of SE 640, year 331 of the imperial calendar, the Goldenbaum Dynasty's Galactic Empire and the Free Planets Alliance had been at constant odds. In that time, no small number of politicians had struggled to establish mutual nonintervention and trade pacts between their respective political systems. These attempts, however, had been thwarted at every turn by zealots and fundamentalists on both sides. One side regarded the enemy as rebels who went against everything

His Imperial Majesty stood for; the other as viewed its adversary an auto-cratic state. By disavowing each other's existence, had they not scattered the bodies of countless compatriots across battlefields through excessive military force in their quests for justice?

Joining forces toward a common goal was a complete turnaround. It was no wonder people were surprised.

Julian quickly ran his eyes across those gathered in the central control room. Even the sharpest of tongues, like those of Caselnes and von Schönkopf, were dulled into awed silence. Yang, for his part, was unsure what to feel, but watched closely as a gray-haired figure appeared on-screen.

"I am the secretary of state of the legitimate imperial government, Jochen von Remscheid. I cannot express the depth of my gratitude to the Free Planets Alliance, by whose humane consideration I have been granted the opportunity and a base of operations to restore justice to our fatherland. On behalf of all our comrades, whose names I will now read, I give you my sincerest thanks."

Count von Remscheid proceeded to list off the cabinet ministers of his so-called legitimate government. Secretary of state was to be von Remscheid's own post, and among the other ministers were names of exiled nobles, but when Senior Admiral Merkatz was named as secretary of defense, all eyes couldn't help but widen at the exiled guest admiral. None, however, was as surprised as the target of their attention.

"Your Excellency Merkatz, this is…" muttered Merkatz's aide, von Schneider, who looked around the room in shock, apologizing on behalf of his reticent boss.

"Please, don't misunderstand. This is absolutely the first either His Excellency or I have heard of this. I, for one, would very much like to know why Count von Remscheid has named His Excellency."

"I know why. No one believes that Admiral Merkatz has sold himself out."

Yang's attempts at pacifying von Schneider kept in check any remarks from his subordinates, who were eyeing Merkatz with suspicion.

Count von Remscheid was unlikely to have asked for Merkatz's consent, convinced as he was that offering the position was enough to seal the deal, thereby precluding the need for negotiations.

"I'm guessing Count von Remscheid would have offered the seat of defense secretary to Admiral Merkatz anyway. I can't imagine a more suitable candidate."

"Agreed."

Yang felt relieved by the good timing of von Schönkopf's interjection. He was nothing if not punctual. Count von Remscheid's list of cabinet ministers had been completed with input from the alliance government, which meant that Merkatz would soon be leaving Iserlohn to organize the legitimate government's army. Yang felt a great advisor being torn from his grasp.

Lieutenant Commander Olivier Poplin was among the many stoked into rage by the chairman's address.

"Here we are, knights of justice, saving that vagrant child-emperor and fighting a usurper who is nothing short of evil incarnate. This is insane! Are we characters in some TV drama?"

Poplin attempted a laugh but failed and threw his black beret to the floor in disgust. His comrade, Ivan Konev, picked up the beret in silence and handed it back. The young ace pilot refused it and continued with his tirade.

"Isn't it enough that we must shed our blood just to protect the Golden-baum family in the first place?! Haven't we been fighting for over a century, since the time of our great-grandfathers, to overthrow the Goldenbaum family and restore freedom and democracy to the galaxy?"

"But if this should lead to peace, a policy shift is inevitable."

"*If* it leads peace. But even if peace comes between us and the Golden-baums, what of Duke von Lohengramm? He'll ever be satisfied. What's to stop him from going mad and taking it out on us?"

"All I'm saying is we cannot turn away the emperor. He's only a seven-year-old child. Humanitarianism compels us to aid him."

"You speak of humanitarianism? Are you saying the members of the Goldenbaum family have any right to ask for humanitarian treatment? Maybe you should crack open your history textbooks again to remind yourself of the billions Rudolf and his descendants have killed."

"That blood is on his forefathers' hands. It's not his cross to bear."

"Aren't you just the sound rationalist? You manage to find fault with everything I say, don't you?"

"I wouldn't go that far."

"Don't get so defensive! I was being sarcastic!"

Seeing no reason to go on, Poplin snatched the offered beret and stormed out. Ivan Konev shrugged and smiled askew as he watched him go.

III

"In other words, the Galactic Empire and Goldenbaum family no longer stand as one body."

Yang let out a sigh, his jaw moist with the steam wafting from his brandy tea. Every other staff officer had a coffee in front of him—not that they had any time to enjoy its aroma. Julian stood next to the wall behind Yang, obediently serving his tea.

"No mere child of seven years defects of his own free will. Call it 'rescue' or 'escape,' but as his self-professed loyal subjects, we should see it as nothing less than abduction," offered Caselnes.

A few voiced their agreement.

"Be that as it may, I'm more concerned about Duke von Lohengramm's next move. What if he comes demanding the emperor's release?"

As Rear Admiral Murai knit his eyebrows, Commodore Patrichev tactlessly shrugged his broad shoulders.

"You heard the chairman's fluent speech. After talking such a big game, there's no way he'd give him up that easily."

Walter von Schönkopf, in his refined manner, returned his coffee cup to its saucer and interlaced his fingers.

"Well, if we were going to play nice, we'd have done better to join forces a century ago. Our opponents have lost their effective authority and run away, and now they want us to be friends. This whole thing reeks of absurdity, if you ask me."

"Joining forces with the lesser of two evils bodes well and good for the Machiavellians among us. But even assuming the timing was right, they'd need real power. In this case, we have neither."

Yang gave his back a good stretch and settled his full weight into his chair. If the alliance was truly of a Machiavellian spirit, the time to take advantage of the dispute between the pro- and anti-Lohengramm factions would have been during last year's Lippstadt War. Had the alliance intervened then, they might have reaped sufficient benefits while the imperials fought among themselves.

Having anticipated that very possibility with his enviable astuteness, Duke Reinhard von Lohengramm had brought about a coup d'état. In so splintering the alliance, he prevented their armies from taking part in the empire's civil war. Now that Duke von Lohengramm's authority was secure, there was practically no chance of his opponents recovering lost territories. Von Schönkopf had hit the mark.

Had Yang expected Machiavellianism within the alliance government, he would have handed the emperor over to Duke von Lohengramm in acknowledgment of his hegemony over the empire and made him promise a peaceful coexistence from thereon out. And while this act would appear inhumane, from where Yang sat, Duke von Lohengramm didn't have it in him to kill the child emperor with his own hands. The elegant young dictator wasn't foolish enough to indulge in thoughtless cruelty. In his shoes, Yang would have thought up a more effective use for the child emperor the moment he was born. Perhaps the alliance government had played its joker expressly for Duke von Lohengramm's sake.

Duke von Lohengramm lost nothing by the emperor's defection. On the contrary, focusing his attention on the emperor's "recapture" or "rescue" gave him ample justification to take military action against the alliance. Amplifying the people's animosity toward the emperor was also an effective barometer to measure national unity. If anything, Duke von Lohengramm had much to gain from the emperor's defection to the alliance.

Yang was terrified by where his thoughts on this were going. Since he thought highly of Reinhard's genius, he didn't believe the young dictator could be so easily taken by remnants of the old regime. When Yang voiced his thoughts on the matter, those present fell into silence, until von Schönkopf broke it.

"You mean to say Duke von Lohengramm intentionally let the emperor get away?"

"It's certainly a possibility," said Yang gravely.

He poured brandy into his empty teacup, ignoring Julian's critical eye. Caselnes took the bottle once it was returned to the table and poured some of its contents into his own cup, and from there it went to Murai by way of von Schönkopf, and so on. As he watched the bottle make its way around, Yang felt somewhat anxious, but Julian's look reined in his thoughts back to Duke Reinhard von Lohengramm.

Assuming Duke von Lohengramm's strategy was as elaborate as he'd made it out to be, a magnificent puzzle was about to be completed. But was this the work of Duke von Lohengramm alone? The alliance and the empire's old regime were both being made to dance. And were they not in agreement with the one making them?

Most terrifying of all was the prospect of Duke Reinhard von Lohengramm joining forces with Phezzan. Would they be joining their military and economic powers, talents, and ambitions out of common interest? Phezzan would never have extended a hand to Reinhard without something to gain. That much was certain. Still, what benefit would rush them into such an agreement? Was it the monopoly of economic interests promised by a unified empire? It was an answer he could agree to, as could Duke von Lohengramm. But was it the real one? Could it not be a trap to force Duke von Lohengramm to agree, and consequently to neglect? Or maybe Phezzan wanted something even bigger, its worship of money nothing more than camouflage to conceal ulterior motives.

All this thinking was beginning to make Yang's head hurt. He tuned in to Caselnes and von Schönkopf's conversation.

"You could say a 'white knight syndrome' of sorts is spreading in the capital: 'Let's fight for justice to protect the young emperor from the hands of the tyrannical and vicious usurper.'"

"They restore the Goldenbaum family's tyrannical power and call it justice? As Admiral Bucock said, we need a new dictionary. Would anyone here disagree?"

"Not that there aren't more conservative theories, but just speaking up about this might be enough to brand you as inhumane. Practically everyone is beside themselves, and over a seven-year-old child, no less."

Caselnes stared disagreeably into his coffee cup, empty yet again. He bent forward to reach longingly for the brandy bottle.

"If it were a pretty girl of, say, seventeen or eighteen years, you can be sure everyone would be all over this. People can't get enough of princes and princesses."

"That's because, in fairy tales, princes and princesses have always been righteous, while nobles have a reputation for wickedness. We cannot judge matters of politics on the level of fairy tales."

As their conversation wandered the labyrinth of his ear canal, Yang cultivated the field of his intelligence for the first time in a long while, hard as it was to yank out the weeds.

Let's sow some politics and diplomacy for now. In military matters alone, the alliance is courting no small risk. No doubt Duke von Lohengramm means to charge us with the crime of abducting the emperor. He might even inspire those common-born soldiers to action by making them believe the Goldenbaum family and the emperor are their enemies. They call themselves republicans, even as they overthrow the Free Planets Alliance, which schemes to shelter the emperor and restore social inequality under an autocratic government. But reality paints a different picture, as accomplices of the Goldenbaum Dynasty overthrow the alliance to protect your rights and privileges. The prospect of such sedition abounds in persuasiveness.

Belief that remnants of the old regime had "rescued" the emperor would result in delusions of chivalrous romanticism and political ambition, but in truth these were empty signifiers.

Duke Reinhard von Lohengramm stood to gain the most from this turn of events. He'd once needed the emperor's power behind him, but now that he'd destroyed the alliance of the high nobles and purged his rival, Duke Lichtenlade, at court, dictatorial power over the empire was firmly in his grasp. A mere seven-year-old child sovereign was the one eroded obstacle that stood between him and the throne. With full authority and military force at his disposal, he would hardly have needed to lift a pinkie to remove that obstacle from his path. But Duke von Lohengramm had standards. If he was going to dethrone the child emperor and receive his imperial crown, he needed just cause to withstand the scrutiny of history. If, for example, Erwin Josef II were a subversive tyrant who killed his own people, Reinhard would be more than justified in dethroning him. However, a seven-year-old child emperor, unlike several emperors before him, was unlikely to snatch away the wives of his retainers for his own pleasure, have his own demilitarized people killed in the name of maintaining order, or murder the successors of rival families as infants.

IV

Among the Goldenbaum Dynasty's succession of emperors, the most treasonous had been August II. Otherwise known as "August the Bloodletter," he had taken the throne in SE 556, IC 247.

By the time he was crowned at the age of twenty-seven, it was said he'd already known many of life's pleasures. Excessive drinking, fornication, and indulgence in fine foods had stricken him with gout, leading to a daily opium habit. His body deteriorated until it was 99 percent fat and fluids. His feeble bones and muscles could no longer support his massive weight, confining him to the down cushion of his electric wheelchair, on which he would transport his bulk of melting lard. Although his father, Emperor Richard III, was ashamed by the mere sight of him, August was still his eldest child and showed intellectual promise, and so the emperor couldn't bring himself to strip him of the crown. In addition, August's three younger brothers were no better in their disposition or behavior. His inauguration was met with indifference, and the greatest tyrant in the history of the Galactic Empire's court and government was only casually welcomed to the throne.

August reveled in the limitless authority now handed to him like a plaything. His first decree as emperor forced his late father's favorite mistresses to transfer to his own harem. It was customary for a late emperor's concubines to be given money and to be released from their bondage, while the new emperor selected new women for himself. August's brazenness shocked his ministers and angered his mother, the Empress Dowager Irene. The young emperor cocked a half smile in response to her condemnation of his insolence.

"Mother, I'm only trying to dispel the regret you felt over Father being stolen from you by those whores."

Grabbing his mother's hand, he dragged her into the inner palace, his eyes gleaming sadistically. Sometime later, her ladies-in-waiting heard a woman's piercing scream. Before its echo had died, the empress dowager came staggering out of the inner room, collapsed to the floor, and began heaving the contents of her stomach. The metallic smell of blood assaulted the nostrils of her ladies-in-waiting as they rushed to her aid.

The empress dowager had seen the corpses of hundreds of concubines in the inner palace. What's more, it was said they'd all been skinned. The deterioration of August's mind had been winning the race against his body, and the one remaining vestige of his reason had narrowed to a single thin line of sanity. But even that had vanished the moment he'd gained unlimited power, as the new emperor's mental kingdom welcomed darkness onto its throne.

From that day forth, with every wave of his fat fingers, this blob of lard clad in extravagant silk reduced the population of the capital city of Odin. His three younger brothers were all killed as conspirators to usurp the throne. Their bodies were cut into pieces with laser knives and thrown into a pit of hornheads. As the one responsible for birthing them into this world, the empress dowager was forced to commit suicide. Just one week after the new emperor's enthronement, not a single cabinet minister was left alive. Commodore Schaumburg of the imperial guard sought out so-called rebels and their extended families, including infants, based on nothing more than the emperor's "intuition." Sentencing and repossession of assets were carried out in the name of "fairness," regardless of status.

True to form, when executing criminals, he made sure to use extravagant, inimitable methods, and countless men and women provided him with no shortage of training materials for his innovations.

Reports among the extant official imperial records pertaining to August II weren't always accurate. On the one hand, there was ample reason to cover up any stain on the Goldenbaum tunic, while on the other it was necessary to record this tyrant's evil deeds by way of extolling those emperors who succeeded him. Because of this, the number of people to die under

August II's reign was estimated to be at most twenty million, and at least six million. But even the smaller figure was rarely mentioned. Like Rudolf the Great and Sigismund I before him, he wielded power as a toy, killing without reason despite his self-righteousness. Rumors of the emperor eating human flesh and drinking wine mixed with blood were clearly exaggerated. It was, however, a fact that he used a technique known to this day as "August's needle" to kill many an unfortunate victim. Said method involved inserting thin needles made of diamond into prisoners' eyes, piercing the skull and damaging the brain, causing death by insanity.

For six agonizing years, the Galactic Empire groaned under the weight of his tyranny. Ironically enough, it was a time when nobles and commoners trembled in fear alike, their mutual antipathy as good as forgotten. Over time, this fear turned them into cornered rats.

It took Marquis Erich von Rinderhof, August's cousin and son of former Emperor Richard III's younger brother, Archduke Andreas, to break the cycle. Seeing that the emperor's sense and reason had jumped off a cliff into a sea of madness, and sensing imminent danger, he absconded with his life from the capital city of Odin and fled to neutral territory. In the end, August killed nearly every member of his family in the capital and, not forgetting his cousin's clever escape, demanded his surrender. Erich refused the guillotine, and with the support of a neighboring imperial military garrison, he flew the banner of revolt. Erich was prepared to die for his freedom and had hidden a poison capsule in his body. In the event he was captured by the emperor, he could take his own life before his cousin could torture him to death.

Despite being prepared for defeat, three young admirals pledged him their allegiance. They had already deserted the tyrant, and one had lost a wife and child to the emperor's despotism. They clashed with a punitive force sent by the emperor in the Trouerbach Stellar Region but easily overwhelmed their passionless enemies. For every dead soldier, twenty chose to surrender and live, and the surviving army was resigned to follow suit.

And yet, even as the battle's outcome was being decided, August was dead. Knowing the end was near, Commodore Schaumburg had pushed

August into his pit of hornheads as he was feeding the dogs raw meat. The emperor let out an indescribable scream on his way to the bottom of the pit, where his fat was torn by fangs and claws and digested in the stomachs of animals well fed.

After an unbelievable triumphal return to the capital amid cries of "Long live the new emperor," Erich immediately summoned Schaumburg, praising him for eliminating the tyrant, and preventing any further harm to the people and their nation, and promoted him to full admiral. He then had an elated Schaumburg apprehended and sentenced to death by firing squad for having massacred so many people as the tyrant's trusted retainer.

The newly enthroned Emperor Erich's subsequent reign was neither particularly resourceful nor civilized. Erich nevertheless earned his place in history as a ruler of great merit by dispelling the shadow of August's terror-based politics, rescuing the empire from a hellish state, and stabilizing the spirits of his people. But, like his descendant Maximilian Josef, he only prolonged a despotic regime that might otherwise have collapsed, being naught but an unwitting criminal in the grander scheme of things.

V

All of which was to say that ousting the child emperor Erwin Josef as a tyrant was a crime they couldn't afford to commit.

Even if he died of natural causes, people would automatically suspect foul play. To avoid being dishonored as a child killer, Duke von Lohengramm had to protect the child emperor's life and health at all costs. It was a suitably ironic position to be in, and no matter how discerning Duke von Lohengramm might have been, one could imagine the burden this child emperor had come to represent. Still, the emperor's defection had resolved one challenge by leaving the throne vacant. Could the former ruler's side blame a new ruler for wanting to fill it?

The old regime's subjective aim was now unburdening its enemy's load. Duke von Lohengramm, in his flamboyant manner, enjoyed a hearty laugh over that one. All paths led to his triumph. If the emperor had defected, abandoning the throne and his subjects of his free will, then Reinhard had every right to criticize his irresponsibility and cowardice. And if the emperor had been abducted against his will, Reinhard would condemn the kidnappers and proceed to "rescue" the emperor himself. Either way, the power of choice was in his elegantly hand-stitched pocket. Meanwhile, the Free Planets Alliance had hopped into bed with the emperor and his self-proclaimed loyal retainers, and could only wait with bated breath to see which card their opponent would play. They'd already missed their chance.

Is this just blind luck on Duke von Lohengramm's part? thought Yang.

The answer provided some consolation: *Fate seems to be sitting this one out.*

Duke von Lohengramm was young, bursting at the seams with ambition and courage, and had never been the type to spend his days pining for good fortune. It was right to see the cogs of Duke von Lohengramm's intentions spinning throughout this latest turn of events. He'd already succeeded in bringing about a coup d'état in the alliance. And while he couldn't claim to have planned it from step one, there was a distinct possibility he'd known of a plan to abduct the emperor but willfully shut his eyes to it. Yang didn't believe remnants of the old regime had the wherewithal to take the emperor out of Odin. How would they infiltrate the capital to begin with? How would they make their escape? And how would they manage to stay hidden from the prying eyes of authorities? It was impossible to imagine anyone other than Duke von Lohengramm abetting this crime. He had in his possession all the necessary resources, capital, and personal connections, to say nothing of a viable motive.

And what about Phezzan?

Had Phezzan struck again? Yang almost reprimanded himself for entertaining the notion. As someone who had never joined a legitimate historical school, he'd never been much of a revisionist. In his mind, one needed more than the plots and schemes of an infinitesimal minority to change the course of things. History just didn't work that way.

At any rate, the alliance government shouldn't be held accountable for the cause, but for the effect.

The Free Planets Alliance had joined forces with the old regime of the Galactic Empire. The aristocrats were clearly reactionaries. By rebuilding the legitimate authority of the Goldenbaum Dynasty, and using that as their backdrop, mustering power through and within it, they'd monopolized wealth in the hopes of turning the tide. Their opposition to Duke von Lohengramm's political and social reform came from a staunch belief in "future democratization." It was the brilliant culmination of foolish decision-making.

Yang felt schools of prejudice swimming through the sea of his thoughts but admirably refrained from casting his net. The Goldenbaum Dynasty had lasted for five centuries since Rudolf the Great, and in that time it had had many opportunities to correct sociopolitical injustices. The elites turned away every time, killing dynastic flowers from root to petal with their poisonous breath of corruption. What could their remnants possibly have anticipated?

Someone once said there were three kinds of thieves: those who rob by violence, those by wisdom, and those by law.

And what of the twenty-five billion people of the empire released by Duke von Lohengramm from the yoke of an aristocratic governmental system? They aren't likely to forgive the alliance anytime soon for allying itself with the worst kind of thief imaginable. That's a given. Does this mean we'll come to fight a "people's army" of the Galactic Empire, as I once suspected? And won't justice be on their side when that happens?

"Well, Admiral Merkatz, what are you going do to?"

A gentle voice pulled Yang's attentions back to the Iserlohn conference room. He scanned the faces of his men until his eyes landed on the speaker: his chief staff officer, Murai. Despite their differences in rank, the other staff officers made no effort to mask their like-minded bewilderment. The attitude of the legitimate imperial government's newly nominated military secretary might very well have meshed with his staff officers, but no one could read his face. Murai had torn up his reserve and hesitation like a sheet of paper.

"Count von Remscheid, as leader of the government-in-exile, surely wouldn't expect Admiral Merkatz to refuse his nomination. I see no use in defying his expectations."

Although there was no cynicism in Admiral Murai's voice, he lacked a certain tolerance for evasion and self-effacement, and made Merkatz feel that his path of retreat had been cut off. The ever-serious Murai had vaulted the wall of guest admiral defectors with the pole of a surface-level criticism. Merkatz turned to his questioner with tired eyes.

"I don't agree at all with Count von Remscheid's point of view. My loyalty to His Majesty the Emperor is every bit as strong as his, but if you ask me, I'd rather see His Majesty lead a carefree life as an ordinary citizen."

The veteran admiral's voice deepened.

"Just because they've set up a government-in-exile doesn't mean they can overrule Duke von Lohengramm's authority. He treats the people as his allies, but only because they support him. What I can't seem to wrap my head around…"

Merkatz shook his head slowly. The shadow of a weariness that was more than physical was tightening its invisible grip around him.

"…is why those who should be defending the young emperor seem to be pushing His Majesty into a maelstrom of political strife and war. If they're going to set up a government-in-exile, they should do it on their own. There's no reason why they should involve a child, even if it is His Majesty, who cannot yet claim power of judgment."

Yang, who'd removed his beret and was fiddling with it impolitely, was silent. He glanced unassumingly at von Schönkopf, who offered his opinion.

"If you think about it, supply and demand don't agree in this case."

"Supply and demand?"

"That's right. Since Duke von Lohengramm's power would be nothing without the people it's built on, he no longer has need for the emperor's authority. On the other hand, by undermining the veracity of his power, Count von Remscheid is forcing him to use his surplus to take initiative over the government-in-exile."

"Admiral Merkatz's position is understood. But I want to ask what Your Excellency plans to do and how you will act."

"Rear Admiral Murai," said Yang, opening his mouth for the first time.

He felt like Merkatz was being put in the defendant's chair. He highly valued Murai's fastidiousness and precision, but sometimes he could be a thorn in the side.

"How nice it must be for those within an organization to be able to manage themselves for their own convenience. I've got a mountain of choice words I'd like to convey to those government bigwigs. What really gets me is how they're forcing us into their arbitrary decisions."

Caselnes, von Schönkopf, and Frederica Greenhill nodded at Yang's reasoning, understanding what he was getting at. Merkatz was by no means seeking to follow protocol and participate officially in the government-in-exile, but had become a scapegoat of ex post facto coercion. It would be unfair to give him an ultimatum at this point. Perhaps aware of this, Murai bowed his head and took his leave.

Fearing the situation would turn into a quagmire, Yang ordered a reprieve. Von Schönkopf turned to the general with a wry smile on his face.

"If you've got a mountain of things to say, then why not say them? Why not just shout 'King Midas has donkey ears!' and get it over with?"

"It's not the place of an active-duty soldier to voice political criticisms in an open meeting, is it?"

"I think those imbeciles on Heinessen *should* be criticized."

"You're free to think, but never to speak."

"I see, so the freedom of debate is narrower territory than the freedom of ideas? Where do you suppose the 'Free' in Free Planets Alliance comes from?"

Yang was certain he knew how to answer that question, but shrugged his shoulders in silence all the same. Iserlohn's defense commander saw this and narrowed his eyes.

"A free country? My grandparents fled to this 'free' country with me when I was six years old. That was twenty-eight years ago, but I remember every detail. The cold winds that cut like a knife and the contemptuous looks of customs officers who treated refugees like beggars. I'll never forget them until the day I die."

It was rare for von Schönkopf to share anything about his past, and Yang's black eyes brimmed with interest, but von Schönkopf didn't feel like going on about himself. He stroked his pointed chin and gathered himself.

"Point is, I'm a man who's already mourned the loss of his homeland. If once becomes twice, I'll be neither surprised nor grieved."

In a separate room, a heated conversation was taking place between a superior officer and his subordinate.

Merkatz looked back at his aide, Lieutenant von Schneider, his face a perfect blend of cynicism and self-derision.

"The power of a man's imagination can only go so far, am I right? Not one year ago, I never would've dreamed fate was setting a place for me at such a table."

Von Schneider was beside himself with disappointment.

"For the record, I pushed for exile, thinking it better for Your Excellency's sake."

Merkatz narrowed his eyes a little.

"Oh? I thought you, of all people, would be pleased. For someone who opposes Duke von Lohengramm, there could be no higher title."

From anyone else's mouth, those words would have felt like barbed wire on von Schneider's skin. He shook his head in disgust.

"Secretary of the military of the legitimate government does have a nice ring to it, but in truth there wouldn't be a single soldier under Your Excellency's command, would there?"

"And if I wasn't there to lead, how would it be any different from now?"

"Point taken. But you *did* take charge by leading Admiral Yang's fleet, if only temporarily. But now even that would be too much to hope for. It's an empty title without a shred of fidelity."

Von Schneider clicked his tongue.

"Count von Remscheid's one thing, but outside of nobles holding rank at court, there's no one of merit on the list. I don't see how anyone among them would be capable of rallying opposition against Duke von Lohengramm."

"There's still His Majesty the Emperor."

Merkatz's voice sank into von Schneider's chest. The lieutenant held his breath. He stared at the veteran general, who'd served as the emperor's retainer for more than forty years, and who by the hunch of his shoulders appeared to have aged quickly. Von Schneider, too, was naturally aware of his service to the emperor but, compared to Merkatz, was more impulsive and prone to following wherever compensation led him. Seeing how stupefied his aide was by the implications of his words, Merkatz smiled.

"I suppose I can't stop you from worrying too much. And in any case, I have yet to formally accept the request. Let's think about it carefully."

The tempest was already sending in its vanguard, and Yang had taken no measures against it. In fact, he had no backup plan whatsoever. If the empire's massive navy was indeed rushing toward Iserlohn Fortress, he could rouse some tactical strategists of exceptional ability, but given their inexperience outside of politics, as uniformed officers they'd be useless. Yang continued to watch from the side lines, unprepared.

"Your Excellency! Duke von Lohengramm is on the comm screen. He's about to deliver an address to the empire and the alliance."

The communications officer brought this urgent report after managing to squeeze in a meal following news of the government-in-exile.

Reinhard's lion-maned figure was transmitted over the main screen of the central command room.

He wore the traditional black-and-silver uniform that distinguished him as head of the Imperial Navy, yet set him off to such advantage that it might as well have been designed centuries before just so that it might one day cling to the body of this young, golden-haired man. His ice-blue eyes concealed a blizzard deep within, and being locked in their gaze was enough to send waves of fear through one's entire being. Whether one liked him or not, he clearly belonged to another realm entirely.

As Reinhard opened his mouth, his fluent, musical voice caressed the eardrums of his listeners, even if the contents of his speech were most severe. After announcing the truth behind the emperor's abduction, the alluring dictator dropped his intangible bombshell.

"I hereby declare: Having abducted the emperor by unlawful, not to mention cowardly, means, the remnants of the high nobility are attempting to turn the tide of history by depriving the people of their hard-earned rights. For this atrocity, they will receive due recompense. As for those overly ambitious people of the Free Planets Alliance who, in their illicit collusion, plot a war of insubordination against universal peace and order, they will suffer the same fate. Their error must be rectified by the appropriate punishment. Criminals require neither diplomacy nor persuasion. They possess neither the ability to, nor do they intend to, understand such things. Force alone will make them see their ignorance. No matter how much blood is to be shed, remember that these foolish kidnappers and conspirators are to blame."

No diplomacy, no persuasion. Reinhard's listeners felt their hearts racing in their chests. The old galactic regime's government-in-exile, in conspiracy with the alliance government, had been rendered a target of military intervention. To be sure, anyone who saw it as "reform" had foreseen this rapid, merciless response.

As Reinhard's figure faded from the screen, von Schönkopf turned to Yang.

"This is tantamount to a declaration of war, is it not? I guess it's too late to worry about it now."

"The pieces are all in place."

"Looks like Iserlohn will be on the front lines yet again. That's the last thing we need. Those cretins do as they please, just because they think they have this fortress. Makes you wonder, doesn't it?"

Yang opened his mouth to say something, then closed it, staring through the grayed-out screen at something no one else could see.

CHAPTER 5:

I

THE FREE PLANETS ALLIANCE was thrown into chaos by Emperor Erwin Josef II's defection and Duke Reinhard von Lohengramm's declaration of war. Naturally, the High Council, with Job Trünicht as its chairman, had expected Reinhard to antagonize the government-in-exile, but it was shocked by the severity of his reaction. So far as councilman Kaplan was concerned, just as they were considering diplomatic negotiations with the government-in-exile, they'd received a preemptory slap in the face, told in no uncertain terms by the enemy that compromise was no longer an option.

"That golden brat has the gall to threaten us, backed by military force," said Kaplan, infuriated.

But no matter how much they might blame Reinhard, culpability was on them for their rash political decisions. They'd practically laid a welcome mat out for Reinhard's strong-arm tactics.

Their choice, foolish as it was, had been unknowingly directed by Reinhard and Phezzan's coproduction behind the curtain. This was a small comfort, given the greater misfortune it had spawned.

Two unaffiliated politicians—João Lebello and Huang Rui—were eating dinner at a local restaurant. Both men, being attached to the hearing, were bound to Yang. And so, for the moment, their conversation was focused on that very subject.

"Yang Wen-li? A dictator? That's a hard one to swallow."

"It's easy to laugh now before it becomes a reality, but I've seen smiles fade more times in my life than I can count, Huang."

Although as a politician Lebello was aboveboard when it came to his ethical duties, he sadly lacked a capacity for humor. It was the one thing Huang felt sorry for in his friend.

"To make this cocktail we call a dictator requires capturing its essential flavor. Dictatorship can be a good thing. Dictators are unwavering in their beliefs and sense of duty, express their own sense of righteousness to maximal effect, and possess the strength to regard their adversaries not solely as their own foes, but as enemies of justice. But I wonder if you can see that much, Lebello."

"Of course I can. And in Yang Wen-li's case?"

"Well, Yang Wen-li makes a delicious cocktail, but as I see it, he lacks the ingredients to make a dictator. It's not a question of intelligence or ethics but of belief in one's own infallibility and a certain infatuation with authority. Maybe it's just my own cocktail talking, but I'd say he's lacking in both areas."

The two politicians went quiet as their whitefish soup was brought to them. Lebello brought the spoon to his mouth, glancing at the waiter as he walked away.

"But does he not have a belief in his own infallibility? At the hearing, he came across as a dauntless accuser and a stubborn orator. You said so yourself."

Huang shook his head, not only to express his disapproval of Lebello, but also, it seemed, to comment on the poor flavor of his soup.

"Ah, you're right, but he had to throw down the gauntlet to thwart his examiners' idiocy. As far as that hearing is concerned, he was an outstanding strategist. But not when it comes to war. As a tactician, he'd just as soon side with any dumb lot to avoid a conflict. Nevertheless, our good old boy Yang Wen-li would never…"

Huang grimaced as he brought another spoonful to his mouth.

"That's why he called those pigs what they were to their faces. People lose their dignity when they're upset. Any number of pitiful examples from history will tell you that. Humanity's dignity and political triumphs sometimes make for a fair exchange."

Huang looked down dubiously at his empty bowl and took a drink of water.

"I see no reason to believe that Yang Wen-li will become a dictator anytime soon. At least he harbors no such ambition."

"Not if the situation unfolds to his liking."

"Granted. And Yang Wen-li's not the only one we should be worrying about. You're no exception, Lebello. You hardly seem anxious about Admiral Yang, but what are you prepared to do if he should grab the dictatorial reins and put an end to democracy as we know it?"

Lebello knitted his eyebrows, not giving an immediate reply. Huang didn't press him for one, either. He was having enough trouble keeping his own sound views and resolutions stowed away.

Choosing between a corrupt democracy or a virtuous dictatorship was one of the most difficult dilemmas faced by human society. The people of the Galactic Empire were fortunate in being delivered from what was inarguably the worst condition: a corrupt autocracy.

. . .

Now was a time when miscalculation and dejection were being mass-produced. The bewilderment of the legitimate imperial galactic government over welcoming a child emperor who should've been worthy of loyalty and devotion surpassed even that.

"Damn that brat! There's nothing redeeming about him. He's arrogant, rude, and harder to deal with than a psychotic cat."

Anger, disappointment, and other unpleasant feelings boiled in their stomachs, pushing acidic saliva up into their mouths. They had known little about the child emperor, except that he'd had the full support of Reinhard and former imperial prime minister Duke Lichtenlade, but had never imagined he would stimulate so little devotion from his subordinates.

Were the young emperor to grow to adulthood without ever learning to control his ego, they could look forward to another August II.

August II had been the biggest pariah in the history of the Goldenbaum family and the empire, and if this child were to successfully claim and hold the imperial throne, August II's name had to be prudently ignored. Per future historians, fortunately his successor had not interfered with any expression of views about August II, allowing the tyrant's deeds to be understood and forestalling the need for a political insurgency.

The current emperor had neither the appearance nor the character of someone who respected the opinions of adults, and so the criticisms of Erwin Josef II were severe. First, one couldn't very well question a seven-year-old child about self-invested responsibility. He was to be kept in check by the adults around him who'd so diligently labored to improve his character. With his parents already dead and Reinhard being in no position to be a father figure, and coupled with the fact that his attendants had all the temperament of petty officials, the emperor exerted himself only in the most minimal of official duties. Not that love necessarily decided all, but a total lack of it meant that positive change was impossible.

Unfathomable ruin was gnawing at the child's mind, and it would continue to expand and intensify. It was enough to steer others away from him.

To the higher-ups of the legitimate government, the emperor needn't have been a hero or a wise ruler in the least. A banal puppet was far preferable. Falling so far below even that standard was troubling all the same. As for the government-in-exile, which had no domain to govern, no citizens to exploit, and no army to rule by organized violence, the protection of the Free Planets Alliance and the assistance of Phezzan were necessary for its existence. They were weighing their options as they went along, but even so, between the goodwill they were burning through and the favor they were currying with their allies, they had to prepare for future opposition and reconstruction by keeping themselves in the good graces of the child emperor.

For that reason, they'd wanted the seven-year-old emperor to be a sweet angel out of some fairy tale. Those hopes were quickly vanquished. It was all they could do to minimize any animosity surrounding him. And so they decided to keep His Majesty from the public eye as much as possible. They ordered a doctor to administer tranquilizers to the child emperor and restricted his world to the bedchamber of his "temporary palace." Although his "court physician" was worried about how the drugs might affect the child's frail body, in the end he had to follow orders.

Thus, all politicians and financiers from the alliance, the press, and those wanting to do their part for the government-in-exile had to be content with staring from the doorway at the face of a child who'd been forced into a kingdom of sleep. Among his visitors were those fascinated by his slumbering face, while others regarded him as the living embodiment of five centuries of ongoing despotic darkness.

It had become a vexing situation, as everyone carried out their decisions based not on reason but on emotion. They supported him through sentiment, opposed him through visceral hatred. Any debate over whether recognizing the emperor's defection as such would bring about the lasting peace of democracy had been abandoned. Both supporters and detractors—the former of which occupied the larger camp—disparaged the foolishness of their opponents and stopped wasting time and effort on futile persuasion.

Emperor Erwin Josef II wasn't the sweet little angel that some fantasized him to be, but an utterly charmless and undisciplined child. This realization put a dent in Caselnes's so-called white knight syndrome, although it had more than enough political cachet to go around. In any case, Duke von Lohengramm, a person of insubordinate ambition, had predicted that most of the officers in the Imperial Navy would hesitate to point their guns at the child emperor. Back on ancient Earth, when Muslims were embroiled in civil war, the opposing army held out an original manuscript of the Qur'an. Seeing that, the enemy threw down their weapons and ran. The parallels were clear, although Duke von Lohengramm's prediction was the bastard child of desire and delusion.

Although burdened with uneasiness and regret, the refugees and alliance government that supported them had been herded past a point of no return. Reinhard's shocking response had roped them from the center of the ring. With no room left for discussion, resolution was reachable only by force. Military fortification and maintenance were now urgent matters. The alliance government's first undertaking was to dispel any modesty in its military authority and to increase its government's political influence by seating military heads with high-ranking officers from the Trünicht camp.

Thus, the director of Joint Operational Headquarters, Admiral Cubresly, retired for reasons of illness, while former acting director Admiral Dawson was promoted in his place. Although Dawson's loyalty found suitable reward in Trünicht's political power, military leaders were at least opposed to appearing as if they adhered to the current administration. The hands of human resources didn't reach so far as the commander in chief of the alliance's space armada, Admiral Bucock, but they did stretch indirectly to Yang and could one day summon a roaring thunder over his head.

"Julian Mintz has been promoted from warrant officer to ensign and is to be appointed to the resident commissioner's office as a military attaché. He will take up his new post on-site by October 15."

When this order was brought to Iserlohn Fortress by FTL, Lieutenant Frederica Greenhill couldn't bring herself to look her superior officer in the eye.

II

Aware that his authority was anything but omnipotent, Yang understood this was part and parcel of being in a democratic republic. Upon receiving the order, he couldn't help recalling von Schönkopf's sarcastic recommendation, when the fortress defense commander had advised with utmost impropriety that they should just become a dictatorship. Acquiescence on their part meant condoning the arrogance of their colleagues.

Lieutenant Frederica Greenhill stood clutching a file to her chest as Yang paced back and forth exactly sixty times. The young commander took off his beret and ruffled his black hair. He let out a breath that sounded like a geyser, casting a foreboding glance at something unseen. He wrung his beret in both hands, not realizing he was treating it like someone's throat.

"Your Excellency," said Frederica by way of diffusing the tension.

Like a misbehaving boy grabbed by the scruff of the neck, he looked at his beautiful aide, stopped strangulating his beret, and heaved a sigh.

"Lieutenant Greenhill, get Julian here for me."

"Right away. Excuse me, Admiral, but…"

"Ah, I know what you want to say…I think. Would you please just summon Julian?"

Yang's choice of words betrayed his insecurity, but it was all Frederica could see in the young commander's heart. She did as she was instructed.

Anyone could see that Julian was a sharp boy, but since Frederica had managed to suppress her feelings, until Julian stood before Yang's curtain-drawn face and was handed the directive, he had no idea of the ill fortune that would soon be upon him.

He read over the directive repeatedly. Once he understood the meaning of its inorganically arrayed letters, his blood boiled with fury. He looked from Yang to Frederica and back again, his vision clouded by distortions of anger. He had an urge to tear up the directive right then and there, but he bit that urge in the jugular with fangs sharpened on the wall of reason.

"Please, you must revoke this order!" Julian shouted.

He knew he was being louder than propriety allowed, but felt justified in his response. Anyone who could keep their cool in his shoes was emotionally defective.

"Julian, when you were a civil servant, appointments and transfers were always up to the on-site commander. But you're a real soldier now. It's your duty to follow orders from the Defense Committee and Joint Operational Headquarters. I shouldn't have to spell it out for you this late in the game."

"Even when the orders are this absurd?"

"In what way are they absurd?"

Yang's retort was so forced that Julian avoided a direct answer and grew defensive.

"If that's the case, I'd rather go back to being a civil servant. Then I wouldn't have to comply with this order, would I?"

"Julian, Julian..." said Yang, sighing.

He'd never once rebuked Julian, but this time the boy was rebuking *him*. Perhaps Yang had overestimated Julian's maturity.

"You should know better by now. No one forced you to become a soldier. You volunteered, remember? You knew that following orders was part of the job the moment you signed up."

Yang's retort was formulaic at best. If there was any power of persuasion in it, it was not in the content of his words, but in something underlying his tone that inspired sympathy in Julian.

While Julian tried to restore balance in his heart, the surface of its waters remained disturbed. His face was flushed from increased blood flow.

"Understood. I'll take up my new post on Phezzan as resident military attaché. Not because it's an order from Joint Operational Headquarters, but because it's an order from Admiral Yang Wen-li. If that's all you wanted to see me about, do I have permission to leave, Your Excellency?"

With an expression that seemed coated in alabaster, Julian performed a perfect salute by rote and left the room with a disingenuous gait.

"I understand how Julian feels," said Frederica at last.

It was only Yang's prejudice that made him detect an element of blame in her voice.

"I'm sure he feels like Your Excellency sees him as expendable."

Frederica looked at the commander with hazel eyes that wordlessly questioned his lack of consideration for the boy's feelings.

"Expendable? It's nothing like that." Offended, Yang attempted an explanation. "So sending him away means he's expendable, while keeping him by my side means he's needed? It doesn't work that way. Even if he wasn't useful to me, I'd keep him by my side. No, his necessity isn't a question of utility."

Losing confidence in the expressive power of his own words, Yang went quiet. He ruffled his hair, crossed his arms, and took a breath. There was plenty to back up his decision, but pushing the boy away without making any effort to understand his side was the last thing he'd wanted.

"I guess I'll need to have a talk with him."

Even as he said it, Yang wondered why he hadn't just done so in the first place. Yang was fed up with his own carelessness.

The grand botanical garden of Iserlohn Fortress was the perfect place to refresh oneself. Frederica had nonchalantly informed Yang that Julian was sitting, deep in thought, on a bench among the jacaranda trees where Yang occasionally napped alone.

Yang had no intention of working overtime and left the central command center at five o'clock.

He sat himself down on the garden bench next to an inconsolable Julian, who lifted his head to see Yang with a can of beer in his hand and an imposing look on his face.

"Admiral…"

"Hey, uh, you mind if I sit here?"

"Help yourself."

Yang sat down somewhat awkwardly, pulled the tab on his beer, gulped down a lump of foam and liquid, and took a breath.

"Look, Julian."

"Yes, Admiral."

"I'm only sending you to Phezzan because I was ordered to. But, if you ask me, having someone on the inside that I can rely on might not be such a bad thing. Either way, I'm sure you'd rather not go."

"With the way things are going, Iserlohn is headed for the front lines again. I think I'd be of greater use here."

"I honestly wouldn't see the point, Julian."

Yang tossed back another swig of his beer and looked at the boy.

"Everyone is expecting the Imperial Navy to invade by way of the Iserlohn Corridor, although neither protocol nor law demands it."

"But if that's the case, then where would they invade from? Will they make some grand detour beyond the solar system? The Phezzan Corridor is all that's left."

"You're right."

Julian gasped at Yang's easy response and waited for an explanation.

"For Duke von Lohengramm, no tactic could be more effective than laying siege to Iserlohn with one fleet while breaking through the Phezzan Corridor with another. Odin knows he has the resources to pull it off. Iserlohn would be isolated, reduced to little more than a pebble on the side of the road."

"But then wouldn't the empire make an enemy of Phezzan?"

"Good question, but I wouldn't count on it. The way I see it, Duke von Lohengramm has two options if he's going to pass through the Phezzan Corridor. One would be to eliminate both Phezzan's overt and covert resistance by force. The other would be to bypass Phezzan's resistance altogether."

Yang explained no further, but Julian knew what the black-haired commander was hinting at.

"Are you saying Duke von Lohengramm and Phezzan are secretly working together?"

"Precisely."

Yang raised his beer to eye level, commending the boy's acumen.

Julian couldn't afford to feel glad about being praised in this case. Collusion between Duke von Lohengramm and Phezzan meant the unification of the greatest military and economic powers in their galactic system, and their spears were sure to be aimed at the Free Planets Alliance. Julian had grown used to the prevailing political and military conditions, but now he was drastically revising his mental diagram of an opposing empire and alliance with Phezzan equidistant between them. It was a lot to take in in one sitting.

"Julian, we humans are hardwired to fall into these kinds of misunderstandings. But think about it for a moment. The Galactic Empire didn't exist five hundred years ago. The history of the Free Planets Alliance is half that length, and Phezzan is barely a century old."

Anything that hadn't existed since the dawn of the universe probably wasn't going to be around for sunset. Change was the way of things. As manifested in the outstanding character of Duke Reinhard von Lohengramm, change had swept through the Galactic Empire and was now spinning its web to ensnare human society.

"Does that mean the Galactic Empire—no, the Goldenbaum Dynasty—will crumble?"

"It will. In fact, it already has. True political and military authority are in Duke von Lohengramm's grip. The emperor has abandoned his country and his people. Even if the name hasn't changed, the Lohengramm Dynasty is already upon us."

"I'm sure you're right. But I wonder, is the probability of Phezzan having allied itself with Duke von Lohengramm really that high?"

"Imagine you have three major powers—A, B, and C—and that A and B are in a relationship of mutual adversity. In this case, C's best course of action would be to save A if A was being threatened by B, help B if B was being pressured by A, or simply prolong the conflict between A and B until both sides destroyed each other. But if A's influence strengthened dramatically, so that even with B's help C would find it difficult to oppose A, wouldn't C be better off attacking B in cooperation with A?"

"But say it did, and the overwhelmingly fortified A capped off its victory of destroying B by attacking C—wouldn't C be heading from independence into certain doom?"

The young, dark-haired admiral looked at the flaxen-haired boy, impressed.

"Yes, that's exactly right, and the crux of where I'm going with this. In offering its wealth and strategic position to Duke von Lohengramm, perhaps Phezzan will lose its independence. And how are they planning on getting out of *that* situation?"

Beer in hand, Yang mulled this over.

"Maybe Phezzan's goal isn't its own preservation…No, that's too big a leap of intuition. To start with, there's no proof whatsoever. I was thinking

Phezzan intended to monopolize economic interests in the newly unified Galactic Empire, but now I'm not so sure."

Julian tilted his head, sending the slightest ripple through his flaxen hair.

"If not material benefit or self-interest, might it be something spiritual?"

"Spiritual?"

"Ideology, for example, or religion."

Now it was Yang's turn to widen his eyes. He turned the beer can around idly in his hand.

"Religion, you say? Why, yes, that's a possibility. Maybe I was overstepping my bounds in thinking of Phezzan as a group of superficial, logical realists. Religion, indeed."

At the time, Julian didn't follow the branch of his own fine logic to pluck the fruit of reality, because he'd simply recited something he'd suddenly remembered, and so Yang's admiration was for him more a source of embarrassment than elation. He gave a cough and confirmed the details of his assignment with the young commander.

"If I can go to Phezzan and uncover even a fraction of their plans and strategies, in addition to determining the Imperial Navy's movements, that would be of use to Your Excellency, right? In that case, I'm happy to go to Phezzan."

"Thank you. But there's another reason why I think you should go to Phezzan, Julian."

"Which is?"

"Well, how should I put this? Looking at a mountain from only one side, you'll never grasp the whole…Scratch that. There's something more important I'd like to ask you."

Yang crossed his legs.

"Sooner or later, you can bet we'll have to risk our lives fighting against Duke Reinhard von Lohengramm. Incidentally, Julian, do you really think Duke von Lohengramm is evil incarnate?"

Julian was stumped by the question.

"I don't think so, but…"

"You're right. Incarnations of evil only exist in TV dramas." Yang paused to laugh at his own observation. "If anything is evil, it's the fact that the Free Planets Alliance aided the old imperial regime. Not only does this accelerate the flow of history, it supports the one contributing to its reversal. Perhaps history will one day portray *us* as the bad guys."

"I don't see how that could ever…"

"It's not uncommon."

Yang tried to imagine a future in which Duke Reinhard von Lohengramm became supreme ruler and brought peace and order to the entire human race. From then on, the Goldenbaum Dynasty would be spoken of in derogatory terms, and the Free Planets Alliance as an enemy who'd stood in the way of unity. Of Yang specifically, history textbooks would say, "Were it not for him and his thirst for blood, unification would have been achieved much sooner."

The idea that absolute good and perfect evil existed would always be a bane to the human spirit. Harmony and compassion were impossible so long as one side thought of itself as benevolent and of its enemy as nefarious. This only justified valorization of the self over a defeated opponent, over whom rule was made manifest.

Yang was no holy crusader ordained by God. As a military man, unjustifiable decisions came with the territory. Had he been born in another time and place, he would, of course, have walked a different path. He wasn't one to delude himself into thinking that, just because he believed in justice, future generations would follow suit. So long as his motives were subjectively correct, their results didn't matter. To him, this was the only beneficial way to think about it.

Human beings weren't built to endure the knowledge that they were evil, and they were at their most forceful, their most cruel, their most ruthless when asserting righteousness. It was only because Rudolf the Great had believed in his own righteousness that so much blood was spilled, and although it bathed his reign in crimson, it was peaceful. Or maybe he had just pretended it was. For when a crack opened in the armor of self-justification with which he had wrapped his granite tower of a body, did the enormity of it become the foundation of his ego?

"Julian, are you familiar with the legend of Noah's flood? It was God, not the devil, who destroyed everyone but Noah's clan. You might say all monotheistic myths and legends verify truth by showing that God, not the devil, rules humanity through fear and violence."

Yang knew it was an extreme example, but one could never overemphasize the exceeding relativity of right and wrong. The best choices of which humans were capable, compared to the countless events reflected in their fields of vision, involved taking a stand for the better. And for those who believed in the existence of absolute righteousness, how did they explain the enormous contradiction inherent in the phrase "fighting for peace"?

"So, Julian, when you go to Phezzan, see if you can't tell the different between their sense of righteousness and ours. That wouldn't be such a bad experience for you. Compared to that, the rise and fall of nations pales in significance. *That's* the gospel truth."

"Even the rise and fall of the Free Planets Alliance?"

Yang ruffled his black hair and smiled.

"Yes, although I can only hope it lasts long enough for me to collect my pension. Even from a historical perspective, the Free Planets Alliance was created as the very antithesis to Rudolf von Goldenbaum's political ideology."

"That I can understand."

"Constitutional government goes against autocracy, progressive democracy against intolerant authoritarianism. We advocate these ideologies as if they were natural choices and put them into practice. But if all things Rudolf are to be denied and buried at the hands of Duke von Lohengramm, I see no reason for the alliance to go on as such."

Julian was silent.

"Look, Julian. No matter how unrealistic the man may be, he doesn't sincerely believe in immortality—and yet, don't you think it's strange that so many idiots out there delude themselves into thinking their nations are indestructible?"

Without answering, Julian, with the dark-brown eyes that even his foster parent had, looked at the young admiral. Yang's thoughts often developed beyond space and time and made use of an extreme frankness of expression, much to the exhilaration not only of Julian, but also of Frederica.

"Julian, nations are nothing more than basic tools. Never forget that, and maybe you'll hold on to who you are."

The worst sickness born in human civilization, thought Yang, was faith in one's nation. It was nothing more than a mechanism by which to efficiently promote complementary relationships between those who lived in it. There was no reason in being ruled by tools. Or, more accurately, the majority allowed itself to be ruled by a select few who knew how to use those tools. Yang didn't think there was any need for Julian to be lorded over by people like that. Yang didn't say as much, but assuming he could find comfort in a life on Phezzan, Julian would be better off shedding the alliance and becoming a Phezzanese. For now, Yang was satisfied that the future was calling to Julian.

At least my senior classmate Caselnes did something right. He brought you to me.

Yang had intended to say this but somehow lost the substance for such words, which vanished like mist. Yang stared in silence at the unnatural twilight above them. On his crossed knees, the empty beer can and black beret seemed to cry for mercy from their handler's numerous abuses.

III

News that Julian Mintz was to leave Iserlohn Fortress, and Yang stay behind with it, came as no small surprise to Yang's staff officers. When Yang's academy mentor, Alex Caselnes, caught wind of the report, he grabbed hold of his old charge during lunchtime at the admirals' mess hall.

"So you finally plucked up the nerve to get rid of Julian? I must say I'm surprised."

He sounded more rhetorical than caring.

"There was nothing I could do about it—National Defense Committee's orders. Besides, I was also sixteen when I left my father and enrolled at the academy. Maybe it's time he went out on his own, too."

"An admirable view, but how will you get on without Julian around?"

This time, Caselnes sounded genuinely concerned, which irritated Yang even more.

"Lieutenant Greenhill asked the same thing. Why does everyone think I'll be lost without him?"

"Because it's the truth," averred Caselnes with such lucidity as to leave no room for objection.

Even as Yang was scrambling for an effective counterattack, Caselnes asked him to bring Julian over for dinner. Once Julian left for his new post on Phezzan, such opportunities for fraternization would be lost.

If anything about Yang gave Caselnes and von Schönkopf cause for resentment, it was how unusually straightforward he became when lecturing Julian. From where Caselnes stood, the one being lectured was a more upright man than the one doing the lecturing.

"Only people without common sense make the mistake of proselytizing others by appealing to common sense."

"That's right, because children don't obey their parents, but they emulate them. It's pointless just talking about it."

Listening to their conversation, Yang felt quite out of place among these self-professed keepers of common sense. At least Caselnes ran a harmonious household, although if you asked Yang, it was the wife, not the husband, who wore the pants. But he saw no reason to be treated like some irrational person by the likes of von Schönkopf, who at three years his senior was still a bachelor and was the very embodiment of the caliph from *One Thousand and One Nights*.

With more important business demanding his attention, Yang wasn't in the mood for this kind of verbal jousting. Joint Operational Headquarters had requested that Yang appoint a guard to accompany Julian to and on Phezzan, and this he could not neglect.

Yang agreed with Frederica Greenhill, who nominated Warrant Officer Louis Machungo for the job. He was an upstanding man who'd served as Yang's personal security guard, and Rear Admiral von Schönkopf gave written guarantee of his loyalty and strength. He was sure to counsel and protect Julian well. Almost all military officers stationed on Phezzan were undoubtedly of the Trünicht persuasion, and Yang's sense was that, in the "enemy territory" of the commissioner's office, Machungo would be Julian's only and most trustworthy ally.

The chief resident officer acted as captain, and under him were six officers and eight attachés in the so-called military attaché division. The chief resident officer held the third highest position in the commissioner's office, after the commissioner himself and his secretary. All six officers were soldiers, three being field officers and three company officers. The eight attachés were low-ranking soldiers, and Yang had been entrusted to refill a vacancy among them. He sensed some underhanded dealings at work and felt uneasy about the whole thing, but since Julian had been confirmed, Yang couldn't pass up an opportunity to surround him with other young men his age. Yang wondered if he was being overprotective, but at sixteen even Yang had never been entrusted with official business and had never left the country.

After deciding on Machungo's deployment, Yang turned to his next order of business: writing a letter to the commander in chief of the space armada, Admiral Bucock. Julian wouldn't be going to Phezzan directly, but would receive official notice of his appointment from Joint Operational Headquarters in Heinessen's capital city, whereupon he would be sent off to his new station. Yang would have Julian hand-deliver the letter himself. Although there was a possibility of the main military faction—that is, Trünicht's drones—getting in the way, if anyone could work around that, it was the ever-resourceful Julian.

In the letter, Yang pointed out the likelihood that Duke Reinhard von Lohengramm and Phezzan were in collusion or had at the very least joined forces after the fact to produce the emperor's abduction. To Yang's chagrin, the evidence was circumstantial. Still, it was favorable to assassination. An abduction was no loss to Duke von Lohengramm's reputation. The kidnappers had taken the emperor and incompetently fled Duke von Lohengramm's faraway system of public order. Immediately following the announcement of the government-in-exile, and with almost clairvoyant rapidity, Duke von Lohengramm had made his declaration of war. This was evidence enough of his foreknowledge.

Duke Reinhard von Lohengramm had declared "discipline by military force" and would likely go on the offensive, backed by his unconquerable army. But Yang didn't for one second believe that it was only under pretense of the emperor's abduction that he would dispatch his troops. It was his foolish plan to bury the Iserlohn Corridor with the corpses of imperial officers.

While making a show of capturing Iserlohn Fortress, he would divert his grand army and penetrate the defenseless Phezzan Corridor to invade alliance territory. And with no-holds-barred tacticians like Wolfgang Mittermeier calling the shots, even if Yang could make a quick break from Iserlohn, the planet of Heinessen would fall into imperial hands long before he arrived. Furthermore, no commanding officers of the Imperial Navy in the Iserlohn area, least of all renowned fleet commander Oskar von Reuentahl, would stand idly by as Yang withdrew from Iserlohn. In the worst-case scenario, the empire's greatest commanders would cut him off in a pincer attack. And even if Yang could engage them, von Lohengramm, the greatest war genius he'd ever known, directly or indirectly, would be lying in wait.

Perhaps he was thinking too far ahead, but the possibility of the Imperial Navy using the Phezzan Corridor as an invasion route was beyond disturbing. In the event that that happened, imperial forces could easily lie and use Phezzan as an enormous supply base. Also terrifying for Yang was the fact that Phezzan maintained a massive database of star maps pertaining to trade and space flight, and by appropriating it for their own use, the Imperial Navy could significantly diminish its geographical handicap.

One hundred and fifty-eight years ago, during the Dagon Annihilation, alliance Commander in Chief Lin Pao and Chief of Staff Yusuf Topparole had lured a navigationally ignorant Imperial Navy into the mazelike Dagon Stellar Region, serving them grand and total annihilation on a platter. But had the invaders used precise star maps along with their fearless leadership and precisely laid-out planning, the server would have become the served.

Yang brushed away his bangs, thinking how much more fortunate those great commanders of half a century ago were compared to him. Lin Pao and Yusuf Topparole had only the battlespace to worry about. Back then, the democratic republic abounded in vitality. Its citizens' faith and reverence was based on a government they'd chosen of their own volition and out of a sense of personal responsibility. The government took care of its functions thoroughly, and there wasn't a single frontier soldier who questioned the efficacy of his government.

Military affairs could never make up for sterile politics. It was a historical fact: there were no examples of politically inferior countries achieving ultimate military success. All great conquerors, without exception, started out as talented politicians. Politics could make up for military failures but never the reverse. Military affairs were one part of politics—the most truculent, most uncivilized, and clumsiest part. Only those who'd become mental slaves to incompetent politicians and arrogant military men conceived of military power as a miracle drug.

When Commander in Chief Lin Pao's resounding success in the Dagon Annihilation was reported to the capital—"Get two hundred thousand bottles of champagne ready!"—High Council chairman of the alliance Manuel Juan Patricio had been playing a round of 3-D chess with National Defense Committee chairman Cornell Youngblood in a room of his official residence. Upon opening the message delivered by the chairman's secretary, the council chairman held his breath, hardly changing his expression, and turned to the young defense chairman, who was eager for an explanation.

"It seems those rascals have accomplished a formidable task. If this conflict is truly over, now I'll have to call about a hundred bars and taverns on the visiphone."

The glory of a bygone, legendary age. Yang held up an invisible champagne glass with one hand. Glorifying the past, someone once said, was like looking at the distant profile of a woman from behind as she walked out and deciding she was beautiful without ever seeing her face firsthand. Setting aside the truth of that simile, the past was nothing one could lasso back to the present. For Yang, dealing with this situation was just another facet of reality.

IV

Julian was likewise busy preparing for his departure, but because his daily management skills far exceeded those of his superior, he was ahead of schedule. Heavier on his mind was Yang's drinking, about which Julian urged caution.

"Alcohol is man's best friend. Can I abandon a friend?" said Yang amiably.

"That's what people say, but what about the alcohol?"

"Alcohol wants nothing more than to be drunk. People were drinking it five thousand years ago. And they're still drinking it now."

"I can see that."

"And five thousand years from now, you can be sure they'll be drinking it still. Assuming there's anyone left to drink it."

"I'm not worried about five thousand years from now, I'm worried about next month and thereafter."

Despite his attempts at blocking the rebuttal, Julian didn't press the young commander any further, not wanting to leave on a sour note. Yang's alcohol consumption had increased dramatically over the years, and it was beginning to affect his health. Julian changed topics.

"And then there's the matter of you waking up in the morning, or lack thereof. Can you even get yourself up promptly at 7:00 a.m. without me dragging you out of bed?"

"Sure I can," Yang declared, reflexively bluffing without confidence.

"Can you really? I wonder."

"Now look here, Julian. If anyone else heard this conversation, they'd think Yang Wen-li couldn't even take care of himself, wouldn't you say?"

Yang was clearly ribbing him, but Julian shrugged his shoulders in anticipation of Yang's self-examination.

"Before you came into my life, I took care of myself just fine. I did a splendid job managing the house and grounds without anyone's help."

"Made friends with mildew and dust, did we?"

Julian chuckled. Yang made to answer with a look of displeasure but failed, responding instead with a nervous laugh. He remembered the first time they had met face-to-face, one early spring day four years before. The morning sun had shown the stubbornness of winter's traces, the air thick and lifeless.

A pajama-clad Yang had lain stretched out on the sofa, wondering how to spend what promised to be a long day off.

Yang's rule was that days off were for catching up on his work—not that he had anyone to go on a date with anyway. Noticing his kettle was empty, he'd gone to pour himself a cup of black tea when a knock came at the door.

After being called on his door phone for the third time, he opened the front door, only to find standing on his porch a dark-brown-eyed boy of around twelve, holding a suitcase with both hands like some oversized accessory. From beneath his flaxen hair, stuck to his forehead with diluted sweat, Julian looked squarely at the young head of the Yang household.

"Captain Yang Wen-li, I presume?"

Yang wondered whether answering was necessary, since the boy's question had answered itself. All the same, Yang stopped himself from irresponsibly sending the boy next door, nodding instead.

"How do you do? My name is Julian Mintz. I've been assigned to take care of your house. Pleased to make your acquaintance."

When Julian was fourteen or fifteen, Yang asked himself whether having his ward take on additional duties would interfere with Julian's love life. His doubt disappeared like the frost in spring sunlight when he heard one name:

"I'm here by introduction of His Excellency Commodore Caselnes."

At that time, Yang was a captain and Caselnes was a commodore. Per the so-called Travers's Law, orphans of those killed in action were fostered by other military families.

"Back then, you'd come out onto the porch with a toothbrush in your mouth," said Julian.

But Yang had no memory of his crude appearance. He assumed the boy was imagining things, but when left to others' judgment, the scales of faith always tilted in favor of Julian's claims. Once, Caselnes had turned to Yang and said that whenever he wanted any kind of information or data about him, he would go ask Frederica Greenhill for anything related to government business and go ask Julian for personal matters. And why didn't they just come to him? The answer was resolute.

"Everybody wants accurate information. But can someone who mistakes left and right in a mirror draw an accurate self-portrait?"

Yang objected to the metaphor, but couldn't help thinking it was his personal duty to take to heart the harder-to-swallow assessments of friends and subordinates. Then again, it could also have been Caselnes's way of mocking his junior classmate.

Julian wasn't the only one preparing for departure. Merkatz, who'd responded to his inaugural appointment to be secretary of defense for the galactic legitimate imperial government, and his aide, Commodore von Schneider, were likewise indisposed. In the end, Merkatz had to accept the position, after which Yang had no choice but to see him off. Von Schneider, for his part, would be standing in Merkatz's shadow wherever he went.

When Julian expressly visited Caselnes to say his goodbyes, the man responsible for introducing the boy to Yang said, "Don't go sleeping around. You'll make Charlotte cry."

It was hard to tell whether he was joking.

Julian smiled uncomfortably, making a mental note of his own reaction.

Julian's expert dogfighting instructor, Lieutenant Commander Olivier Poplin, went against Caselnes's grain.

"If only you'd stayed on here at Iserlohn another year. There's so much left for you to do."

"Yes, I wish I could've learned more from you."

"Yeah. And not just about spartanian piloting. I would rather have taught you more enjoyable things," said the young ace pilot, knowing Yang would have had a hard time holding his tongue during this conversation.

"When I was seventeen, I took down my first enemy plane *and* my first woman. I've been racking up victories ever since. Both are now in the triple digits."

Julian voiced his dry amazement and made no signs of wanting to say more. Had von Schönkopf been there, he would have offered some cynical comment—"It's always been quantity over quality with you"— but the sixteen-year-old Julian didn't have the wherewithal to voice it. By no influence of Yang's, sometimes Julian blushed just being in the presence of Frederica Greenhill. He was still that way. Poplin felt like he was losing a protégé.

Poplin's comrade, Lieutenant Ivan Konev, first answered Julian's farewell with a "Take care of yourself out there," adding, "I think I've got a cousin on Phezzan. I've never met him, though. Phezzan is enormous." He shook Julian's hand and wished him well one last time.

Chief of staff and rear admiral Murai, a meticulous man endowed with a fine intellect and meticulousness, as well as noble management skills, was in a league of his own. He rather had the air of a bureaucrat, and Julian had never gotten close to him, but Julian couldn't afford not to give him parting regards. Welcoming the ceremonious boy into his room, Murai changed his tone after giving the usual formal encouragement.

"Well, I guess I can say it now. It was my job to make Admiral Yang look better. Oh, don't give me that look. I'm not trying to complain or be self-deprecating here."

Even as Murai was smiling, Julian realized he'd probably accused him with his eyes of being unfair to Yang.

"Admiral Yang is that rare individual who combines both the temperament of a commander and the talent of a staff officer. If such a person needed a staff officer, what would other people think? Knowing that, I just consulted with him about tactical operations."

Isn't that *the truth*, thought Julian, but this time buried that thought behind a neutral expression. Murai smiled again.

"When I aspired to serve as staff officer to the hero of El Facil, I asked myself, what is the role I must carry out? I didn't have an answer until after the fall of Iserlohn. Only then did I understand my role. I deliberately recited commonsense arguments and went against Admiral Merkatz. It was a tough time. You understand what I'm getting at?"

"Yes, I understand. But why tell me this now?" Julian couldn't help but ask, shedding the skin of his surprise.

"Why, indeed. It may not make much sense to talk like this, but it means there's something in you that makes others trust you. I suppose both Admiral Yang and the rest of the gang tell you all sorts of things. Don't ever lose that. It might just be your greatest asset down the line."

Although that last bit had come off as a stale sermon, Julian knew it was given in good faith. He gave his thanks, thinking he knew one possible reason why Murai had made such a good staff officer for Yang. Yang had justifiable reasons for choosing Murai as his chief of staff. But until hearing it from Murai himself, Julian had never thought he needed such insight into Yang.

Julian said his goodbyes to Rear Admiral Fischer, Commodore Patrichev, and Rear Admiral Attenborough in turn. Each expressed regret in his own way. Fischer clasped Julian on the shoulder in silence, as did Patrichev, if a little too forcefully, and offered a few token words of encouragement. Attenborough gave him a rusty old copper key, saying it was a good-luck charm. When Julian asked what kind of luck it had brought him, Iserlohn's youngest admiral gave him a broad smile.

"Well, back when I was in my first year at the academy, whenever I used to break curfew and climb the fence, a certain on-duty upperclassman by the name of Yang Wen-li looked the other way."

And now that same insolent upperclassman was worried about Julian's safety and was making von Schönkopf laugh.

"That's why Machungo's going with him. You won't find a more reliable bodyguard."

"But not even Machungo can be with Julian twenty-four hours a day."

"Don't worry—Julian's combat skills, with or without a sidearm, are better than yours, Your Excellency."

"When you talk about me like that…"

"Does it make you uncomfortable?"

"No, just confused. Should I admire him or be worried that it doesn't take much to be better than me?"

"Let's go with the former."

Yang gave up on the matter and took his leave.

That evening, at dinner, Yang had a gift for Julian.

"Take this with you when you go. It may be of some use."

Yang held out a debit card from Polaris, one of Phezzan's five banks. The moment he took it, Julian was shocked to see that a new account had been opened in his name and that it contained an amount equivalent to half of Yang's yearly salary. He tried to give it back, but the young black-haired admiral held up his hands in gentle refusal.

"Really, I insist. Just take it with you. At least you'll never have to worry about how to spend your money."

Yang, of course, made a good living for himself. Not only because he earned a high salary for his age, but also because he had a sense of economy that Julian himself had never developed. When Julian became a civil servant, Yang had expressed his doubts over, and dissatisfaction with, the wage system when his taxes suddenly spiked. Julian, in his own carelessness, had never realized he was no longer a dependent. It was only Yang's frugality that saved him from bankruptcy. When it came to household supplies and attire, Yang was content with cheap goods and faded cotton shirts, so long as they weren't in bad taste. When shopping for sunglasses, after listening to his employees rattle on for half an hour about niche brands, he had bought the most common mass-produced ones he could find. As far as he was concerned, sunglasses and other like accessories were fine so long as they had a little color. Neither did he care about first editions when buying books, and as far as alcohol was concerned, he didn't have the palate to distinguish between a vintage wine from 760 years ago and one from 762 years ago. He had a weak attachment to material things. When it came to food, he did eat often at restaurants designated for high-ranking officers, but this was only so he could enjoy a certain freedom of conversation.

Yang had gotten the idea for this sensible gift by borrowing from Frederica's wisdom, and wasn't so narrow-minded as to feel ashamed at having done so. One could, however, trace this motivation back to his father. "Having as much money as you can control," he used to say, "guarantees uninterrupted freedom."

"Thank you very much. I won't waste a cent of it, Admiral."

Acceptance of Yang's good favor was the best way to reward it.

"I don't doubt it. Use it whenever you feel it's necessary. One more thing. Would you deliver this letter to Admiral Bucock for me?"

Yang gave Julian a handwritten letter.

The letter would later become recognized proof that Yang Wen-li was no run-of-the-mill strategist, but an unimaginably significant one. It was, of course, impossible for Julian to see that far into the future. Its importance didn't need to be stressed either way.

"I'll be sure to deliver it to him personally."

"See that you do."

Yang smiled before his expression changed.

"Listen, Julian, this isn't just anybody's life we're talking about here. It's *your* life. Always remember to live for your own sake first. Beyond that…"

Yang seemed poised to say more, but the well of his words ran temporarily dry. When he spoke again, it was impersonal.

"Don't catch cold. Stay healthy."

"And you as well, Admiral," said Julian, shoring up the waves of his emotion. "Please try to cut down on the drinking if you can, all right? And eat more vegetables."

"Man, you never quit, do you?"

Yang winked twice and took Julian's hand. Yang's was warm, dry, and soft to the touch. Julian would vividly remember that sensation for a long time to come.

At noon on September 1, Julian Mintz left for Iserlohn Fortress aboard *Thanatos III*, along with Guest Admiral Merkatz, Lieutenant von Schneider, and Warrant Officer Machungo.

Neither Julian nor Merkatz, nor even the fortress's so-called master, Yang, were fond of ceremony, but the send-off was conducted on a scale some might have called grand. Admiral Yang, known for his "two-second speeches," broke precedent by giving one a hundred times as long. Within what common sense still deemed a very short time, his innermost, if somewhat childish, thoughts became transparent to everyone in attendance.

The departing received bouquets from ladies, but Julian Mintz, youngest ensign in history to become a resident officer on Phezzan, had the honor of a bouquet from Caselnes's daughter, Charlotte Phyllis. This gesture garnered enthusiastic applause.

The uniquely Iserlohnian event was not advertised to the public. Yang and Caselnes were at first opposed to the tradition of giving flowers. "You can't eat bouquets," they'd said.

What settled it once and for all was something the commander's aide,

Lieutenant Frederica Greenhill, said after hearing out numerous irresponsible ideas from the other men.

"For this kind of thing, a ceremony is necessary, but formality not so much."

Against this calmly delivered assertion, they had no objection.

"And so, I ask you, my comrades, who is the wisest man in our lofty fortress of Iserlohn?"

The story that ended with this very rude question made those who heard it laugh; those who brought up the subject barely tittered.

Caselnes and the others decided that either Rear Admiral von Schönkopf or Lieutenant Commander Poplin, if not both, were guilty of spreading the rumor throughout the fortress, although there was no way to prove it. The episode itself was not entirely believed to have taken place. In any case, Yang and, oddly enough, Caselnes felt increasingly useless. They were so impressed by the efficiency with which Frederica Greenhill managed everything, inspiring Poplin and the others to get their acts together.

After the ceremony, when Frederica was called to Yang's private room, the black-haired commander sat rudely with his feet stretched out on his desk and, with a brandy glass in one hand, gazed at the great ocean of stars outside his observation window in a funk. The brandy bottle, now two-thirds empty, sat proudly on his desk.

"Admiral," said Frederica softly, after a moment's hesitation.

Yang turned around with the expression of a boy caught misbehaving, but Frederica wasn't in the mood for games today.

"He's gone now."

"Yeah."

Yang nodded, placed his empty glass on the desk, and started to pour another before putting it back. Frederica couldn't tell whether his restraint was for her sake or for that of someone who was no longer there.

"I suppose he'll be a bit taller the next time we meet," he said to himself.

Little did he know how true that would turn out to be.

CHAPTER 6:

I

"ORDER OF ONE HUNDRED MILLION people and one million ships."

Those words were being whispered throughout the halls of Imperial Military Command Headquarters after the stern declaration of war on the Free Planets Alliance and the legitimate imperial government by the fleet's supreme commander, Duke Reinhard von Lohengramm. After "discipline by military force" was declared, those young commoners not on the military roll came running in droves from their jobs and schools to the navy's recruitment offices. Among them were many who'd quit the service and returned temporarily to their hometowns and were now throwing their tranquil lives away to resume their place in the ranks.

Reinhard had succeeded in fomenting among the common man a hatred for the Goldenbaum Dynasty's elitist despotism, and leavened it with a fresh enmity toward the Free Planets Alliance.

"Down with the remnants of the high nobles! Don't let them take over again! Protect the rights of the people!"

"Down with the high nobles' coconspirators, the so-called Free Planets Alliance!"

Within a week's time, these slogans were on everyone's lips. Although Reinhard had played a part in drawing them out, they grew on their own. By his declaration of war, Reinhard hadn't necessarily urged his people into action in any direct way. If anything, he would have preferred to conceal the fact that the Free Planets Alliance had passively allied with the high nobles, so that it might seem a more deliberate act. Above all, he would have covered up his own complicity in the plot to abduct the emperor. The people harbored their own sense of danger. Social and economic justice had been snatched right out of their hands, and they couldn't help but fear restoration of the privileged class.

For the first time in a while, Admiral Neidhart Müller of the Imperial Navy showed his face at the Sea Eagle admirals' club on the first Saturday of September. That morning, having just been released from a long hospital recovery, Müller had finished his speech to Reinhard's council, received his notice of return to active duty, and then gone straight to the club where his comrades were sure to be hanging out. He was the best of the Imperial Navy's admirals and, apart from Reinhard, the youngest. He was also a bachelor and had no need to rush back to his official residence.

"I was starting to think I'd be chained to that hospital bed forever. Hope you weren't too worried about me."

He smiled as Mittermeier and von Reuentahl stood up from the small poker table to welcome him. The Gale Wolf ordered a coffee from the academy student working as the club's waiter and offered Müller a seat.

"I still had a hard time getting discharged. Hearing all that talk of the 'order of one hundred million people and one million ships' was just the kick in the pants I needed."

"It's spreading like wildfire," said Müller, taking a seat. "But is it the only way to mobilize the people?"

Von Reuentahl had a twinkle in his heterochromatic eyes.

"Well, it's quantitatively possible. But in coordinated practice, that's a different story. First, there's the problem of supply. It's not easy feeding a hundred million people."

"Practice is always harder than theory."

Mittermeier was well received. Vexed by repeated delays and interruptions in supplies on the front lines, they knew all too well that war wasn't manageable on paper alone. It was difficult to express the magnitude of their anger and regret whenever they saw mountains of provisions spoiled by neglect, after plans of production were thwarted by lack of transport. Provision shortages had caused them to abandon preciously fortified bases and return home more times than they cared to admit.

After a few conversational rounds, von Reuentahl got up and bid farewell to his two comrades. Watching his sleek figure as it disappeared through the door, Müller smiled at the Gale Wolf.

"I hear that Admiral von Reuentahl has taken a new lover."

"Looks that way," answered Mittermeier with a wry smile, but his expression told of far less mundane thoughts behind it.

It was clear to see that von Reuentahl was a philanderer, but he also had the unusual quirk of being a serial monogamist. Although none of his relationships had ever lasted long, whenever he made a woman his partner, his mismatched eyes never looked another woman's way. Maybe it was for this reason that the women he'd so indifferently tossed aside still believed his heart belonged to them, and so cases of resentment were surprisingly few and far between. Not that he cared what the other men thought of him.

"Von Reuentahl has indeed changed girls."

"It's been five months already."

Mecklinger was the literatus of the group and was prone to writing cynical phrases like "Last year's flowers shall not be this year's flowers" in the margins of his notebook. Of course, von Reuentahl never paid any mind to cynicism or criticism. Mittermeier knew his comrade's debauchery was the result of the severe trauma of his mother gouging out his right eye, but he wasn't about to go spilling that secret. As far as that incident was concerned, he could only obscure the situation with vague statements like "Any woman who falls in love with him is just as bad as he is."

"Why do women cling to their pillows during a thunderstorm anyway?"

He'd once asked this question with a straight face. Even Mittermeier was stumped.

"I assume because they're scared," was all he could muster.

Von Reuentahl disagreed.

"Why would they cling to their pillow when they could cling to me? Do you think a pillow's going to save them?"

Although it was useless asking for a rational explanation, as with military tactics, the young admiral with heterochromactic eyes insisted on rationality.

"That's how women are. It's pointless to ask. They don't even know themselves."

Mittermeier yielded. He couldn't hold a candle to his comrade's conquests off the battlefield. At any rate, he had a family at home, but at that time von Reuentahl wouldn't recognize the authority of a married man.

"Don't put on airs. There's no way you understand women better than I do."

From there, the atmospheric pressure began to drop.

"I understand Evangeline. Evangeline's a woman."

"Your wife doesn't count."

"And how is it you know such things?"

Putting down his beer mug, von Reuentahl lowered his voice.

"It's always Evangeline this and Evangeline that. Do you enjoy being tied to one woman? All it does it limit your options. I don't get it."

To say these conversations between commanders praised as the best and brightest of the Imperial Navy were lacking in dignity would be an understatement. The last one had apparently turned into a fistfight. Not that they remembered anything about what had transpired. Witnesses, too, kept their mouths shut, and so the next day they could only guess as to why their bodies hurt all over.

"With Admiral von Reuentahl hogging all the merchandise, there aren't enough beautiful women to go around," said Mittermeier without the least bit of spite, and took a sip of the coffee brought over to him by the student waiter. There were rumors that he'd gone through a bad breakup in his sublieutenant days, but he just smiled quietly, and in an incongruous manner, neither confirming nor denying those rumors. Of the young man who would come to be known as "Iron Wall Müller," it was a different side to fame on the battlefield.

II

Initially, seventeen names attended the Supreme War Council held on September 19 at the Lohengramm admiralität: Imperial Marshal Reinhard von Lohengramm; his chief aide Commodore von Streit; secondary aide Lieutenant von Rücke; chief secretary Countess von Mariendorf; senior admirals von Oberstein, von Reuentahl, and Mittermeier; and admirals Wahlen, Müller, Fahrenheit, Lutz, Kessler, Wittenfeld, Mecklinger, Steinmetz, Lennenkamp, and von Eisenach.

Kessler was responsible for maintaining public order in the capital, and in that capacity had been asked about his involvement in the emperor's defection. He had been slapped with a warning and a pay cut and had been placed under temporary house arrest, but that had been lifted and his formal seat restored.

The Imperial Navy's entire armada was on full standby for first launch, and if given the order by Imperial Marshal von Lohengramm, a grand fleet numbering approximately 150,000 warships, big and small, could be at the planet Odin within twenty-four hours.

Reinhard's tall, elegant figure took the seat of honor. His golden hair glistened luxuriously like a lion's mane as he received the salutes of his admirals.

"I've gathered you all here today to hear out your opinions concerning these rebels calling themselves the Free Planets Alliance and a concrete method of reprimanding them using military force."

So prefacing the meeting, Reinhard made his important, if also detached, declaration.

"But first, let me tell you my plan, which is to not worry about taking down Iserlohn Fortress as we have in the past, but to use another corridor as our route of invasion. To put it simply, we will be invading alliance territory via the Phezzan Corridor. Phezzan will renounce its political and military neutrality, and join our camp."

For a moment, a voiceless commotion stirred the air in the conference room. Reinhard signaled gently with a hand for order.

The admirals glued their eyes to the door, each making an expression in accordance with his respective character.

Standing next to the captain of Reinhard's personal guard, Günter Kissling, was a very familiar face: Phezzan's commissioner, Nicolas Boltec.

"He has agreed to help us. Not without compensation, of course."

After formally introducing Boltec to all present, Reinhard suppressed all skepticism. Reinhard had made a secret pact with the vigilant commissioner. Seeing the advantage of Boltec using every means possible to grant the Imperial Navy passage through the Phezzan Corridor, Reinhard would dismiss Landesherr Rubinsky as soon as he received Boltec's appeal and would seat him as Rubinsky's replacement. Although Reinhard hadn't said as much, it didn't take long for the admirals to put it all together.

"You mean to say he's selling out his own nation?" asked Wittenfeld, only thinly veiling his disgust for Boltec.

The commissioner sympathized and made a pained expression.

"With all due respect, the only thing I'm selling is Phezzan's nominal independence. This action says nothing about Phezzan's true intentions or profits. By doing away with such a useless formality, Phezzan stands to gain substantially."

"Dress it up however you like. You'll find a reason to sell your parents or betray your friends eventually."

"That's enough, Wittenfeld." With that, the golden-haired imperial marshal dulled the brave admiral's sharp tongue. "If not for his cooperation, we'd have a difficult time fitting our fleet through Phezzan's doors. I fully intend on repaying his assistance with commensurate remuneration and courtesy. I've gathered you all here today to hear out your opinions, of course. What say you, von Reuentahl?"

"Pardon me for saying this, but I'm not so sure about putting our unconditional trust in a scheming Phezzanese," asserted von Reuentahl with polite indifference. "As soon we've passed through the Phezzan Corridor and invaded alliance territory, if they decide to change their tune and seal off the corridor, we'll be sitting ducks. Without knowing the layout of enemy territory, we'd be putting our supplies and communications at too great a risk, don't you think?"

Wittenfeld objected. "Von Reuentahl's worries are only natural, but even if Phezzan resorted to such cowardly measures, wouldn't we have enough brute force to put them in their place?"

"Are you saying we'd have the fleet reverse course through the Phezzan Corridor?"

"Yes, Phezzan's military strength is no match for ours. I'm sure we could frustrate their schemes adequately enough."

"And if the Alliance Armed Forces attacked the moment we turned our backs, what then?" asked von Reuentahl. "That would put us at a disadvantage. Not that I think we'd lose, but we can't overlook the sacrifice."

The soldier reciting this conservative theory had often been unable to escape the slander of being a coward, but neither was there anyone in the entire Imperial Navy who could cause von Reuentahl to incite such rejections from others. Wittenfeld was glum yet silent, and none of the other admirals were willing to dispute him. Reinhard opened his mouth.

"Von Reuentahl's remarks make sense, but I fully intend to invade the alliance through the Phezzan Corridor. Assuming that the Iserlohn Corridor is our only route of invasion, reducing the scope of our own strategic choices would reproduce the folly of the Alliance Armed Forces, which paved the way to the fortress with the corpses of their men. It's by human design that we cannot pass through the Phezzan Corridor, not some law that has existed since time immemorial. We're under no obligation to share in the alliance's illusions. Passage through the Phezzan Corridor is our best option, if only because it grants us the element of surprise."

Reinhard looked around, making sure his point was getting across before he continued.

"Now then, first we'll advance our troops in the direction of the Iserlohn

Corridor, just as they expect. Far more troops than were moved under Kempf and Müller this spring. This will, of course, be a diversion."

Reinhard's white cheeks were flushed. It was neither politics nor subterfuge, but strategy and tactics that filled his prodigious self with exaltation.

"With the alliance's focus concentrated on Iserlohn, our main force will pass through the Phezzan Corridor on its way to invading alliance territory. Yang Wen-li is at Iserlohn. Any of the alliance's other military forces and commanders aren't worth our breath."

"It is, I think, as you say," said the Gale Wolf, looking slightly doubtful, "but there is the matter of Yang Wen-li. We must consider the possibility that he'll make the long haul from Iserlohn to retaliate against our main force's movements."

"In that case, we should attack Yang Wen-li from the rear, making him a martyr for his democratic cause."

To Reinhard's proud declaration, most of the admirals made expressions of assent, but von Oberstein was staring into space with his artificial eyes.

"Do you think it'll be that easy?" said von Reuentahl.

Wolfgang Mittermeier shot him a glance. For one so blunt, it was unlike him to give in to anxiety. No one seemed to notice.

"I would like to make it go well."

Whether consciously or not, Reinhard had nimbly engaged von Reuentahl's remarks, forcing a transparent smile to his elegant lips. From past to present, those who harbored hatred for Reinhard and denied his abilities hardly recognized the beauty of that smile.

"As would I."

The young heterochromatic admiral smiled in kind. Mittermeier loosened the belt of nervousness constricting his heart. Immediately after Karl Gustav Kempf had died in battle at the Iserlohn Corridor, von Reuentahl had surprised Mittermeier by voicing his distrust for Reinhard. The next day, he'd joked it was the alcohol, but although Mittermeier was sympathetic toward that excuse, he couldn't prohibit a vague anxiety from patrolling his inner streets. Von Reuentahl didn't like holding grudges, nor did he like letting other people in on them. At least he could be content in knowing he'd never spoken or acted out of turn.

"And what shall we call this grand operation?" asked Müller.

Reinhard smiled with satisfaction. He threw up a lock of his golden bangs, speaking almost musically.

"I dub it 'Operation Ragnarök.'"

"Ragnarök?!"

The admirals muttered to themselves. The reverberations of that name made them tremble with perverse excitement. If these long-serving, brave soldiers had for one moment feared the demise of planetary civilization as they knew it, neither could they imagine a more perfect name for their conquest. The name itself guaranteed success, or so their momentary delusion assured them. They knew the journey ahead wasn't going to be easy, and soon their faces grew stern, but their ambition and ardor as soldiers in troubled times was revived. That much was real.

The admirals spoke up in succession. Each demanded participation in this unprecedented operation, knowing his name would be forever written into the final chapter of the Free Planets Alliance's 250-year history.

III

After the admirals had adjourned, Senior Admiral von Oberstein stayed behind to go over details of their next meeting.

"We'd do well to err on the side of caution as far as Boltec is concerned, Your Excellency."

Reinhard lifted his shapely eyebrows.

"At least Boltec will be easier to keep under control than that Black Fox, Rubinsky."

"Granted, but suddenly we have a different problem on our hands. Namely, whether Boltec will be able to keep Phezzan under control. He's capable enough as an assistant but is otherwise nothing more than a shrewd mouse siphoning the power of a black fox."

"Are you saying he lacks the ability to rise above the others?"

"I'd be just as troubled if he had *too* much ability. But if he can't muster enough power to suppress all those dissidents, he'll end up standing in the way of our fleet."

Reinhard dismissed his chief of staff's pessimistic opinion with a laugh.

"We might as well expect him to have that level of power. However much he has, he'll have to run around like mad to keep those dissidents down if he's going to hold on to his position and authority. Naturally, he'll be the target of hatred and opposition. If I take care of him myself before things get to that point, then I can effectively handle whoever replaces him. And without fear of how others might react."

"I see, so you've thought ahead that far?"

The artificial-eyed chief of staff made no effort to hide how impressed he was.

"Forgive me. I should never have doubted for a moment. Please, proceed however you see fit."

Von Oberstein's admiration meant nothing to the elegant imperial marshal. His thoughts were already somewhere else.

"This is how I'm thinking we can use him once we've subjugated the Free Planets Alliance. Don't you think so, Chief of Staff?"

"I do." Von Oberstein nodded. "There will surely be those who desire the position of secretary-general of the alliance in support of the new empire's authority and military power. Shall we seed a candidate now?"

Reinhard gave a silent nod, cupping the wings of his imagination around a lone figure.

Yang Wen-li. The youngest and most resourceful general of the Alliance Armed Forces. Military men decorated at such a young age tended to be jealous of smaller achievements. Assuming he was content with being forced into the position of secretary-general of the new empire, would he be able to steadfastly maintain loyalty to his democratic nation? It was a significant proposition.

He had to stop letting others play around with his destiny and make them rule over their own destinies instead. Reinhard had thought this way ever since he'd been a boy, when things were stolen from him that should never have been stolen. Reinhard could no longer justify these infractions unconditionally. He'd discovered any number of reasons to ostracize himself from the old regime of the Galactic Empire and the Free Planets Alliance, and grab all the power for himself. The imminent Lohengramm Dynasty would stop at nothing to bring about universal peace. His reign, compared to that of the old regime, was fairer and, compared to the Free Planets Alliance, far more efficient. At least he would never entrust a large fleet to those debauched high nobles, who could only boast of their pedigree and family connections or shake the power of agitating politicians who moved an ignorant populace with their sophistry and pandering to public interests. Even to a man like Yang Wen-li, the path to might was wide open. And yet, no matter how his numerous talents came together, Reinhard knew he could never make up for the loss of his late redheaded friend a year before.

Hildegard von Mariendorf had lingering misgivings about Reinhard's strategy for full-spectrum hegemony. She said as much when they were alone.

"Is there no way to a peaceful coexistence with the Free Planets Alliance?"

The question was a rhetorical one, devoid of value beyond the asking.

"No. They had their chance," said Reinhard a little too indifferently, so that Hilda wondered what was weighing on his mind. "True Machiavellians would've seen no point in getting sentimental over the emperor's age. If only they'd apprehended and deported the emperor and his kidnappers, it would have been beyond my power to take either political or military action against them. They've signed their own death warrant."

Reinhard believed that second-rate Machiavellians holding a monopoly on power was the sign of a ruined country. In his mind, he'd arrived at a crucial point when, in conjunction with the inevitable and the historically indeterminate, the Goldenbaum Dynasty and the Free Planets Alliance were squandering their own destinies. Nevertheless, Reinhard couldn't stand to think of himself as a mere tool of history. He had every intention of bringing the Goldenbaum Dynasty to ruin and lifting Rudolf's tenacious five-century curse from humanity's shoulders. But still…

"Fräulein."

"Yes, Duke von Lohengramm?"

"Do you find my ways unscrupulous?"

Hilda was at a momentary loss. The look in those ice-blue eyes was a little too serious.

"And if I said no, would it please Your Excellency?" she said at last, not knowing the answer he was fishing for.

The young duke adorned his face with a wry smile.

"I'm grateful to you, fräulein. Truly. Had I gone to that mountain villa myself, I'm sure my sister wouldn't have seen me. She never would've agreed to my guards if you hadn't persuaded her."

Hilda sensed a difference between Reinhard's way of doing things as a ruler and the boyish frankness of this fraternal regret. She knew it was silly to wonder which was the real Reinhard, but couldn't help but imagine which of those skins he'd end up wearing.

"Although my sister hates me, I would never undo what I've done. If I divert from the path to leadership at this stage in the game, who else will restore unity and harmony to the universe? Am I to entrust the future of the human race to the Free Planets Alliance or to those demagogues of the old regime?"

Thinking he'd made his point well enough, Reinhard was suddenly perturbed. His ice-blue eyes were filled with a hard and furious light, and he recovered an expression worthy of a dictator ruling over twenty-five billion citizens.

"Tomorrow, we announce the emperor's dethronement," declared Reinhard.

The seven-year-old emperor, Erwin Josef II, would be deprived of the throne, and in his place the eight-month-old Katharin, daughter of Viscount Pegnitz, would take over as empress. She would be the Goldenbaum Dynasty's youngest and final ruler. The moment he put an infant on the throne, Reinhard could easily imagine the outrage and hatred with which remnants of the old regime would response to this fearful spectacle.

"That golden brat profanes our power and tradition."

Such slogans of revenge were inevitable, but their "power" and "tradition" were nothing more than two towers of a castle in the sky invented by Rudolf von Goldenbaum five centuries earlier. And when those two pillars lost their structural integrity, the whole thing was sure to come crashing down. Reinhard felt oddly sorry for the old regime, delusions and all.

IV

Until nearly two years ago, Heidrich Lang had held an important bureaucratic position. As chief of the Bureau for the Maintenance of Public Order, his duties had involved rounding up political offenders and thought criminals, monitoring or suppressing free speech activities, and even dabbling in education and the arts. He was a fulcrum of authoritarianism within the imperial government, and as such exploited the full range of his power and influence. He stood to one day become secretary of the interior.

Lang had not been put to death as a member of the old regime by von Lohengramm's new order. There were two reasons for this: First, as chief of secret police he'd excelled at intelligence gathering and had amassed much in the way of valuable information on the nobles. Second, as a business specialist he possessed an awareness and loyalty all his own, and had expressed his intention to follow the new ruler after the former high nobles—whom Mittermeier maliciously dubbed the "shepherds"—fell. Lang saw no reason to despair over Reinhard's abolishment of the bureau, and he believed in himself enough to wait patiently for the day when the sun would again dispel the darkness.

His patience had paid off sooner than he'd expected. The military police, whose self-imposed disgruntlement was an apparent obligation of their work, were ordered by Senior Admiral von Oberstein's office to release him from house arrest.

Fortunately for Lang, von Oberstein's thorough investigation turned up no evidence to suggest he'd abused his authority in any way for personal gain. He was, among the higher-ups of the old regime, uniquely flawless in his personal conduct and was treated like a darling of the nobility despite disliking their company. He put all his diligence into his duties and was, not without reason, known as the "Hunting Dog."

Just looking at him, von Oberstein wanted to laugh—not that he would have said as much to his face. Lang's outward appearance was incongruous with his talents and achievements. Although he wasn't yet past forty, 80 percent of his brown hair had vanished. What little was left clung for dear life around his ears. His ashen eyes were big and restless. His lips were thick and red, although his mouth was small. His head was relatively big for someone of his short stature. His entire body was more than plump, and the skin covering it pink and glossy. In short, Heidrich Lang gave the visual impression of a healthy baby full of mother's milk, and guessing his professional duties by his appearance alone wouldn't have been easy for anyone with an active imagination. As chief of secret police, he stood out for not having a more coolheaded, grizzled exterior.

But it was his voice that showed just how unique he was. The average person would have thought such a man to have the high-pitched voice of a child. What came out of Lang's mouth was instead a solemn bass, like that of some ancient religious leader preaching the gospel to his believers. Those who stood ready to stifle their laughter were bowled over. Taking advantage of this contradiction caught his opponents off guard, and his bass had served him well as a weapon of interrogation.

But the man before him now, whose artificial eyes stared at him inorganically by way of a light computer, would decide whether Lang deserved consideration and then report back to the imperial prime minister, Duke von Lohengramm.

"Your Excellency Chief of Staff, you can spin it however you want, but government has only one reality."

Lang spoke emphatically, and von Oberstein had already been evaluating Lang's speech from word one.

"Oh, and what might that be?"

"Control of the many by the few."

Lang's voice was so much like that of a solitary man appealing to God that one almost expected a pipe organ to accompany him. Then again, holding full life-or-death authority as he did over Lang, von Oberstein was like God in that no matter how sincerely one spoke to him, it was never enough.

"We insist on democracy being rule of the many by free will, but I'd like to know your thoughts on that point."

"If the people number one hundred, fifty-one of them can claim majority rule. And when that majority is divided into so many factions, it only takes twenty-six of those to rule over that same hundred. In other words, it's possible for a mere fourth to rule the many. A conventional and reductionist view, I admit, but one that shows just how useless majority rule is as a democratic principle. I know a man of Your Excellency's intelligence will understand."

Von Oberstein ignored the knee-jerk flattery. Like his master, Reinhard, he couldn't help but notice that those who brownnosed him were always the ones who despised him. Ignoring that he was being ignored, Lang went on.

"Since the reality of government is control of the many by the few, I'm sure you'll agree that people like me are indispensable for keeping things in line."

"You mean the secret police?"

"Someone to maintain a system of public order."

It was a subtle turn of phrase, but von Oberstein again disregarded the man's modest self-assertion.

"The secret police may be convenient for those in power, but their very existence becomes a target of hatred. Although the Bureau for the Maintenance of Public Order was only recently dismantled, there are many who would punish you for overseeing it. People like that reformist Karl Bracke."

"Mr. Bracke has his own ideas, but all I've ever done is devote myself to the dynasty, never once exercising the limits of my authority for personal gain. Should you take my loyalty as cause for punishment, it won't turn out well for Duke von Lohengramm."

From beneath the clothes of this goodly intentioned advice, a holster of threat was beginning to peek out. If he was being accused not only for past misdeeds but also for his tenure at the bureau, then did he have something else in mind?

"It would seem Duke von Lohengramm doesn't care much for your existence, either."

"Duke von Lohengramm is first and foremost a soldier. It's only natural he'd try to subjugate the universe through grand battles. But sometimes the smallest false rumor may outrival a fleet of ten thousand ships, and defense becomes the best form of attack. I would expect nothing less than the utmost discernment and forbearance from both Duke von Lohengramm and Your Excellency."

"Never mind me. How do you intend to repay Duke von Lohengramm's forbearance? That's the crucial point here."

"Of course, by summoning my unconditional loyalty and all my meager talents in cooperation with the duke's military rule."

"That's all well and good, but it's pointless to restore the bureau, now that it's defunct. It would be tantamount to a retreat from our reform policies. We'll have to come up with another name."

Lang's childlike face was shining.

"I already have one in mind," he declared in his captivating bass, sounding for all like an out-of-place opera singer.

"The Domestic Safety Security Bureau. What do you think? Has a nice ring to it, no?"

Although he wasn't particularly inspired, the artificial-eyed chief of staff nodded.

"Old wine in a new skin."

"I'd say the wine also wants to be as new as possible."

"Very well. Give it your best shot."

Thus, Heidrich Lang redefined himself from bureau chief for the Maintenance of Public Order to chief of the Domestic Safety Security Bureau.

In anticipation of Operation Ragnarök, the Imperial Navy's top brass had secretly set things in motion. Von Reuentahl still had misgivings about making an ally of Phezzan. The thought of being so close aroused especial caution in him.

"His Excellency von Reuentahl is a worrier," said Mittermeier with a smile.

Their partner wasn't some naive young girl, but the old fox of Phezzan. Mittermeier, for his part, much preferred a swift military victory over giving Phezzan any room to lay a trap, but in the unlikely event that they failed, they would, as von Reuentahl had said, become sitting ducks.

"In that case, we'll have to procure our food supply right then and there if we're to feed our troops. And even if we succeed in that, we'll be branded as marauders."

Mittermeier felt compelled to disagree with his own sentiments. Nothing but dry, verbal decorations.

"I can handle being despised as conquerors, but being scorned as marauders is less than ideal."

"Even that depends on whether they're worth plundering in the first place. It would be merciless to be taken by those same scorched-earth tactics that bested us a year ago. You'll remember what a sorry state the Alliance Armed Forces were in then."

No matter how much, and by what rhetorical flourishes, he advertised his self-justification, when the reality of pillaging was close at hand, the people would never support their conquerors. Once they decided on a temporary destruction, developing their conquest into permanent unification would be far too disadvantageous if founded on the people's animosity.

"On that point, however, Lohengramm's thoughts on the matter override anything we say."

Neidhart Müller had humbly proposed that they refrain from discussing the matter to clear their heads. Mittermeier and von Reuentahl nodded, abandoning an argument that bore no signs of consummation, and shifted to more practical matters. Müller's remark had nonetheless provoked a private thought in von Reuentahl: *So it's all up to Lohengramm, is it?*

When it came to domestic affairs, the young, golden-haired imperial prime minister had always stood for righteousness. At least Reinhard's rule outrivaled the nobles' old regime in fairness. And perhaps he would see it through, down to every citizen in enemy territory.

Von Reuentahl was a man of ambition. He had the ambition of a hero of turbulent times who was already pondering the next step before finishing the one before. For the past year, a desire to overthrow his superiors and take their place had begun stirring in his heart like a dormant leviathan come to life. There was nothing inherent or delusional about it. If it turned out that Reinhard's abilities and luck exceeded his own, von Reuentahl would graciously give up his seat of supremacy, proof that only Reinhard was suitable to be their supreme ruler. But if he did anything to neglect that…

V

Although news of the imperial fleet's imminent large-scale dispatch was communicated to Phezzan via multiple channels, most people's reaction was "Here we go again." Even Phezzan's shrewd merchants had for more than a century been accustomed to a three-cornered contest and were convinced that nothing would change. They'd papered over the crack of needless killing, hoping against hope that it would foster their accumulation of wealth as they competed in their respective fields of investment, finance, production, and distribution. To them, it seemed unlikely that the Galactic Empire's grand fleet would fill in the Phezzan Corridor with an ocean of peace and prosperity, or that they would hold Phezzan's self-reliant merchants captive in some immaterial cell. Surely such plans had been devised on countless occasions in the past, to no avail. The landesherr's government managed everything for them, which was why they paid their taxes in the first place. They worked, and earned, for themselves. The bulk of Phezzan's general population shared that sentiment.

But one couldn't say the current landesherr embraced any selfless loyalty toward that same opinion. Since founder Leopold Raap, successive landesherrs had worried about whether the Phezzanese people and Earth would swear their devotion, and with Adrian Rubinsky, an end to all of this was at last foreseeable. But Rubinsky's heart was multidirectional, as suited him well.

"Where hardware is concerned, Iserlohn Fortress is impregnable. Furthermore, the best commander in the Alliance Armed Forces is there. It's just like those mediocre politicians to be so complacent."

Rubinsky was speaking to his aide Rupert Kesselring about the state of the alliance.

"But that sense of security has robbed the alliance's governing bodies of healthy judgment and brought about the worst decision they could've made. A quintessential example of a past success leading to present mistakes and robbing any hope for the future, if you ask me."

Rupert Kesselring wondered whether such moral instruction was of benefit to anyone. The landesherr was quite the laughingstock for convincing himself that he alone was an exception. His estranged son had been diligently digging his father's burial plot, but these days it seemed he wasn't the only one with a mind to grab a shovel.

"Commissioner Boltec's movements are of great interest to me."

A stinger was planted in Rupert Kesselring's voice. It was useless to try to conceal his malice anymore. For Rupert, the thought of that buffoon Boltec joining in the digging made him want to kick them both into the hole in one go.

"Boltec flashed his trump card too early. This allowed Duke von Lohengramm to turn the tables on him. I guess he was too eager for success."

"A surprisingly incompetent man."

The landesherr wasn't bothered by the implication that *he* had been the one guilty of appointing said incompetent man.

"Duke von Lohengramm one-upped him. Boltec is a hard worker and until now has been immune to failure, but he slipped off the last step."

"How do you propose we deal with him?" asked the young man, doing his best Mephistopheles impression, but there was no answer.

The thoughts of these three parties—Rubinsky, Rupert Kesselring, and Boltec—had entangled themselves into a giant helix.

It wasn't easy to choose the most offensive traitor among them. One thing was for certain: any one of them would sell out the other two in a heartbeat. That didn't mean they were keen on selling out Phezzan. Phezzan's wealth and vitality, to say nothing of its strategic position, would guarantee their present and future. With it they could level the playing field between the imperial prime minister, Reinhard von Lohengramm, and the Grand Bishop of Terra. No wonder they were reluctant to sell.

Rubinsky changed the subject.

"Incidentally, I understand that Ensign Julian Mintz has been appointed to the alliance commissioner's office."

"I hear he's Admiral Yang Wen-li's favorite errand boy. I wonder just how favored he was."

Rupert's scorn was even more garish than his father's large-scale reproductions.

"Anyway, he's just a sixteen-year-old brat. He can't do much of anything."

"When Duke von Lohengramm was sixteen, he'd already earned his stripes as a lieutenant commander. Julian Mintz is only moving at a slower pace."

"Isn't he just riding his guardian's coattails?"

"Perhaps, but his accolades are only increasing. Personally, I'd rather not be the one who mistook a tiger's cub for a cat."

Rupert Kesselring agreed. Looking back, at sixteen, had he not already resolved to bring his father down and seize his status and power? Would he not take by force that which his father would never give him? As an ancient wise man had once said, talent was like a stone thrown in water—its ripples magnified as they grew. Ambition and desire were no different. If so, then Rubinsky was naturally on his guard. But was similar suspicion, he wondered, being directed at him as well?

Rupert Kesselring turned the blade of his cold stare to his father's profile but looked away at once. As his father, Rubinsky still had power over him. Lust for power, fear of suspicion: Rubinsky embodied both, and both were worthy of Kesselring's hatred.

CHAPTER 7:
MILITARY ATTACHÉ ENSIGN MINTZ

I

COUNTLESS PETALS DANCED in a sea of faint light…

Before waking, Julian Mintz's entire body was overtaken by precious memories.

When I get up, I need to take a shower, brush my teeth, and prepare breakfast. Black tea of Shillong and arusha leaves, with milk. Three pieces of rye toast, cut in half. For spread, butter mixed with parsley and lemon juice. Next, sausage and apples pan fried in butter would be nice. Fresh salad and a simple egg dish. Yesterday was fried eggs, so today I'll make them scrambled, with milk…

Bubbles of light continued to float and pop, spraying the breath of reality on Julian. When his eyelids opened, his view was filled with morning, populated with the furniture in his room. Looking at his bedside clock, he saw that it was 6:30. It seemed that habit had permeated the boy down to the cellular level. He could've slept for another hour, but…

"*Oh seven hundred hours, Admiral, seven o'clock. Please get up. Breakfast is ready.*"

"*Please, five more minutes. No, four and a half minutes is enough. Make that four minutes and fifteen seconds.*"

"*Really, Admiral, you're so stubborn. Aren't you setting a bad example for your subordinates by sleeping in?*"

"My soldiers get along just fine without me."

"The enemy is closing in! If they take you by surprise and kill you where you lie, future historians will ridicule you for ages."

"The enemy is still sleeping, too, and future historians haven't even been born yet. Good night. At least it's still peaceful in my dreams…"

"Admiral!"

Four years ago, "admiral" had been "captain." Regardless, hadn't they had that same conversation a thousand times over? And in all that time, Yang had made no progress when it came to getting out of bed.

Julian sat up in his own bed and stretched. It felt strange being by himself and not having to worry about preparing breakfast. Julian jumped out of bed, anticipating his adaptation to the life of a soldier.

He took a shower, vigorously flexing his young muscles. He changed into uniform and carefully righted the angle of his black beret. With everything in order by seven o'clock, he still had time to kill. Getting up first always bothered the noncommissioned officers and soldiers, or so Yang had told him, but that was probably only partly true. Four hours remained until arrival at Phezzan, and his last meal aboard the ship had yet to be announced.

Julian stayed in the allied capital of Heinessen for a mere three days. During that time, he was shuffled every which way throughout this nucleus of the government and military. He felt like he was being led to the pinnacle of an exclusive, powerful society. Not unlike Yang, advancing beyond his age invariably upset others, and so he was more often poorly received than not.

Among the Defense Committee subbranches were Joint Operational Headquarters, Rear Services Headquarters, the Science and Technology Headquarters, and eleven others, including the departments of defense, field investigations, accounting, information, human resources, provisions, engineering, health, communications, and strategy. In cases where the department head was an active-duty soldier, high-ranking officers like admirals and vice admirals were appointed beneath him or her. The late Admiral Dwight Greenhill, father of Yang's aide Lieutenant Frederica Greenhill, had been a onetime director of field investigations. Julian was required to meet with the head of the human resources department, Vice Admiral Livermore, to receive an official notice for his military attaché assignment on Phezzan. His rank would be no higher than ensign, and once a military attaché, his status would fall under Livermore's direct purview.

Julian stuck to his appointment, but the preliminaries took longer than expected, resulting in a two-hour wait. He wondered if this was intentional but had enough to worry about—Yang's recent hearing, for one—without falling prey to useless suspicions. The inflexibility of a powerful society robbed human beings of their mental verve and weakened their naive loyalties to the state. As Julian was mulling over these somewhat exaggerated concepts, his name was called by an aide, and the boy was ushered into the vice admiral's office.

His time inside the office wasn't even one-fiftieth of the time he'd been kept waiting. He was greeted unceremoniously and handed his notice and insignia, after which he bowed to the slightly hunchbacked vice admiral and left.

Visiting space armada Commander in Chief Admiral Bucock was like crawling out of a sewer into fields of green. In addition to feeling relieved about safely delivering Yang's handwritten letter to its recipient, Julian was fond of the old admiral, as were Yang and Frederica, and it lifted his spirits just being able to meet with him again. Although Bucock was also in the middle of something and made him wait for an hour, this time Julian wasn't bothered by it in the least. Worrying was one bad habit he'd picked up from Yang.

"My, how you've grown," said the old admiral, welcoming him warmly. "Only natural, I suppose, considering I haven't seen you for a year and a half. You're at that age when you must be growing a centimeter every night."

"Commander in Chief, I'm glad to see you looking so well."

"What? Every day brings me closer to the gates of hell. I can't wait to see Emperor Rudolf boiling in a cauldron for all eternity. Which reminds me, did Vice Admiral Livermore have anything to say?"

"No, nothing. There was no informal talk whatsoever."

Bucock smiled, expecting as much. As a man affiliated with the Trünicht faction, Vice Admiral Livermore was always wanting to strengthen his own convictions and saw no reason to curry the favor of a sixteen-year-old boy. On the other hand, he was thought childish for resorting to abusive language and took pride in the fact that he said nothing that wasn't necessary in the context of official business.

Julian shook his head.

"Why would currying my favor improve Chairman Trünicht's impression of him?" said Julian with a slightly prankish glint in his dark-brown eyes. "I'm on Yang Wen-li's side, not Trünicht's."

"So you are. Perhaps you weren't aware of this, but the high council chairman asked for you personally. Chairman Islands is Trünicht's third arm, and that would seem to indicate his interest in you."

"I never asked for this!"

"I thought you might feel that way, but don't go shouting it from the rooftops. The last thing I'd want is for you to pick up any choice habits from me or Admiral Yang."

The old general smiled as if to a favorite grandchild and explained to him the chain of military command in which Trünicht's faction was involved. It wasn't fundamentally limited to Trünicht, nor to the Free Planets Alliance. What had always weighed heavily on the minds of civilian authorities was that ships in territories far from the capital might turn into the commander's private fleet or military clique, in defiance of central government control. Such a possibility was their constant nightmare. As a preventive measure, they considered using their own authority to keep key members of those forces from staying in one place. They had to be careful not to upset equilibrium between their military power and human resources.

"So my position here is part of that plan?"

"Yes, I'm afraid so."

Bucock stroked his chin.

"And when headquarters pulled Admiral Merkatz away from Admiral Yang, was that part of the same plan?"

Impressed by the tactical sense of Julian's question, the old admiral gave a deep nod.

"Yes, it was, at first."

From here on, the government was likely to pull advisors Caselnes and von Schönkopf away from Yang as well.

"But what's going to happen then? By weakening Admiral Yang, won't they just be strengthening the Imperial Navy's position?"

The foolishness of those in power trying to deal with situations through factional politics alone, and with such a flagrant disregard for logic, was beyond upsetting to Julian. Seats of power were, in and of themselves, cancers waiting to happen, and so long as men were content to sit in them, would not their limited field of vision and self-interest grow into an inevitable disease?

Bucock opened Yang's letter, nodding a few times as he read it. The possibility of imperial fleets passing through the Phezzan Corridor, from a purely tactical standpoint, had been considered. But long-term stability had diluted people's sense of danger to almost nothing, and countermeasures sat gathering dust, forgotten. From the start, both the alliance and the empire had drafted plans based on the assumption that each had comparable military strength and munitions-production power and that in their present state they were useless and ineffective.

Bucock summarized the contents of Yang's letter for him.

"Admiral Yang's proposal is as follows: If the Imperial Navy should pass through the Phezzan Corridor, thus preventing an invasion into alliance territory, we'll have to rely on the civil resistance of the Phezzanese people."

Specifically, that meant first rendering useless Phezzan's social and economic systems through systematic sabotage and general strikes on the part of Phezzan's civilian population. Via these means, they could stall the Imperial Navy's designs to make a supply base of Phezzan. Second, they would block the Phezzan Corridor with rows of civilian merchant ships, making it physically impossible for the Imperial Navy to advance.

"Do you think it will work?"

"Not necessarily. Admiral Yang himself says as much in his letter. In which case, placing the citizens of Phezzan before the Imperial Navy as a shield for the alliance would be a crime far greater than killing each other in the battlespace."

Julian was struck silent by this prospect.

"The people of Phezzan act on their own beliefs, and if forced, the strength of their convictions would never allow them to accede to another nation's military force. But if they waited until the Imperial Navy occupied Phezzan, effective and systematic resistance would be next to impossible."

At that point, wrote Yang, it would be necessary to start groundless rumors within Phezzan. The rumors would go something like this: Phezzan's government, conspiring with the empire's own Duke von Lohengramm, was attempting to sell away territory, people, and autonomy to the highest bidder. As proof of this, the Imperial Navy had stationed itself in Phezzan, and the Phezzan Corridor was being offered as an invasion route against the alliance. To prevent that, they had to topple the current administration and forge a new regime that would adhere to a neutral national policy. If Phezzan's public sentiment could be aroused by these rumors, the Imperial Navy's occupation might not be so easily realized. If forced, the people of Phezzan would block it. In the end, even if the Imperial Navy was in successful in its occupation, there was the possibility of the alliance supporting Phezzan's own anti-imperialists. Of course, such Machiavellianism would never escape moral reproach.

Bucock shook his aging white head.

"Admiral Yang sees the future very well, but unfortunately there's nothing we can do about it. Not that it's his fault, of course. He has no authority to take decisive action to such an extent."

"So it's the system's fault?"

The old admiral lifted his grayish-white eyebrows, thinking Julian's question was more daring than the boy realized.

"The system?" There was a hint of remorse in his voice. "I could easily blame it on the system. I've come to take pride in being the soldier of a democratic republic for so long. In fact, I've felt that way since becoming a private at about the same age you are now."

Bucock had watched his own progress for over half a century, even as democracy succumbed to weakness and deterioration, an ideal being eaten alive by cancer cells dressed in truth.

"I think it's right for democratic nations to limit military power and authority. Soldiers shouldn't be able to exercise those privileges anywhere but in the battlespace. Also, no democratic government can be of sound body when its military grows obese by ignoring the criticisms of its own society, effectively becoming a nation within a nation."

The old admiral's words seemed like the work of one revalidating his own value system.

"It's not the democratic government system that's wrong. The problem is that the system has become dissociated from the very spirit that holds it up. For now, the existence of our public facade barely forestalls the degeneration of its true intentions. I wonder how long we'll hold out."

Julian could only react to the gravity of the old admiral's sentiments with silence. His was an inexperienced and helpless existence, and at times he felt powerless to hold *himself* up.

After taking his leave of Bucock, Julian headed for the galactic legitimate imperial government building to offer his formal salutations to Merkatz, newly instated as the government-in-exile's secretary of defense. But the building was nothing more than a former hotel now overrun with exiled nobles. Merkatz was nowhere to be found. It was only by chance that he happened to run into von Schneider just outside the door.

"This place is swarming with hyenas dressed in tuxedos. They seem to vie for position and rank, even in a government without citizens and a navy without troops. I'll be amazed if they settle on six or seven cabinet ministers. Just hurry up and join the Imperial Navy already, Julian. You'd be a shoo-in for lieutenant commander."

Julian couldn't tell whether von Schneider's sharp tongue came naturally or whether nearly a year of life in Iserlohn had tainted him.

"Admiral Merkatz, too, must be working extra hard."

As von Schneider so scandalously explained it, he'd heard that Merkatz would soon be granted the rank of imperial marshal by the "legitimate government." For the time being, there wasn't a single soldier for someone in his position to command. He would have to start by receiving provisions of capital and old warships from the alliance government, recruiting from among the refugees, and building a fleet from scratch.

"Do they honestly believe they can rally enough forces together to compete with a political and military genius like Duke Reinhard von Lohengramm? If so, they're either overly ambitious or totally delusional. I'd put my money on delusional. It's no fun being caught up in all of this, either way."

If Merkatz were promoted to marshal, von Schneider would become commander—not that that was good enough for him.

"If there's one saving grace, it's that, although Lohengramm is a genius, history has more than a few examples of geniuses losing out to the ordinaries. Still, I don't see how we can win without hoping for a miracle from the start."

Julian couldn't keep his thoughts from barreling over a waterfall of pessimism. Had he said as much to Merkatz, it would have sullied his government-in-exile position. There was no one with whom he could even talk about such things. Despite being treated like a receptacle for all these complaints, at least he knew that von Schneider's loyalty to Merkatz was genuine. His sympathy for Merkatz being unable to gain a position worthy of his abilities was insuppressible. Just the thought of Yang getting the same kind of position as Merkatz made Julian feel the innermost soil of his heart freeze solid. Whatever the outcome, of course Julian planned on going with Yang.

In the end, Julian entrusted von Schneider to give Merkatz his regards and left Heinessen in a hurry without being able to meet him.

II

As the ship approached, the planet of Phezzan took shape as a delicate blue orb and was a sight for sore eyes. In the space behind them, silver particles of light danced boisterously against a black backdrop, while the planet in the foreground appeared for all like a piece of music visualized in all its variations of light and darkness. From within its fluctuations of intensity, études of tones and wavelengths spun outward.

As Julian Mintz gazed at the planet from the observation window, a pair of hazel eyes superimposed themselves over its light as he thought of Lieutenant Frederica Greenhill. She was eight years his senior, which put her about halfway between himself and Yang Wen-li. Had it not been so obvious that Yang was the object of Frederica's affections, Julian's own might have been a little stronger and, if only subtly, clearer. Their last conversation before his departure replayed in his mind. It began with her story of meeting Yang on the planet of El Facil.

"Admiral Yang was a sublieutenant back then. He never got used to that black beret."

The citizens of El Facil had no reason either to respect or trust this wet-behind-the-ears officer, but their open hatred of him nevertheless filled Frederica with righteous indignation. She felt obligated to do whatever she could to help him.

"I thought about it a lot. He was an unreliable, pompous sort of man who slept on the sofa in his uniform, didn't wash his face in the morning, and nibbled on bread without even putting any butter on it, muttering to himself all the while. I knew that if I didn't love him, no one would."

Frederica laughed. The ripples of her laughter were never monotonous. Many things had happened in the decade since, and each had faintly yet deeply cast its shadow.

"I didn't fall in love with him because he was a hero or a famous commander. Maybe I just have a knack for investing in the future."

"You sure do," Julian answered, although he couldn't be sure if this was the response Frederica had wanted to hear. Had Frederica's impression of Yang changed?

"No, Yang Wen-li hasn't changed. The surroundings have changed, but he himself not one bit."

During his days as sublieutenant, Yang felt ill-suited for the job, as he did also for his admiralty. If and when he ascended to marshal, he was sure to feel just as incompetent. Yang gave the impression that, whatever his rank, he would never quite get accustomed to the duties of his station. Yang had never once actively considered becoming a military man, and even now had his heart set on becoming a historian. But picturing him as a teacher, Frederica imagined he'd be as much of a sore thumb standing at a podium as on a battlefield, and in this respect Julian understood her thinking full well. More difficult to understand, of course, was Yang's emotional side, and Julian wanted to know what it was in Yang's mental labyrinth that made him seemingly oblivious to Frederica's attentions.

The visiphone chirped, and the boy was informed they would soon be arriving on Phezzan.

By Phezzan standard time, it was noon, and for the first time in his life, Julian Mintz was about to set foot on the surface of this distant planet. His new life had begun.

III

Although Julian had heard that Captain Viola, chief of staff and military attaché of the FPA commissioner's office on Phezzan, was relatively tall and obese, in Julian's eyes he didn't fit that description. He was more hefty than obese, had no traces of either fat or muscle beneath his pallid skin, and if anything looked like he was bloated with gas. Julian guessed he weighed less than expected and wondered if he was going too far in thinking of him as a walking airship—until the next day, when he discovered the existence of the nickname "Grounded Blimp."

"You have a lot to learn, Ensign Mintz. I understand you've made a name for yourself in the battlespace, but here that means nothing. First off, if you have any feelings of dependence, get rid of them."

The implication was clear: any benefits he'd received by dint of Yang Wen-li's patronage were no longer valid.

"Yes, sir, I'll be sure to keep that in mind. I am fully aware of my inexperience and trust you to guide me well in all matters."

Julian sensed this Captain Viola was going to be a tough nut to crack and felt miserable inside. Back on Iserlohn Fortress, he'd had some unpleasant exchanges, but such hollow diplomatic etiquette was almost entirely foreign to him. Maybe there were too many wildflowers in the greenhouse and its external environment was harsh, but Iserlohn was a world unto itself.

"Hmm, you speak well, don't you? Your silver tongue belies your age."

Although those words indicated the captain's narrow-mindedness, Julian was pained by their apparent insincerity. The captain's slightly high-pitched voice and thin, epicanthic eyes only served to emphasize an underlying malice in his remarks. It seemed pointless to waste any emotional energy trying to get on his good side.

One thing was for certain: Phezzan was enemy territory. Whether inside the commissioner's office or outside it, the air was filled with a colorless, odorless hostility that might catch fire at any moment. Julian resigned himself to the fact that the only person he'd be able to trust from now on was his warrant officer, Louis Machungo.

Any internal hostility directed at Julian was ultimately a reflection of the Trünicht camp's feelings toward Yang Wen-li. If any of it was personal, it was doubtless because of a certain jealousy and enmity over his reputation as the youngest military attaché in history. All told, he was nothing more than an ensign, and as such would never exercise much of an influence over his surroundings. Julian understood that, seen from the outside, he was Admiral Yang Wen-li's property, and that if he ever made a mistake, it would reflect badly on Yang. He had to be careful.

Neither could he just curl up into a little ball like a hedgehog and isolate himself. He had duties as a military attaché, and even if the outcomes of the Trünicht faction's schemes should became an unexpected part of his work, that didn't mean he would be justified in defying his station.

Julian had never cared too much about his dress. On formal occasions, he got along just fine in uniform. Whenever Yang took Julian clothes shopping, a lack of fashion sense prompted Yang to drag him inside and leave everything up to a more knowledgeable sales associate. He'd been content having cheap things for himself but always sought out goods of higher quality for Julian, perhaps as a way of showing his admiration. As Alex Caselnes put it, Yang and Julian were of different classes. Julian didn't need to attract other people's attention, so naturally he didn't care, and in Yang's case it was just a nuisance.

A military attaché was tasked with the important duties of gathering and analyzing information and observing people's lives out on the streets. It was credible work. Dressed like a civilian in a thin cream-colored turtleneck and jeans, and with his characteristically flaxen hair grown long, Julian, like Yang, looked nothing like a military man. Machungo, who was accompanying him, tried to hide his muscles beneath a thicker sweater, without success, and looked like some dark, giant turtle sheltering a mythical vagrant prince, but his round eyes brimmed with respect and helped to diffuse some of the danger in the air.

Once their procedures were finished and they were released from work, they walked together out into the streets of Phezzan. Office buildings lined the streets as far as their eyes could see, places where they would be treated as obstacles by superiors and colleagues alike. As outcasts, they weren't about to be invited out for dinner anytime soon.

Julian and Warrant Officer Machungo walked the lively, bustling streets at a leisurely pace. A group of half a dozen girls around Julian's age sized him up on their approach. When Julian looked up at them, they shrieked with laugher and ran away at a half gallop.

"He's kind of cute, isn't he?" they said. "Doesn't look like he's used to it, though."

Julian turned his flaxen head sharply around. In contrast to the power politics that went on behind closed doors, Julian understood nothing of women. Had Poplin been there, he would have given him a lecture for sure.

Spotting a side street, the two of them went into a clothing store. The shopkeeper ran up to them, plied them with courtesies, and recommended a few items after seeing where Julian's eyes were traveling.

"This one would look great on you. Not everyone could pull it off, but with your features and sense of style, it would be a perfect fit."

"It's expensive."

"Are you kidding? I'm making a big sacrifice selling it to you at this price."

"I thought it was twenty marks cheaper last month," lied Julian.

"You must be mistaken. In any case, check the electronic newspaper. It tracks fluctuations in the price index down to every cent."

Julian nodded, seeing that the shopkeeper had other fluctuations in mind, and answered enthusiastically.

"I'll take it, then. Can I get a receipt?"

He paid ninety Phezzan marks and grabbed a sweater while he was at it. An unexpectedly extravagant price to pay for a little information gathering. Later, at a terraced café, he checked out a few electronic newspapers to verify the shopkeeper's assertion.

"The prices are stable, and the quality of goods is high. Financial troubles are rare, which means the economy here is quite robust."

"A far cry from back home, wouldn't you say?" lamented Machungo openly.

Compared to the alliance, which was falling into ruin, Phezzan's economic strength appeared solid from head to tail, down to every little shop.

"Those who shed blood, those whose blood is shed, and those who engorge themselves on the shed blood…Takes all kinds, eh?"

Julian's voice trembled with a hateful brilliance. He'd never once heard Yang speak of Phezzan in prejudiced terms, but when he compared those who suffered calamity in battle to those who boasted of their prosperity and the profits they gained from it, Julian could see no reason to feel good about the latter. Try as he might, Julian couldn't squeeze his sensitivity through his military filter.

When they left the café, Julian and Machungo made their way to the commissioner's office in the city proper. They didn't go inside, of course, but only gazed at its facade.

"Strange, isn't it? Housing enemies and allies in the same place."

Julian nodded to Machungo's obligatory observation, casting his gaze on the white-walled commissioner's building, half-hidden by a grove of trees. Perhaps they were also being watched by the infrared camera system, the butt of some grandiose Phezzanese joke.

I ∪

The next day, a party was held at the Hotel Batavia to welcome the new attaché. Julian heard they'd decided not to use the commissioner's office building to avoid the danger of attendees setting wiretaps inside. But then, he couldn't help but wonder, what would happen if the hotel itself had been bugged in advance? In either case, as the guest of honor Julian was obliged to attend. Formality was formality.

He knew well from Yang's example that being a guest of honor meant having to stand constantly like a statue entitled *Starving*. Moreover, due to being exposed to everyone's scrutiny, it took a certain amount of effort just to smile. As Yang had once told him with a sigh, a life in which one could get by without doing things one didn't want to do was as rare as pure metallic radium.

If someone observed him, it was also an opportunity for Julian to observe in kind, and as Yang's representative, it was necessary for him to disseminate the virus of a groundless rumor involving Phezzan's occupation by the Imperial Navy. He had no choice but to plant the virus, let it gnaw at people's hearts as it bred its powerful toxins, and wait for symptoms to show. If it exhibited its biggest effect, it would spawn antagonism between Phezzan's people and its autonomous government, and the government, pressured by the people, would reluctantly repeal its secret pact—assuming there was one—with the empire, while the alliance thwarted any invasion by the Imperial Navy from the Phezzan Corridor. Even if there was no secret pact, he had to confirm whether this would sow suspicion of the empire among Phezzan's people and, regarding their feelings toward the autonomous government, whether they would still grant imperial passage through the Phezzan Corridor. The alliance stood to gain either way.

Yang's worry was that, if the Phezzanese people panicked and sealed off the corridor by their own means, bloodshed was possible between the autonomous government and the empire's occupational forces. Such was the pinnacle of Machiavellianism: peripheral countries being tricked into

sacrificing themselves for the sake of the whole. What helped Yang overcome this hesitation was that, when the Imperial Navy's passage through
the Phezzan Corridor went from hypothesis to reality, it was clear that
the Phezzanese people would come out en masse to prevent bloodshed
at all costs, groundless rumor or no.

Yang said as much in his letter to Bucock:

"As stated above, while I do think that Phezzan's autonomous government has made a secret pact with Duke von Lohengramm of the
empire, and that they mean to sell out the corridor, how will Phezzan's
people, proud as they are of their independence, react? I predict it will
never come to a showdown with either the empire or the autonomous
government. Although it would be a chance to act, that doesn't mean
they would make the impossible possible. In the end, they are who they
are. If they cannot avoid shedding blood to protect their own freedom
and dignity, then blood will be shed. And if not, the Imperial Navy will
not occupy peacefully. The problem is that Phezzan's people might start
acting when this information is leaked, thereby giving imperial forces a
giant head start. If that happens, this will backfire in the worst possible
way. Moreover, the Imperial Navy is already on the move. It's too late to
work out a secure countermeasure."

This last bit made Bucock and Caselnes feel that sometimes Yang saw
too well into the future. He saw everything at its worst.

Yang was clearly endowed with talent as a strategist, but talent wasn't
everything. Character and intention, as well as being successful in carrying out one's strategies, in and of themselves had no meaning. To him,
the highest sense of value was not the pursuit of national benefit through
war and strategy—unusual for a career soldier who'd risen to such a high
position at his age. There were those who criticized Yang, as there always
would be, for lacking honesty of conviction, noting that although Yang
never saw righteousness in war, the more decorated he became, the more
enemies he killed. Julian, of course, didn't share that criticism, and Yang
himself would have responded with little more than a bittersweet smile.
Even then, he'd probably be criticized all the same for neglecting his duty
as a human being to assert his own righteousness.

Julian was standing in the middle of the crowd, dressed in the white formal dress reserved for officers. His long, somewhat unruly flaxen hair, graceful features, animated dark-brown eyes, and upright posture attracted the attention of everyone in the room.

Had it been Reinhard, he would have overwhelmed his surroundings with his magnificence, as if he were the only chromatic thread in an otherwise achromatic tapestry. Julian might not have possessed that kind of intensity, but he did give the impression of someone who was exactly where he needed to be, the indispensable corner piece to a larger puzzle.

Phezzan's gentlemen and ladies were bubbling with conversation around the youngest military attaché in history, and every time one of those bubbles popped, a wave of laughter radiated across the room. As Julian predicted, the constant smiling was already getting to him.

"How are you finding Phezzan so far, Ensign?"

"Well, I'm impressed by how clean even the back alleys are. That, and there are so many pets, and they're all so well fed."

"My, you do have some eclectic interests, eh?"

Julian shrugged his shoulders on the inside. He was being metaphorical anyway. The cleanliness of the back alleys was another way of saying that Phezzanese society was running smoothly, and many well-fed pets meant that Phezzan's people enjoyed a material surplus. Although Julian had hinted that, from these snapshots of daily life, he'd observed one facet of Phezzan's perfect national power, no one picked up on it. Julian felt like he was being fired at with blanks. Had Yang been here, he would surely have winked and called him a show-off, making Julian turn and blush.

"And what do you think of the girls here on Phezzan, Ensign?"

His conversation partner, experienced enough with these sorts of functions to lend the rookie guest of honor a helping hand, had changed the subject.

"They're all so pretty. And lively, too."

"How tactful of you to say so."

Just saying the right thing, however insincere, would allow him to coast through the evening unscathed.

"Phezzan's got everything, from pretty girls to terraforming systems. Everything you could possibly need. You can get anything with the right resources. In your case, Ensign, you could probably buy a girl's heart with just a smile, no money. I'm so jealous."

"I'll see what I can do."

Julian flashed an unseemly expression, which made him feel even more out of place. He couldn't help but think he was overreaching.

"Incidentally, speaking of buying," said Julian, casually switching on his detonator, "I'm concerned about these rumors I've been hearing regarding the Imperial Navy buying out the Phezzan Corridor and Phezzan's independence."

"Come again?"

It was a forced, hackneyed way with which to answer a question with a question. Julian followed suit by rephrasing. Did Phezzan mean to sell out its corridor to the Imperial Navy like a piece of merchandise?

"My, our little ensign has quite the imagination. The Imperial Navy, of all things!"

The man's voice undulated with laughter.

"Are you saying the Imperial Navy will pass through the Phezzan Corridor and invade alliance territory? No, that would make for a great story, but…"

The man was getting preachy.

"Isn't that just a little too far-fetched? The Phezzan Corridor is a veritable ocean of peace. Only passenger and merchant ships sail through there. Any vessel flying a military flag would never get very far."

"Who decides that?" asked Julian with an unbefitting lack of civility.

"Who decides?" asked the man in return, trying to laugh but failing.

The others around them became aware that Julian had raised the question in earnest. Standing amid all those stares, Julian raised his voice to be heard.

"If the people established that law, I think those same people could also revoke it. Given the way Duke Reinhard von Lohengramm of the empire operates, I don't see him following the old customs. I don't know that any reigning emperor has ever defected from his homeland."

His audience was stunned.

"Does not Duke von Lohengramm calmly destroy tradition and unwritten laws to command and conquer? I doubt anyone would argue otherwise."

Everyone was talking quietly among themselves. Even if there was opposition to Julian's remarks, no one could voice it.

"But let's say Duke von Lohengramm does harbor such ambitions. I doubt the people of Phezzan would sell him their pride so easily."

Behind his air of nonchalance, Julian's heart was trembling. Having no idea how his own provocations would be received, he was swimming in dark waters.

A trim young man engaging in friendly chatter with a nearby group cast a sharp glance at the young guest of honor. *Such a keen-witted boy*, thought the landesherr's aide, Rupert Kesselring. Nonetheless, it was strange for the boy to have derived such a well-formed conclusion on his own. Yang Wen-li was most certainly behind this. He bowed curtly to his fellow guests and joined the circle of people gathering around Julian. Not a minute later, he was standing in front of the boy to grab the reins of this conversation.

"Even so, Phezzan selling itself to the empire is quite a daring conjecture, isn't it, Ensign Mintz?"

"Is it really? I don't think that independence, even formal independence, is Phezzan's highest priority."

"But it's close to the highest. You mustn't underestimate that, Ensign Mintz."

The way Rupert Kesselring put emphasis on Julian's name gave him the chills. His scornful superiority billowed in the air, seeming almost to blow Julian's voluminous bangs.

There was seven years' difference between Kesselring and Julian, but an even bigger gap besides—not of intelligence but of independence.

As Kesselring saw it, Julian had yet to take a single step off the palm of Yang's hand.

Thankfully, Captain Viola came rushing in with his booming, classical voice to dispel this noxious atmosphere.

"Ensign Mintz, you came here to be welcomed, not to argue. Have you forgotten your place? My apologies, everyone. Please excuse him. I'm afraid he's let his youthful ardor get the better of him."

Sometimes even this kind of snobbery was effective. The music played on, and vacant conversations bubbled once more above the attendees.

∪

Rupert Kesselring heaved a sigh in the driver's seat of his landcar. His breath was warm more from the alcohol flowing in his veins than as a reflection of his frustration. The car's interior was dim, illuminated only by the light coming from the four-centimeter-square screen of his visiphone, on which the face of the bald, vigorous man who'd been listening to Kesselring's account of the party's progress still glowed: Landesherr Rubinsky.

"All of which can only mean that Yang Wen-li has probably seen through the Imperial Navy's strategic plans. What now?"

"Even if that's true, there's nothing he can do about it."

"Isn't there?"

Kesselring feigned mockery but was having trouble picking out the fly of suspicion from his mental soup. Ensign Julian Mintz wouldn't present a problem, but he wasn't so thickheaded and presumptuous as to think he could turn his back on Yang Wen-li for a moment.

"Nevertheless, that boy certainly spouted some choice words to the people at that party. Sure, they're all drunk, but I wonder how many of them will remember it in the morning. And if their interest should turn into political speculation, what then?"

"It's too late. Whatever their doubts might be, there's no time to act on them. I wouldn't worry about it."

Switching off the visiphone, Rupert Kesselring kept his eyes fixed on the cloudy screen, muttering to himself, "Even if I am worried, it's not about you."

Getting out of his landcar at Coburg Street, Rupert Kesselring briskly entered an old building. A genderless mechanical voice confirmed his identity. The bare concrete steps leading underground were steep, but his perfectly controlled pace kept him from stumbling. The hallway made a turn, and Kesselring opened the door at its end, bathing his body is a sickly orange glow. He looked down at the figure cowering like some dying animal on the sofa.

"And how are we feeling today, Bishop Degsby?"

He was met with a pathetic, curse-filled wheeze. Kesselring lifted a corner of his mouth in a derisive smile. The smoke of half-lit pleasures drifted about the poorly ventilated room.

"Alcohol, drugs, women. You've indulged in every sin under the sun, despite being a religious man who preaches abstinence. I wonder if His Holiness the Grand Bishop back on Earth will be so lenient regarding your promiscuity."

"You forced me to take those drugs!" said the young bishop, wheezing. His capillaries had burst, giving his pale irises the appearance of swimming in a red sea.

"Did you not slip me those drugs and kick me into the depths of depravity? Blasphemer! One of these days, the time will come when you realize the folly of your actions."

"By all means, make me. Will I be struck down by lightning? Or maybe a meteor?"

"Do you not fear righteousness?"

"Righteousness?" The young aide laughed sardonically. "Rudolf the Great didn't become ruler of the universe thanks to a surplus of righteousness. Neither did Adrian Rubinsky gain the landesherr's seat by his impeccable character. They got to where they were because they *were* the higher power. The principle of control is might, not right," Rupert Kesselring pointed out indifferently. "There's no such thing as absolute righteousness to begin with, and so judging anything on that basis is pointless. The many millions of people killed by Rudolf the Great got their comeuppance for insisting on righteousness despite their lack of power. If you had power, you could live without fearing the Grand Bishop's wrath. Which brings me to my point."

He took a breath.

"I care nothing for religious authority. You can monopolize it all you want. If each of us becomes the guru of his respective world, we won't have any need to be jealous of each other."

"I don't get your meaning."

"Don't you? I'm saying I'll give you Earth and the Church of Terra."

The bishop said nothing.

"I take Rubinsky down. You take the Grand Bishop's place."

Degsby still said nothing.

"This is no longer their era. Eight hundred years of hatred on Earth will make a fine meal for the devil's table. From here on out, you and I…"

He closed his mouth, furrowed his brow, and looked at Degsby, who was laughing.

"You forget your place, you fool!"

Degsby's eyes were a blast furnace boiling with unbridled emotion. His thin lips turned upward, and from within his throat exploded a staccato of wrath. The young bishop, clad in black, trembled from head to toe.

"With such ambition and shallow thinking as yours, you actually mean to defy His Holiness the Grand Bishop? Laughable isn't the word. It's beyond ridiculous. Dream your canine dreams, you cur. But don't go trying to stand up to an elephant. It's for your own good."

"I think you've laughed enough at my expense for one day, don't you, Bishop?"

That Rupert Kesselring's script was so common in and of itself delineated a frame around his uncommon spirit. By remaining calm, he allowed himself to respond from a place of personal truth. He wasn't used to being ridiculed. Neither did he want to get used to it. Only victors should have that privilege.

"I've got all of your disgraceful escapades with alcohol, drugs, and women on tape. If you don't cooperate with me, I'll use them as I see fit. A clichéd tactic, I admit, but tried-and-true. The clock is ticking."

"You filthy dog," answered the bishop, although by now his voice was weak, stripped of its zeal.

Julian Mintz tossed and turned in his bed many times that night, which was unusual for him. Something bitter from the party had left such a bad taste in his mouth that he even got up once to rinse it out. He flipped through his mental file, wondering if he could have done things better. He felt the sting of his own inexperience and blushed alone in the darkness.

There were many different types of combat. That he knew, and knew very well. But there was something he knew even more to be true: the type of combat spawned by his little exchange with Rupert Kesselring was not something he liked. If he was going to fight at all, he wanted it to be with ingenuity and bravery, in the vast expanse of outer space, stars at his back, against the heroic Reinhard von Lohengramm. It was an outrageous ambition, of course. Julian didn't have the energy to enumerate all the ways in which Reinhard surpassed him. Not even Admiral Yang could hold a candle to Reinhard von Lohengramm's genius. And here he was, barely worthy of kissing Admiral Yang's feet. But, as von Schneider had said, sometimes it took a common man to defeat the smartest one. This tangle of thoughts had pulled him far from sleep's embrace.

Julian suddenly wanted a drink, and was only now beginning to understand the force of Yang's habit. It was, perhaps, his biggest epiphany of the night.

Beyond Julian's bed, the world continued to rumble noiselessly.

CHAPTER 8:

INVITATION TO A REQUIEM

I

NOVEMBER CAME, and with it the knowledge that a lit fuse was rapidly being consumed as a spark headed toward a point of ignition. The Imperial Navy was performing true-combat drills and all manner of simulations daily, stockpiling material resources, shuffling around units, and carrying out arms inspections in preparation for an unprecedented campaign. On the fourth of that month, Commander von Reuentahl, in the capacity of inspector general, conducted large-scale maneuvers with fleets of thirty thousand ships. These practice sessions were so intense that training exercises alone sustained more than a hundred casualties.

Manufacturing on the nonmilitary side of things was proceeding smoothly. The empire's attaché on Phezzan, Commissioner Boltec, sent word to Phezzan on Reinhard's orders that the Imperial Navy would soon deploy for Iserlohn.

In return, Boltec requested to be the new landesherr of Phezzan. Reinhard was no miser, and naturally Boltec believed his request would be honored, but Reinhard's reply was quicker than he expected. Once he conquered the alliance, Reinhard had no intention of placing anyone in a position of indirect authority when combining newly acquired territory with the old. Phezzan was best placed under his direct control, and he would rather give Boltec a leisurely post, along with a high salary, and be done with it.

Although this was a righteous path to rule, it hardly seemed worth the Machiavellian effort of concentrating the hatred of the Phezzanese people on Boltec. Ultimately, as he had once said to von Oberstein, he expected Boltec to fail early on in his attempts at maintaining public order, and so Reinhard had promised him succession of the landesherr position. But Boltec would need to take full responsibility for maintaining Phezzan's public order in cooperation with the Imperial Navy.

Thus, Boltec continued feeding false information to his native Phezzan. It was, of course, necessary to conform as much as possible to the information being sent out by civilians. In a state of mind he could not have imagined having a year ago, he already regarded his once-unconditional loyalty to Rubinsky as the actions of another self in another life. Originally, Boltec had unexpectedly sold himself, beginning with his mishandling of Reinhard, but to justify his guilt, he found fault in Rubinsky and resigned himself to the fact that he would lose his authority. Boltec's successor, chief aide Rupert Kesselring, was hardly ever on his mind anymore. He wasn't the only one to think of Kesselring as a satellite feeding off the landesherr's gravitational orbit.

On November 8, Reinhard made his final assignments for Operation Ragnarök.

First, he would mobilize a large vanguard fleet toward Iserlohn. And while all eyes and ears were on Iserlohn, he would thread that needle to dominate the Phezzan Corridor in one swift motion. The orders to invade Phezzan would be the jurisdiction of Senior Admiral Wolfgang Mittermeier and him alone.

The wounded Admiral Neidhart Müller would act as commander for the second formation after the Gale Wolf. Müller was a feather in Reinhard's cap who'd fervently hoped to participate in the capture of Iserlohn Fortress as a means of vindicating his past, but on this occasion had to curb his instincts for revenge.

Commanding the third formation was the Imperial Navy's highest commander, the imperial marshal himself, Reinhard von Lohengramm. Under his direct command he placed five vice admirals: Aldringen, Brauhitsch, Carnap, Grünemann, and Thurneisen. Chief of Staff Senior Admiral von Oberstein, chief aide Rear Admiral Admiral von Streit, and secondary aide Lieutenant von Rücke, along with chief secretary to the imperial prime minister Hildegard von Mariendorf and head of the imperial guard Captain Kissling, would be on board the flagship *Brünhild*. It would be the first time a woman had held rank on that warship.

To the fourth formation, Reinhard assigned Admiral Steinmetz. As a high noble with a long and decorated career in frontier defense, he'd held rank as vice admiral. After the Lippstadt campaign, he'd handed over the frontier, pledging loyalty to Reinhard, earning him the full admiral rank he desired.

As a last defense, the fifth formation would be led by Admiral Wahlen. He had counseled the redheaded Siegfried Kircheis in the Lippstadt War, in which he had fought bravely. He was a great general who balanced courage and tactics, and was this time entrusted with the heavy responsibility of connecting the Phezzan Corridor with the imperial mainland.

All told, Reinhard's forces were twelve million strong, including four million essential personnel to defend on land in occupied territories of Phezzan and the alliance, and a total of 87,500 ships in the fleet.

Meanwhile, a formidable battalion was mobilized as the Iserlohn District Army. Although fundamentally purposed as a diversion, their apparent weakness would not be perceived as such. For this, the appropriate balance of military strength, human resources, and materials was arranged. Depending on the circumstances, this unit would be entrusted with the grand and tactically important duty of penetrating the Iserlohn Corridor, infiltrating alliance territory, and then merging with their comrades invading from the Phezzan side. Leadership, large-scale tactical acumen, and the ability to assess things coolheadedly: all these and more were demanded of the commanding officer Senior Admiral Oskar von Reuentahl.

Admirals Lutz and Lennenkamp would serve as vice commandants. Lutz, like Wahlen, had once worked as a vice commandant for Kircheis.

Lennenkamp, like Steinmetz, had become Reinhard's staff officer after Lippstadt and a full admiral thereafter. Although he'd held seniority as a superior officer when Reinhard was still a boy, by outward appearances he was nothing more than a thin middle-aged man.

Admirals Fahrenheit and Wittenfeld, as heads of reserve forces, were ordered to be on standby. Both were great generals, strong in the face of aggression, and more than up to the challenge of holding their own in a decisive battle. Wittenfeld's fleet, notoriously known as the *Schwarz Lanzenreiter*, or Black Lancers, was a bonus.

Admiral Kessler would stay behind on the planet Odin as commander of capital defenses, and, along with Admiral Meckinlger, was to await further orders. In addition to sanctioning business administration at the Ministry of Military Affairs, he would be tasked with the important duty of supply and organization of reinforcements as rear services manager.

The Iserlohn forces were widely announced, and many were notified down to the exact date and time they would be heading for the imperial capital. That, in and of itself, was part of their strategy.

"We can expect the Imperial Navy, led by Senior Admiral von Reuentahl, to head for Iserlohn."

In contrast to the Imperial Navy's ostentatious provocation, the alliance's information network communicated that danger to the capital conservatively at best.

The alliance capital of Heinessen was shocked, if only because its citizens believed in the continued existence of a preestablished harmony. Just as spring followed winter, they never doubted that peace would be revived. And why should they have doubted it? For insofar as Iserlohn was an impregnable fortress and had an invincible young commander on its side, there was no reason for the Imperial Navy to attempt an invasion of alliance territory.

In this case, it seemed government officials were banishing any memories of having ever treated the eminently accomplished Admiral Yang from a factional perspective.

When top government and military brass met to hold a Defense Committee meeting, the commander in chief of the space armada, Admiral Bucock, requested to speak. After being ignored several times, he was finally given the floor. The old admiral was of the opinion that any attack on Iserlohn would be nothing more than a diversion while the enemy's main forces set their sights on Phezzan.

Bucock's observation surprised the high officials in attendance, but the deep impression it made worked against him. Opposition filled with derision and cynicism erupted.

"Commander in Chief Bucock's concerns are uniquely his own. I can't think that Phezzan would be so willing to resign its political neutrality, and more than a century's worth of tradition, in conspiracy with the empire. To begin with, if the empire were to get any stronger because of this, Phezzan's survival would be compromised. Surely they've taken that into consideration."

"Phezzan continues to reap major profits by investing generous amounts of capital in our alliance. Were the alliance to be subsumed into the empire, all our efforts would come to naught. Would they do something so counterproductive?"

The old admiral was unfazed by this concentrated fire.

"Indeed, Phezzan is investing in the alliance, but all of that goes into mines, lands, and enterprises of the alliance's respective planets, not into the alliance government itself. If the capital invested in Phezzan was secure, I doubt they'd lose much sleep over destruction of the alliance's national infrastructure, which for them would be little more than a ceiling collapse."

After inflicting this rebuke, Bucock went in for the kill.

"Or maybe it's also true that Phezzan is investing in the alliance government."

"Admiral, you'd do well to be more discreet," said Defense Committee Chair Islands in a high-handed tone, reining in the old admiral's censure.

Bucock's remarks pointed out the possibility that high government officials had been secretly taking bribes in the form of kickbacks from

Phezzan. Some of those same officials would have pledged on their own conscience that nothing of the sort had taken place. Although it would have been unthinkable among founding fathers like Ahle Heinessen for high officials to imitate the worst parts of the Phezzanese spirit and exchange power and duty for money, for the past century no one had ever worried about their successors. Moreover, mass media collusion with the political sphere assured that nothing beyond political strife between factions had ever surfaced in the public imagination as a subject of concern.

Bucock's remarks were dismissed as pure speculation, and the assembly opted to strengthen vigilance in Iserlohn and to prepare for the eventuality of transporting munitions once an appeal went out. With that, all members of the assembly, save one, adjourned to their satisfaction.

II

Commander Nilson was captain of *Ulysses*, a warship belonging to the alliance's Iserlohn-garrisoned fleet. The past few days had been miserable ones. Since he breathed not a word of it to anyone, his subordinates exercised their freedom—that is, their freedom to speak when their superior wasn't around—to fill in the blanks. Perhaps he'd been passed up for a promotion or lost a fight with his wife? One of the men heard he'd been crushed at poker by Lieutenant Commander Poplin. Another said he had lost at poker, but against Rear Admiral von Schönkopf. Among these voices of speculation was that of Sublieutenant Fields, who claimed first prize when it came to rumors.

"Actually, the captain is in love with Julian Mintz. But, as everyone knows, he's gone to Phezzan to become a military attaché. Losing his unrequited love has pushed him into the depths of despair. Let's go easy on the poor captain."

His audience laughed themselves into convulsions, but Commander Nilson was a tough old man, and everyone knew full well he didn't have a pedophiliac bone in his body. Still, laughter always helped to pass the time. The real reason for Commander Nilson's depression was that, after passing forty, suddenly an old wisdom tooth had been giving him trouble. None could have been the wiser.

Nearly all the surveillance satellites that Yang had set up in the corridor had been destroyed in a raid by Kempf's fleet earlier that year. His inability to replace them because of budget cuts had been a considerable blow to his ability to track the enemy. Yang had repeatedly requested a supplementary budget from the National Defense Committee, but the accounting department had yet to finish the required auditing, and so, in keeping with regulation, it had never been given.

This wasn't a deliberate harassment directed at Yang on the council's part, but simply the side effect of a lackluster national bureaucracy. The situation was looking more dire by the moment.

There was no way they were going to suspend surveillance until a supplementary budget was granted, and so a manned patrol was conducted among the fleets. And now it was November 20, two days since *Ulysses* had gone out on patrol.

Captain Nilson kept rubbing his right cheek in discomfort, and when he received word of enemy signs from his navigations operator, he wasn't the least bit surprised. Although far from a timid man, the pain was draining him, and any spare emotional energy he had was beset with dread and fear.

"It's an unbelievable number of ships—impossible to count them all."

The operator had experienced this kind of situation many times before, but this time made him shudder just as much as the first.

"What should we do? Fight?"

The captain called him an idiot. Iserlohn's garrisoned fleet was undefeated and had stayed that way because it never once engaged an enemy it had no chance of defeating. There was no place in Yang's fleet for the foolishness of fighting against a sure victor.

"Can't you retreat any faster?! What are you waiting for?!"

Von Reuentahl's fleet detected the alliance's battleship as it manically cast off its fighting spirit and fled.

When asked if they should pursue, the heterochromatic admiral ordered them to hold off for the time being.

He would rather Nilson went back to Iserlohn Fortress and spread the word about the Imperial Navy's approach. Like his comrade Mittermeier, he wasn't the type who took pleasure in going after small fish. His sole opponent was Yang Wen-li, the most resourceful general of the Alliance Armed Forces. Should he not be focusing on gathering his courage to fight the greater enemy?

The first shot of Operation Ragnarök had been fired. It was also the first bar of a requiem for the Free Planets Alliance.

After receiving word that the battleship *Ulysses* had wisely retreated, Yang gathered his staff officers in the fortress conference room.

Caselnes rubbed his stomach in discomfort, remembering the hardships of the first half of the year.

"Admiral Kempf had great military strength, too, when he raided us this past spring, but this time will be even worse."

Frederica shook her head.

"I'm assuming this is all part of Duke von Lohengramm's grand scheme?"

Yang nodded. This was merely a local manifestation of the strategic epic that had begun with Emperor Erwin Josef II's escape. If Reinhard was the type to imitate futile actions of the Alliance Armed Forces, Yang had nothing to fear.

Chief of Staff Murai crossed his arms.

"From now on, we should refrain from sending *Ulysses* on further patrols. Every time it goes out, it brings the enemy back with it."

Yang shot his chief of staff a sidelong glance, unsure whether he was joking or being serious. He hoped it was the former, but Murai's expression proved otherwise.

"Well, let's keep it in the back of our minds. We could just up our alert level by one anytime we send *Ulysses* out on patrol."

Yang ordered defense commander von Schönkopf and Iserlohn's administrative director Caselnes to make all the necessary preparations as protocol demanded.

The allies behind him, four thousand light-years away in the capital, were more cause for headache than the enemies before him. For now, fire was limited to the Iserlohn Corridor, and the elite officials of the capital were relieved to know they could count on Iserlohn Fortress's impregnability and Yang's tactical experience. But when the Imperial Navy disturbed their respite by barging through the immaterial door by which the Phezzan Corridor was sealed, it would plunge them into certain panic. And if they were ordered to ignore the situation at Iserlohn Fortress and rush to the capital's rescue?

They would have no choice but to help. He knew that. As Julian had said, soldiers followed orders. Choices weren't up to them. The renowned heterochromatic admiral, von Reuentahl, who, along with Mittermeier, was one of the Twin Ramparts of the Imperial Navy, had once again piqued Yang's direst imaginings. With von Reuentahl in the way, it would be difficult for Yang, despite his intentions of rescuing the capital, to follow through.

In the worst-case scenario, Iserlohn Fortress would be recaptured—it had originally been the empire's property—and they would end up being overtaken from behind, as good as defeated. Securing Iserlohn and dispatching a fleet to rescue the capital from crisis, all while facing an imperial strike, would be nothing short of a miracle. If they made demands, would the high government officials feel satisfied? To make matters worse, he had too much integrity to think that he would be treated amiably.

Yang's plan to defend the fortress was as follows. Before the enemy's arrival, he would dispatch a fleet from the fortress to lay ambush in the corridor, rush in on the enemy from the rear while it attacked the fortress, and crush them with the fortress's aid in a pincer attack. Although this was generally an effective tactic, the Imperial Navy's actions were rapid and systematic, and Yang would have no opportunity to scoff at their clever scheme. How many plans and ideas in this world were over and done with before they even began?

Yang sent word of the raid to Heinessenpolis. In addition, he was of the mind that this was no isolated attack, but one link in Duke Reinhard von Lohengramm's grander tactical chain, which, when completed, would lead to an assault via the Phezzan Corridor. Yang told them to concentrate on fortifying their defenses on the Phezzan side.

Though they knew it was probably futile, it was all they could do. Commander in Chief Bucock was likely fighting alone in the National Defense Committee, and at the very least needed the support.

III

Von Reuentahl spread out the fleet under his command in front of Iserlohn Fortress, making sure to be out of range of Thor's Hammer, the fortress's main gun.

Yang couldn't help but be impressed by the magnitude of von Reuentahl's formation. The clusters of luminous points reflected on his screen were systematic, overwhelming Iserlohn with their thickness and depth.

Which meant the enemy wasn't cutting any corners, even in their diversions. Yang had no doubt that, at the first opportunity, they would gain control of the corridor with their colossal military force, hail their friendly troops invading from Phezzan, and close in from both sides. In which case it would become eminently difficult for Yang to make a move. Von Reuentahl was likely waiting for him to do just that. If only there were a way to use that against them…

With his heterochromatic eyes, von Reuentahl peered at the silver globe reflected on his screen. His subordinates, their number equal to the population of a large city, waited tensely for the command to bombard it. At last, it came.

"Fire!"

More than three hundred thousand gunports hurled their spears of light at once. The fortress's outer walls, made from a four-fold composite of superhardened steel, crystalline fiber, and superceramic interlaced with mirror coating, emitted a white incandescence from a showering of reflected beams. The fortress sparkled like some giant gemstone in the darkness of space, outshining the stars behind it and sending a silent signal light-years away.

Although a considerable number of gun batteries and emplacements were destroyed by this grand fusillade, the fortress itself withstood the raging billows of energy, hanging almost proudly in space.

"It won't budge."

Chief of Staff Vice Admiral Bergengrün was impressed by what he saw on the screen.

"No reason it should. But it's our duty to make a show of things. Let's give them something to feast their eyes on, shall we?"

Although the future was uncertain, von Reuentahl was dedicated to the mission at hand, having no intention of being branded as incompetent. For when a man who out of mere self-interest failed to execute the duties allotted to him rose against the supreme ruler, who would follow him? Popularity was cultivated through actual achievements. It may have been a diversion, but if he could carry out this one mission to its fullest, it would net him an actual achievement, and if he toppled the most resourceful admiral of the Alliance Armed Forces and recaptured Iserlohn Fortress, his popularity and renown would know no bounds.

"Get me Admiral Lutz. Proceed as planned with a semi-enveloping formation."

Like Kircheis before them, he relied on both von Reuentahl and Lutz. Although not the most dynamic of men, they followed orders with utmost efficiency. In the Battle of Kifeuser, too, they had carried out orders well, contributing to Kircheis's grandiose tactics and dramatic victory.

Eddies of bursting, dancing brilliance filled the Iserlohn Fortress command center's giant screen.

As was his habit when issuing battle commands, Yang sat on the commander's desk, put a knee on his lap, an elbow on that knee, and rested his chin in his hand, looking at the screen. Although Yang didn't think his pose necessarily had any effect on his mind, it nevertheless calmed his body and, above all, put his subordinates at ease. And yet, seeing him sitting there, his eyes bloodshot from all the excitement, for once brought about a disturbance in his subordinates' indestructible faith. Their commander sometimes had to put on a show for them, but this time he was truly exhausted.

"The fleet could launch at any time."

It was closer to an appeal than a report, but Yang was having them hold their current position and stay alert. They'd already been forestalled by the enemy's advance, and Yang wanted a little more time to watch things unfold.

Incidentally, while considering possible interactions, a section of the imperial fleet cleverly detached itself and adopted a semi-enveloping formation within range of the fortress's main gun. If they ignored it, the enemy might take advantage of a blind spot in their firing range.

Yang authorized the launch. But, seeing as he himself was confined to the fortress, he was entrusting Fischer and Attenborough as frontline commanders to inform him of the state of the war. Fischer, uninterestedly, and Attenborough, in high spirits, had been preparing to launch from the main ports, but just then Yang, in a stroke of brilliance, allowed von Reuentahl to take the initiative. The heterochromatic admiral waited for Yang's go-ahead, responding within seconds.

His timing couldn't have been more exquisite. As Yang rose to his feet on the command desk, fleets on both sides fell into a melee within range of the fortress's cannons. The enemy and allies were jumbled together like chess pieces, and even as they tried to attack the enemy, they detected the figure of a consort ship approaching from behind. It was all they could do to chip away with small-caliber artillery. Many of the ships were no match even for that, and they dispersed in all directions to avoided collision and contact with the enemy.

Under these circumstances, it was impossible to fire the fortress cannons, which would destroy more friendlies than enemies.

"Not bad, not bad at all."

Yang was impressed. Having witnessed such refined tactical ability, he had no reason to be resentful. He sat himself down again on his desk and thought of how best to make use of this situation. Even as he was convinced von Reuentahl had the upper hand, he wondered if there wasn't an opportunity of which he might take advantage.

Meanwhile, von Reuentahl was calmly watching over the battle's progress.

If the Alliance Armed Forces attempted to rescue their own, they would be unable to rely on guns and would have to deploy reinforcements from the fortress. And if they grew, von Reuentahl would need to grow his ships in kind.

If only they could draw the alliance into a war of attrition, von Reuentahl would be in an infinitely better position. Then again, in dealing with a man variously called "Miracle Yang" and "Yang the Magician," he suspected his opponent might yet pull a rabbit out of his hat. Naturally, von Reuentahl was looking forward to it.

IV

Yang's fleet, dispatched from the fortress under Fischer's navigational control and at Attenborough's tactical command, narrowly avoided annihilation. At the outer rim of a melee storm, fleets on both sides exchanged fire, and balls of light appeared successively in the darkness of space.

An incandescent downpour enveloped the imperial warship *Schoenberg*, and the moment it compromised the ship's composite armor and energy-neutralizing magnetic field, the *Schoenberg* itself added to the light. It expanded and became an ephemeral, small-scale fixed star before scattering soundlessly in all directions. No sooner had its pulsing afterglow vanished than a fresh ball of light appeared next to it before being reduced to atoms.

The alliance sustained damage as well. The battleship *Oxiana* was surrounded by three nimble destroyers, tossed about by deft, tightly knit teamwork, and bombarded with nuclear shrapnel in the firing hole. The large warship was split from the inside, twisting in the explosion before at last being obliterated. The battleship *Ljubljana* was struck by two beams from the front, and the ship split in two when their breaches combined. Within a circle made by the joined hands of death and destruction, both fleets danced in combative struggle, spewing fire.

Into that maelstrom, Yang's fleet launched fresh forces. On the bridge of von Reuentahl's flagship, *Tristan*, the operator widened his eyes when he saw the model and ship's name on his computer.

"It's the battleship *Hyperion*!"

The operator almost doubted himself, even as he said it.

The young heterochromatic admiral was surprised all the same. Of course, he expressed none of that in his speech and conduct. It was unthinkable that the enemy commander had come out himself. He'd heard Yang was resourceful, but did he have what it took to lead an army?

Yang and von Reuentahl were both thirty-one years old. Although this was mere coincidence, that fact that they had both came to be associated with the battlefield and could boast of high ranks and distinguished service at such a young age was harder to believe.

"All ships, charge! Full speed ahead!" von Reuentahl commanded.

They could decide the outcome in one stroke. Every imperial officer wished to be the one to capture and kill Yang. It was a monumental accomplishment, and the young von Reuentahl felt his fighting spirit stoked by the prospect.

The flagship *Tristan* spearheaded the imperial fleet rushing toward *Hyperion*. But when it was just within firing range, the operator shouted, and the ship was rocked by a dull impact as an enemy ship rammed it from an oblique angle.

An assault landing craft had attached itself to the belly of *Tristan* using a strong electromagnet, fired a heat drill, and sprayed an oxidizing agent. After about two minutes, a two-meter hole had eaten its way through both ships' inner walls, through which a landing unit clad in armored suits poured into *Tristan*.

So *that* was Yang's game. Had he just tripped up a first-rate, if not even more capable, commander like von Reuentahl using a second-rate trick? Using his flagship, on which he was not even present, as a decoy, he'd lured von Reuentahl forward, crashed an assault craft into him, and infiltrated his ship, perhaps with the intention of making him a prisoner of war. The plan had been proposed by von Schönkopf.

"Intruder alert! Intruder alert! Prepare for emergency counterattack!"

Amid the blare of warnings and sirens, firefights and hand-to-hand combat had already escalated along the ship's central passageway. The Rosen Ritter regiment, equipped with composite-mirror shields that reflected laser fire, rushed enemy soldiers with reckless heroism and by their carbon-crystal tomahawks left a mosaic of fresh blood on the floor, walls, and ceiling. The imperial defenders were no less brave than the intruders. Even as soldiers crushed by tomahawk tumbled into death, they gripped their laser rifles, using their remaining strength to fell enemies with relentless fire before falling into pools of their own blood.

"Never mind these minions. Our objective is their commander. Find the bridge," ordered von Schönkopf to his subordinates.

As he stood there wielding his tomahawk, enemy soldiers lay dead at his feet, never to move again.

"Don't let anyone leave this ship alive. Make them realize their reward for recklessness!"

This was the command of Vice Admiral Bergengrün, who'd made a name for himself under Siegfried Kircheis. After Kircheis's death, he'd become von Reuentahl's chief of staff, but as a diligent man of high intelligence, he'd taken it upon himself to command this counterattack.

On the chief of staff's orders, the imperial soldiers assumed a pincer attack formation on either side of the passage. Von Schönkopf charged, felling two enemy soldiers with a swing of his tomahawk. Showered in his comrades' blood, with another blow he took down three more men who sprang at him. Only he and two other soldiers made it through, leaving the others entangled in a free-for-all.

Whether he would call them comrades or not, fortuity was on his side. Seeing a group of soldiers running his way, he opened a side door and jumped inside. There were cries of surprise as two soldiers attending an officer unholstered their blasters.

Beams crossed in the ten-square-meter room, and two men on each side fell to the floor amid short-lived screams. Left standing in the room were von Schönkopf and one imperial soldier, who still held the suit he had been putting on to join the fight.

Seeing that the intruder was fully armed, he didn't cry for help but instead cocked an eyebrow and turned to face him instead. In addition to his extraordinary boldness, his magnificent black-and-silver imperial uniform, and particularly the golden desk that only an admiral would have, strengthened von Schönkopf's convictions.

"Admiral von Reuentahl?"

The young admiral, being addressed in the imperial manner, nodded at his unmistakably brazen intruder.

"Yes. The alliance's scouting dog, I presume?"

His voice was calm, which pleased von Schönkopf greatly. He tightened the grip on his tomahawk. He offered no surrender, knowing it was futile.

"I am Walter von Schönkopf. I'll have you remember that in these last brief moments."

No sooner had he spoken than his tomahawk cleaved the air.

Von Reuentahl wasn't foolish enough to block the slashing attack. His long, well-proportioned body, under perfectly conscious control, flew two meters backward. The tomahawk swung parallel to the floor where his head had been just a moment before. When von Reuentahl aimed his blaster, the tomahawk seemed to defy the laws of inertia as it came swinging from the other direction with even greater speed. Von Reuentahl ducked. The carbon-crystal blade shaved a few strands of dark-brown hair off the top of his head. Von Reuentahl rolled on the floor and jumped as he pulled the trigger. A glittering saber of light would have pierced his opponent's helmet had he not blocked the beam with his tomahawk. The tomahawk's handle split under its force.

Reduced now to a broken handle, the tomahawk flew from von Schönkopf's hand and knocked the blaster from von Reuentahl's. Both men, now barehanded, glared at each other, nodding in unison. Von Schönkopf pulled a long combat knife from his belt. Von Reuentahl jumped for the corpse of an allied soldier that had caught the corner of his eye and snatched a bloodstained knife from it.

He kicked off the floor, and the knife glinted in a vertical arc. The superceramic blades clashed, burning their wielders' eyes with sparks. They stabbed, slashed, knocked each other down, and stopped each other's blows in an equal dance. Try as they might to bury their knives in each other's flesh, the impeccable balance of their offense and defense was not so easily broken.

There was a rush of footsteps as the Rosen Ritter regiment came rushing in, having found their commander. Imperial soldiers weren't far behind.

Captain Kasper Rinz mowed down several imperial soldiers from the side, bathing in a mist of their blood. He rolled onto the floor. More soldiers fired at the intruders, using their fallen comrades' bodies as shields.

Angry bellows, fresh blood, and flashes of light filled the room. With no outcome yet decided, von Reuentahl and von Schönkopf were absorbed into a wave of soldiers.

Within three minutes, the alliance soldiers had been driven from the room, and Vice Admiral Bergengrün could at last make out his commander's figure.

"Your Excellency, are you all right?"

Von Reuentahl nodded silently. As he straightened his disheveled hair with a palm, his mismatched eyes glistened with self-deprecation. What a joke this had turned out to be. Here he was, a fleet commander, having just engaged in hand-to-hand combat. Despite having fought bravely against his enemy Senior Admiral Ofresser last year, he didn't feel much like smiling.

"So those are the infamous Rosen Ritter?"

"Yes, it would seem so."

"Stop the fight and withdraw. I was too eager to win and ended up following the enemy's lead. And now, because our timing was off, a regiment has invaded the flagship."

"There's no excuse for this."

"It was never your responsibility to begin with. I was too hotheaded. Let me cool off a little and we'll start afresh."

When Yang heard of this, he recognized that von Reuentahl was not only talented, but a capable, first-rate commander.

Von Schönkopf, who had returned to Iserlohn Fortress on the assault landing craft, appeared before Yang in full armor, helmet in hand, to give his report. His blood-splattered suit, coupled with his fearless expression, made him seem like a knight of the legendary Round Table.

"I almost had him, but the big fish got away. We did succeed in invading the flagship, so not all was lost."

"That's regrettable."

"Indeed, and perhaps they're thinking the same thing. He was a most worthy opponent—an even match at every turn."

"So we failed to change history after all."

Yang smiled, and von Schönkopf grinned back. Both men knew Yang was only joking.

Von Reuentahl had shown extraordinary ability. He had withdrawn his forces from the melee formation and reorganized a systematic file of troops. Moreover, he had succeeded in doing this while continuing to fight against Yang's fleet. Of course, Yang had tried to take advantage of the enemy's retreat, but with no gap in sight to afford pursuit, he had abandoned the idea and received his fleet at the fortress. The battle had ended in a draw.

Yang sat cross-legged on his commander's desk, sipping unpleasantly from his cup of black tea. The reason for his sullen expression was not the state of the war before him, but the taste of his tea. The leaves were fine, but he'd steeped it too long, and so it left a bitter taste on the tongue. Remembering how skilled Julian had been at brewing tea, letting go of Julian weighed even more heavily on his mind. Yang knew he was selfish for thinking this.

"Superior enemies are everywhere you look," commented Caselnes, taking a sip of coffee that was clearly not to his liking.

Yang dangled one leg from the desk, kicking it lightly.

"He shouldn't have let up on his attack, but he *is* one of the Imperial Navy's Twin Ramparts. There's something different about him."

Yang was never sparing when it came to complimenting his enemies. Von Schönkopf asked a pointed question: Although the present situation was developing toward a battle between fortress and fleet, would von Reuentahl put him in check when it came to a game of chess between fleets?

"I don't know. Kempf should've been inferior to von Reuentahl in terms of tactical flexibility, but we came out on top, albeit barely. Who knows how the chips will fall?"

"Please don't say things to disappoint me. I've said it before and I'll say it again: I believe you can defeat Reinhard von Lohengramm. What'll happen if you can't defeat his subordinate?"

"You're free to think whatever you like, but subjective confidence doesn't necessarily lead to objective results."

Yang was speaking as much to himself as to Caselnes. When he'd faced the brave general Karl Gustav Kempf of the Imperial Navy, he'd thought for sure he'd lose to Reinhard's subordinate, but somehow things had grown even more severe and, as Caselnes said, formidable enemies had abounded.

In the wake of this confrontation, imperial forces discreetly kept their distance from Iserlohn Fortress.

If the Imperial Navy came anywhere within range of the fortress's main battery, the fortress could fire its guns or engage the enemy in close combat with a surprise attack, but the enemy gave no response to their silent invitation. Yang had tried the orthodox method of deploying his fleet in small increments and sustaining enemy fire in the hopes of luring them within firing range.

But von Reuentahl's authority was being followed to the letter, without a single kink in the Imperial Navy's movements. By repeatedly advancing and retreating with almost artistic timing, they sowed anxiety into the hearts of the fortress operators.

More than ever, von Schönkopf regretted not killing von Reuentahl when he'd had the chance.

* * *

On December 9, the Imperial Navy launched a surprise offensive. They stopped their patrol outside the range of the fortress's main gun. Of those ships, a group of five hundred employed a hit-and-run tactic, attacking from close range.

It was a kamikaze mission. If hit directly by the 924 million megawatt energy beam of Thor's Hammer, those five hundred ships would be instantly vaporized. No amount of speed or mobility would be enough to escape it, as the fortress's peripheral guns and emplacements were set up to combat precisely these types of evasive maneuvers. Despite being aware of this, von Reuentahl launched his attack. Thus, the battle began anew with even greater intensity and swiftness.

The fortress's turrets took several direct hits, glowing white and dissolving like pillars of salt. Those left pointing skyward fired rapid arrows of energy. The smaller ships did a nosedive. Unable to shake the grip of Iserlohn's artificial gravity, they spun into the fortress's outer wall and exploded. As one wave withdrew, the next rushed in to take its place, assaulting the outer wall with a continuous downpour.

Thirty minutes later, the Imperial Navy had lost more than two thousand vessels, while Iserlohn had recorded more than two hundred damage reports. Von Reuentahl's commands were subtle. With enviable ingenuity, his ships approached a blind spot of the fortress turrets and made a small breach in the fortress's outer wall by concentrating the full extent of their firepower. They sliced it open, scalpel to wound.

Although not a fatal wound, it was enough to damage the nerves of the defending side. Yang was tactically overwhelmed.

Although Yang had been expecting this battle, von Reuentahl had taken initiative from the start. Von Reuentahl's attacks withstood anything that came their way, and the deftness with which he nursed his wounds was unrivaled. This was not the work of a creative artist but a meticulous engineer tidying up the blueprints laid out on his desk. Frederica was secretly worried, for Yang was clearly deficient in his usual brilliance and vitality. Although failure wasn't certain, neither was it far off.

"I've never fought such a boring battle before," said Lieutenant Commander Olivier Poplin, as he took a meal in the pilots' mess hall, still in his uniform.

When they launched, the enemy didn't approach, and if the enemy attacked, it wasn't their turn. It was nothing more than an artillery battle left to the solid outer wall. There was zero enjoyment in this for a man of Poplin's disposition.

"I can't wrap my head around the enemy's behavior. Aren't they just toying with us?"

Ivan Konev looked at his comrade, hoping his doubts would be validated. Poplin impolitely downed his bread and pork sausage with some light beer before responding.

"I rather prefer a man who treats war like a game."

"This isn't a question of your preferences. I'm worried about what the empire has up its sleeve."

"I know that, but however much you're worrying, you can be sure our commander has been worrying about it much longer. He gets zero points as a lover, but as a strategist no one can top him. That boor."

"As opposed to you?"

Konev thought this cynicism might upset him, but the young ace who boasted more of his piloting in bed than in the air laughed calmly.

"I'm not *that* conceited. I'm more of a quantity over quality kind of guy. Philanthropism is a demerit for someone like me."

⁙

As Poplin pointed out, Yang knew the Imperial Navy's true motives. But knowing he was helpless to do anything about it sank his heart to the bottom of a heavy ocean. Just as Yang had discerned Reinhard's strategy and tactical plan during last year's coup d'état, so had he done this time. But to what effect? Wasn't it better to be the actor than the predictor? Didn't that guarantee a far more meaningful life?

Had Julian been there, he would have told him, "There's no use in being depressed." And Yang was indeed depressed. So much so that he wanted to scream, "Don't you know what's going to happen to the Free Planets Alliance?!" He wanted that flaxen-haired boy by his side more than ever. He deeply regretted letting go of Julian. Even more vexing was that he had no way of measuring whether his regret was well-founded.

VI

Von Reuentahl's attack on Iserlohn ended in failure on December 9. Damage notwithstanding, Iserlohn once again proved its impregnability, and von Reuentahl withdrew his fleet. But this was a superficial development, and one that had been anticipated. The Imperial Navy's objective all along had been to bring about a large-scale attack on Iserlohn, then make its failure known throughout the alliance and Phezzan.

Here, an epic yet bitter play was being staged. The alliance government and its people would delude Phezzan and, in a performance intended to cause misjudgments, write a script that would accelerate a historic change.

Commander of the Imperial Navy's Iserlohn invasion forces, Senior Admiral Oskar von Reuentahl, relayed the immensity of Iserlohn's defenses and resistance to the capital, and requested reinforcements from Reinhard von Lohengramm. Reinhard expressed his regret over von Reuentahl's hard fight and conveyed to the Imperial Navy's highest-ranking staff officers his intention of capturing Iserlohn in one swift action. Senior Admiral Wolfgang Mittermeier, Admiral Neidhart Müller, and the others on standby in the stellar regions surrounding the capital were given orders to launch.

"Head for the Iserlohn Corridor and carry out your duty as efficiently as possible. Should you need any further manpower, I will personally depart from the capital and join your ranks."

"As you wish. We'll give it our all."

The admirals knew that Reinhard's command contained a false proper noun. He was heading for a different corridor altogether.

Reinhard saw off Mittermeier and the others as they headed out from the military spaceport. Standing beside him was his secretary, Hildegard von Mariendorf, or Hilda, who watched Mittermeier's flagship, *Beowulf*, blotting out the stars as it pushed its way through the upper atmosphere.

"It's begun, hasn't it?"

Seeing Hilda standing there, clad in her black-and-silver uniform, and treated for all like a commander, Reinhard nodded with boyish enthusiasm.

"Yes, it's the beginning of the end, fräulein."

As she studied Reinhard, the image of her cousin Baron Heinrich von Kümmel immediately came to mind. The eighteen-year-old noble suffered from a disease known as congenital dysbolism and was, like Reinhard, incapable of getting his designs for the universe off the ground. On the contrary, he could barely support his own life by himself. Before her departure, Hilda had promised herself to pay Heinrich a visit. She followed Reinhard's line of sight again, looking up at the night sky.

Far beyond where their eyes could see, an ocean of soon-to-be-conquered stars spread out limitlessly before them.

CHAPTER 9:

I

THE FLEET OF SENIOR ADMIRAL Wolfgang Mittermeier left the capital of Odin, presumably for the Iserlohn Corridor. Most of the officers and men were convinced of this, but as their march progressed, some began to have doubts. It was becoming clear to the navigations control officer that they were moving *away* from Iserlohn with every warp. And while at first it seemed they were hurling themselves aimlessly through space, gradually the letters in their heads formed a single name: Phezzan. It was the only place outside of Iserlohn that was beyond imperial territory. They couldn't believe it.

On December 13, their suspicions were confirmed when the full story of Operation Ragnarök, known until then only by the admirals, was announced to the troops. From the bridge of the flagship *Beowulf*, Senior Admiral Mittermeier made his announcement to the entire fleet via comm screen.

"We are not going to the Iserlohn Corridor, but to the Phezzan Corridor."

When the two million soldiers listening to the Gale Wolf's voice grasped his meaning, they stirred with feverish commotion. Mittermeier went on, as if to suppress this.

"Our ultimate objective, of course, goes beyond the occupation of Phez-zan. We will use Phezzan as our rear base, pass through their corridor, and overcome those rebels who presume to call themselves the Free Planets Alliance, thus putting a stop to a divisive conflict that has rocked human-ity for centuries. That is why we have launched. We're not here simply to command and conquer, but to turn a page in our collective history."

He took a breath, then continued.

"Of course, it's not going to be easy. Alliance territory is vast. They have many troops stationed at the ready and an outstanding commander to lead them. But taking control of the Phezzan Corridor puts us in an over-whelmingly advantageous position. I have great faith in your courage."

And so, the Mittermeier fleet set a course for Phezzan, riding the wave of its own exhilaration.

Phezzan's dedicated mineral freighter, *Easy Money*, was, for the first time in six years, fully loaded with precious cargo and heading for home. The crew, fourteen strong, entrusted its operation to a navigational computer, and as they amused themselves playing cards and chess, from their mouths wafted the odors of alcohol and dreams. Among them was a man, paycheck in hand, who planned on marrying his lover after they returned. Their idleness and calm, however, were shattered by a startling sight on the operator's main screen: clusters of man-made points of light that seemed to go on forever.

The crewmen looked at each other, but on no face was written a satis-factory answer. Three minutes later, the operator made an announcement to his comrades.

"An imperial fleet! Ten thousand, no, *twenty* thousand ships. But why would an imperial fleet be all the way out here? This is supposed to be a demilitarized space zone."

The crew erupted in a chorus of agitated voices. The normally reticent astrogator was the first to propose an explanation.

"The enemy means to invade the Phezzan Corridor. We all thought they were going to Iserlohn, but it looks like we've been had."

He almost sounded like someone telling a bad joke, but beneath the thin crust of his anger bubbled a magma of uneasiness and fear.

"So they intend to occupy Phezzan by military force?" someone asked, hoping for a no that would never come.

"What else could it be?"

"How can you be so calm?! This is an emergency. We must alert Phezzan right away."

But by then, more than ten destroyers and high-speed patrol ships were steering their bows toward *Easy Money*. They sent out orders to stop their ships as they approached. An unthinkable dilemma awaited them. Even the people of Phezzan, who were supposed to be gifted with more than enough audaciousness, were frightened by these unforeseen circumstances and could determine no immediate countermeasure.

"It'll be a while before the destroyers open fire. There's no time to lose. Let's make our getaway while we can."

"Impossible. They'd catch up with us in a heartbeat," said the astrogator, refusing to entertain optimism. "And even if we do manage to escape, we'll end up having to reunite with the Imperial Navy on Phezzan anyway. In which case, we'd do better to make a compliant impression."

"But why has it come to this? I used to think that Phezzan and the empire would continue to coexist, but…"

"I guess times have changed."

They were forced to admit they were nothing more than the estranged audience of a historical drama. After diligently and conscientiously working without faltering, amassing their wealth, and heading home in hopes of living their lives to the fullest, things had now taken a different turn. History had changed and the times with it. As their nation had risen, so would it fall.

Although control of *Easy Money* had been revoked, its safety was guaranteed as the crew returned to a Phezzan surrounded by Imperial Navy ships. If they tried to escape, they would be decimated in an instant. No one outran the Gale Wolf. The prospect of being protected by the imperial fleet's twenty thousand ships was nothing to be happy about. Half a day later, Phezzan's merchant ship *Caprice* also became entangled in the Imperial Navy's surveillance network and was hailed to stop:

"If you don't, we will fire."

But the crew of *Caprice* was much braver than their allies aboard *Easy Money*. Or far more foolish. Disregarding the signal, they commenced their escape in earnest.

When the signal was ignored for the fourth time, even Mittermeier couldn't decide what to do. Thirty seconds later, pure-white striations of light tore through the everlasting darkness, incinerating *Caprice*.

The crewmen watching on the main screen of *Easy Money* hung their heads in disappointment. Knowing they'd made the right choice just as well as they knew *Caprice* had made the wrong one, they'd nevertheless prayed for the success of *Caprice*'s commendable escape attempt.

On December 24, Mittermeier's fleet reached Phezzan's satellite orbit.

On its way, it captured sixty merchant ships it encountered in the Phezzan Corridor and was forced to destroy about half as many. To the Gale Wolf, who'd hoped for a more heroic enemy, it was an entirely unsatisfying expedition, but he could look forward to ones of far greater magnitude. Despite the diversionary tactics, it was hard to make a snap judgment about who was luckier—he or his comrade Oskar von Reuentahl, who'd danced with Yang Wen-li. In any event, Wolfgang Mittermeier would go down in history as the first to invade this corridor since the establishment of Phezzan.

On the bridge of his flagship, *Beowulf*, Mittermeier observed the landing procedure to the planet's surface on his enormous screen. Warnings came from Phezzan's control tower.

"This is Control. Please comply! You are in restricted airspace. I repeat: This is Control. You must comply!"

Those warnings were ignored. The fleet under Vice Admiral Bayerlein's command had already breached satellite orbit and was plowing through the atmosphere toward the surface. Bathed in sunlight, the fleet sparkled in a tight spiral that looked for all like a pearl necklace coming apart around the planet. It was strangely beautiful.

"Contact the landesherr's office at once! The imperial fleet has breached the atmosphere. It's an invasion!"

Phezzan's control tower was beset with panic, thus revealing the fragility of a society that, nonaggressive for more than a century, had been built by those who in their complacency had forgotten what a crisis looked like. Amid the hysteric screams and disorderly footsteps, one of the controllers threw his headphones on the table, tearing at his hair and cursing to himself.

"Why the hell weren't we made aware of this situation?"

Many Phezzanese below likewise cursed the sky. Like throwing one's arms around a hologram, it was instinctive yet pointless behavior.

On Phezzan's surface, even to the half of the globe plunged in the darkness of night, pandemonium set in. Children pointed to the sky with cries of incomplete understanding, while the adults followed suit, their eyes fixed upward.

Julian saw it all as countless points of light overwhelmed the deep indigo sky on a diagonal plane. He'd just stepped out onto the streets in plainclothes when it happened. He sensed he was being followed—whether by a Phezzanese, someone from the commissioner's office, or a comrade, he couldn't tell—but that didn't matter anymore.

It had begun at last. Julian knew this. The Imperial Navy was going to occupy Phezzan and use it as a rear base to invade alliance territory. Admiral Yang's prediction had come true after all. He'd tried to stop it, but to no avail.

As people's screams of commotion were filtered by his eardrums, Julian turned on a heel and, trying not to bump into anyone, ran to the commissioner's office.

II

"The Imperial Navy has invaded Phezzan. The central spaceport has already been occupied."

When that news reached the city, Landesherr Adrian Rubinsky was at neither his office nor his official residence, but his private residence. The ceiling was high in the spacious second-floor salon, a few oil paintings hung on the walls, and the fixtures were all done up in an antique rococo style. Set into one wall was an enormous mirror that measured two meters per side. Extravagant, yes, but one couldn't deny it reflected a personal flair.

Even after facing certain defeat by Reinhard's swift and decisive invasion of Phezzan, Rubinsky looked like anyone but a loser, relaxing as he was on a sofa, calmly drinking from his wine glass. The man sitting on the opposite sofa opened his mouth.

"Have you heard, Landesherr, Your Excellency?" said Rupert Kesselring.

"I heard."

"Phezzan's final hour is close at hand."

No one ever dreamed this would happen, thought Rupert Kesselring. In fact, even he had never imagined that in this year, SE 798, he would see imperial officers setting foot on Phezzanese soil.

"We can expect Boltec to come riding in on his horse at any moment, backed by the Imperial Navy, to snatch away your position and take on a power of authority he isn't built to handle."

Rupert Kesselring smiled coldly at the familiar face reflected in his wine.

"Your time is up. You held your post for seven years, which makes you the shortest-lived landesherr of all time."

"Is that a guarantee?"

"On that point alone, I'm of the same mind as Boltec. Actors who've played their roles yet continue to hog the stage get in the way of those who follow. It's time you made your exit."

Had anyone else spoken to him like that, Rubinsky would have considered plunging a dagger into him right then and there. Adrian Rubinsky was unfazed. The Black Fox of Phezzan put his wineglass back on an end table and stroked his lean chin with one palm.

"You're also of the same mind as Duke von Lohengramm, who thinks I'm harder to deal with than Boltec. I should be honored."

"I didn't think you'd try to glorify yourself so much."

Rupert Kesselring's voice and words had gone from resentful to vulgar. From his expression, too, he'd peeled off the guise of courtesy, and the unbridled hatred boiling over from his internal crucible flushed his graceful face venomously. Had Kesselring been a timid man, he couldn't have looked Rubinsky in the eye. The worst of human emotion had been catalyzed in both parties and seemed to be undergoing a chemical change into something even darker. Smiling, he thrust his hand into his jacket pocket and removed something from it, slowly and deliberately. Gripped in Rupert Kesselring's hand was a blaster, its muzzle pointed at Rubinsky. The landesherr regarded it with a look of contempt.

"I really had no idea. Having such an interest in a corpse is rather morbid, don't you think?"

"I see—so as soon as the chance arrives, you bare your fangs?"

Rubinsky seemed rather impressed.

"Well, I can't say you weren't clever for seizing an opportunity, but let's not get ahead of ourselves, okay?"

"You thought that, even if you gave me a chance to change things, there'd be no need to hesitate over amending the original plan, didn't you, Landesherr, Your Excellency? You probably would've said that success depends entirely on correction."

"Maybe so, but there's no need to dirty your own hands, Rupert."

At being called by his first name, the young aide's face went red. His anger and discomfort stimulated every vein on the surface of his face. He took a breath to steady himself. It seemed the words he wanted to say in retaliation to his abusive father would not come out so easily.

"I'll bring down Boltec's idiocy somehow. But you're in the way of me becoming master of Phezzan, nonetheless. You're a man who lives to deceive others. If I settle things with you right here, not only will I be at ease, I'll also be contributing to the welfare of the public at large."

He'd considered capturing Rubinsky and handing him over to the Imperial Navy, but Duke von Lohengramm, who already had Boltec in the palm of his hand, would have no use for Kesselring. He was more likely to be treated as a traitor, along with Rubinsky, and dealt with accordingly. He wanted to rally the people of Phezzan in the name of rebirth. In which case, the existence of Rubinsky, who was more popular than him, would get in the way. By the time he reached this conclusion, his self-interest was solid, and he could no longer doubt the negative feelings he held toward his father.

"But Rupert…"

"Shut up! Don't get all familiar with me."

Rubinsky calmly recrossed his legs, staring with expressionless eyes at his own flesh and blood.

"I'm your father. You'd do well to let me call you by your first name."

"Father, is it…?"

Rupert Kesselring almost choked on the word. He coughed and cleared his throat.

"Father? If you're going to say father, then you might as well…"

The raging stream of emotions inside him had robbed him of his words. The young aide squeezed the trigger on his blaster.

The mirror on the wall let out a sharp cry as its surface shattered, sending glittering shards flying in all directions. With a look of surprise, Rupert Kesselring turned back to face it. Three rays of light shot out from that brilliant glitter and were absorbed by Kesselring's body.

The young aide, blaster still in hand, performed a short yet violent dance. A moment later, Rupert Kesselring fell to the floor and went still as if some giant invisible hand had swatted him.

"It seems you underestimated me a little, Rupert."

Rubinsky stood up from the sofa and looked down at his son, unimpressed yet slightly pensive.

"I knew you had every intention of killing me. That was your objective in coming here tonight, wasn't it? That's why I was prepared."

"Why…?"

"I always said you were naïve. Did you really believe Dominique was on your side?"

"That whore!"

It required a colossal effort on Rupert's part just to spit out that curse. In his field of vision, which was losing light and color, several indistinct figures stepped out from where the mirror had been, as if they were denizens of some fairy-tale land behind it. They'd been concealed by a one-way mirror, waiting for the right moment to protect their landesherr. Rupert had made the mistake of fighting on his father's turf.

"You always did resemble me in the worst ways. If only you'd curbed your ambition and greed a little more, I might've handed over my position and authority on my deathbed. You knew it all, but you just didn't know to wait for your chance."

The energy of his malice shone faintly in the young man's eyes.

"I never thought I'd get you to hand over a single thing."

The red froth bubbling from a corner of Rupert's mouth made his voice almost unintelligible. The places where he'd been wounded were strangely hot, while a chill crept like some nocturnal animal from the tips of his limbs to the center of his body. When it reached his heart, his future would be lost to him.

"I would have taken it from you. I would have taken everything. That was my decision. I won't leave you anything. Not even myself…"

His hate-filled muttering stopped, and Rupert Kesselring went still. Leaving many strategies and plans unfinished, Rubinsky's son had exited the stage before his father.

"Landesherr, Your Excellency, what shall we do now?" asked one of Rubinsky's guards with some hesitation.

They didn't know the true colors of the one they'd killed. From behind the mirror, they hadn't known the nature of their conversation. But they couldn't help but be vaguely aware of an uncommon relationship between the two. It was enough to make them ill at ease.

Rubinsky turned to the one who'd asked. Feeling an almost physical coercion in being looked at so, he moved his hefty build one step back. A glint in Rubinsky's eye gripped an icy hand around the guard's heart, but a moment later it faded, and Rubinsky returned to his brazen yet trustworthy self, his voice filled with conviction.

"Free Planets Alliance chairman Trünicht hid himself safely until the coup d'état was over. Let's follow his example."

III

Mittermeier had set up temporary headquarters inside Phezzan's central spaceport building.

"I've received word from the imperial commissioner's office," his aide, Lieutenant Commander Kurlich, announced. "It fears retaliation by insurgents hostile to our fleet's occupation. They're requesting a guard unit."

"We've barely arrived, and already they're making requests? Fine, then, have a battalion of ground troops sent their way. If they're so afraid to show their faces, there's no need for them to come greet us," said Mittermeier with a wry smile.

He assembled his staff officers to hand down his first command on Phezzan.

Targets for suppression were reconfirmed. The landesherr's office, the alliance commissioner's office, the Navigation Bureau, the Public Broadcasting Center, the Central Communications Bureau, six spaceports, the Goods Distribution Control Center, Security Police Headquarters, the Ground Traffic Control Center, and the Hydrogen Power Center were the primary targets. With these under control, they would have possession of Phezzan's brain and heart, to do with as they pleased.

"The most important of these are the landesherr's office, the alliance commissioner's office, and the Navigation Bureau. We must gain access to those computer systems and get our hands on their data. Failure is not an option. Understood?"

Bayerlein, Büro, Droisen, and Sinzer nodded nervously in response to the glint in their commander's eye, understanding well the gravity of their mission.

In the past, any number of expeditionary forces had been driven to withdraw in defeat due to inadequate information regarding alliance territory geography. But if they could gain control of the Navigation Bureau and alliance commissioner's office computers, they would neutralize fighting with an enemy who boasted of local advantage over the planet's vast, unknown terrain. With Phezzan as a rear base and this information in hand, they could wage war on equal terms. For Reinhard, who aimed for mastery over the entire universe in one fell stroke, this was a prerequisite.

Neither could one ignore the mental dimensions at play. If such significant information about their own nation's geography and military and economics fell into enemy hands, even the alliance wouldn't be able to stop a disturbance.

By completing its invasion of Phezzan, the empire had decided a strategic victory against the alliance, which had been focusing its attention on the Iserlohn Corridor. Even if the alliance's Yang Wen-li was a tactical genius, at least they had control over their immediate environment.

Mittermeier further declared that murdering civilians, sexual violence against women, and looting of any kind were prohibited, and that any offenders would be sentenced to death by firing squad following a summary trial.

"Don't think that Wolfgang Mittermeier will go back on his word. Anyone who dares wound the honor of the Imperial Navy will receive their just reward. And don't forget it."

His staff officers did as they were told. To his subordinates, Mittermeier could be lavish and welcoming, but he was a superior who knew no mercy when it came to delinquency. The thought of punishment made them shudder. At the time of the old regime, he himself had executed a subordinate who'd murdered a civilian during a robbery. This had been considered a problem, and he had been court-martialed by people jealous that someone of his common origin could grow to be so distinguished. Reinhard had lifted the suit and advanced him, absorbing him into the admiralität. Mittermeier was obliged to do good as recipient of the young master's favor.

His command was favorably executed as, one after another, Phezzan's key locations were suppressed by the Imperial Navy. The Navigation Bureau was the first to be taken over and its computers confiscated, extensive navigations database and all.

Next to be occupied was the landesherr's office, although the master of the building was nowhere to be found. And while a detached force was dispatched to his private residence, this yielded only a young man's dead body in the second-floor salon and a broken one-way mirror. They identified the man as the landesherr's aide, Rupert Kesselring, but would have to wait before they could piece together the circumstances surrounding his killing.

A group of land forces numbering six hundred, led by Captain Gläser and divided into 120 mobile armored vehicles, set out to occupy the Free Planets Alliance commissioner's office on Phezzan. They barreled down the city's main thoroughfare at full speed. Normally there would have been a lot of pedestrian traffic, but most of the stores were closed, and they were met only with stares of fear and anger from the sidelines.

When they reached the alliance commissioner's office, the captain had the building surrounded on all four sides. He descended from his vehicle and stood before the front gate.

Just then, a charged particle beam shot from the building into the ground at his feet, kicking up white smoke and fragments of ceramic pavement.

"Well, that was pointless," said Gläser with a cold smile.

He lifted a hand and signaled one of his armored vehicles to aim its double-barreled heat gun at the building. Once aligned, it fired two roaring arrows of orange flame into the building's ground level. Hard glass shattered, and smoke and fire seemed to battle each other for dominance as they arose from the hole left behind.

No return fire came. If anyone was inside, they were being unusually quiet. Gläser, true to his training, considered the possibility of an ambush, but an infrared measuring device would be useless with all the fire.

After a careful approach, his men rushed inside, but not a minute later one of the soldiers came running out.

"Captain, the building is totally deserted."

When asked who had fired on them, the soldier pointed to the second-floor window.

The captain clicked his tongue when he saw the automatic firing mechanism. A charged particle rifle had been rigged to the window, operated by a timer switch. The captain cursed the clever person they were dealing with. He ordered his men to put out the fire and made for the computer room with his engineer in tow.

After fiddling around with the computer, the engineer's face went pale as he turned to the captain. The moment he saw this, the captain knew he'd failed to carry out this mission's most important task. The sound of his gritting teeth filled the air with futility, then dissipated.

Being a natural-born military man, Mittermeier was ignorant when it came to economics, but he knew enough to tread carefully. For the time being, banks stayed open and businesses ran as usual, much to the relief of the people. Despite their animosity toward the Imperial Navy, they had to go on living, and their current economic circumstances were preferable to the alternative.

By the same token, Mittermeier sent out an ordinance, declaring that anyone who engaged in hoarding or price gouging would be severely punished. Not one hour after the announcement, many of the new price tags that shops had just made became obsolete. With one motion, Mittermeier had crushed the Phezzanese people's robust commercial spirit.

On the twenty-eighth, Neidhart Müller of the second regiment arrived on Phezzan. Mittermeier's subordinates jubilantly welcomed their ally. The more spirited of Phezzan's citizens watched with hatred, the less spirited with resignation, as more than one million imperial troops were freshly added to the occupation. Müller shook hands firmly with Mittermeier, who came out to greet him.

Meanwhile, Phezzan's spaceports had fallen under imperial control, and all passenger flight operations were suspended. No one could leave the surface of Phezzan, at least officially, which meant that Landesherr Rubinsky and the commissioner were hiding somewhere on the planet.

Mittermeier's record as a military governor was almost perfect, but that didn't mean it was without flaw. Just before Müller's arrival, an incident arose involving the rape of a civilian woman by a small group of his soldiers. Along with her dignity, the victim's star sapphire engagement ring had been stolen. By command of an enraged Mittermeier, the perpetrators were ferreted out at once. The Gale Wolf apologized to the victim, returned the ring, and with the power invested in him as commander, sentenced the three men to death.

The public execution was carried out in Saint Therese Square. Extreme, perhaps, but it had to be done. Openly rescinding the execution would mean losing the trust of the citizens under occupation, and if the execution were carried out in secret, people would wonder if the perpetrators hadn't been quietly let off the hook. In any event, he had to placate the people's nerves and eliminate any possibility of civil resistance.

The leader of the perpetrators' unit timidly begged for leniency, but Mittermeier held firm.

"I said I'd never go back on my word. Or does my word mean so little that you weren't listening?"

After witnessing the execution firsthand, Mittermeier headed for the central spaceport to welcome his comrade in arms. Müller was thankful to be greeted by someone of higher rank like Mittermeier, and commended him for being so prudent in his governance.

"Well, so far," the Gale Wolf answered.

Phezzan was behaving itself because of the extreme circumstances. But sooner or later he could expect dissenters to come out of the woodwork. In that case, Duke von Lohengramm was sure to take appropriate measures.

"At any rate, I'll be ill at ease if I don't fight," concluded the natural-born military man.

IV

A boy, dressed casually in a sweater and jeans, ran through a back alley, where his kind were never seen. His longish flaxen hair, facial features that made girls of his age turn their heads, dark-brown eyes, and a well-proportioned, fit body painted the unmistakable picture of Julian Mintz. As he opened the door to a nondescript low-rise building and slipped inside, three men were waiting for him, including Warrant Officer Machungo and Commissioner Henslow, both of whom had escaped from the commissioner's office. The third person was unfamiliar to him. Had Machungo found his independent merchant?

Four days earlier, while running back to the office after seeing the imperial invasion with his own eyes, Julian had picked up a landcar with Machungo, but the chaotic crowds made driving impossible.

"There's nothing we can do, Warrant Officer. Let's get out."

"Shall we walk?"

"No, run."

Machungo followed close behind. He thought the world of this boy and would do anything he could to protect him. It was Admiral Yang's personal request.

When they got back to the commissioner's office, Julian found everyone gathered in the hallway. He walked up to Commissioner Henslow and saluted.

"Your Excellency, please hear me out. We must erase your computer's drive at once."

"Erase?"

The commissioner's reply was so obtuse as to be demented.

"If we leave it as it is, all the data will fall into the Imperial Navy's hands."

Commissioner Henslow gasped and averted his eyes aimlessly, as if hoping to pin the responsibility on someone else. No one met his gaze.

"Please, the time to make a decision is now. Imperial forces will be here any minute."

Julian looked around. He wondered if no one was going to agree to this, for everyone was silent, almost apathetic. Even chief of staff and military attaché Captain Viola just stood there, glaring at him spitefully.

"I won't take orders from the likes of you!"

Surprised at the volume of his own voice, Henslow wiped his sweat with his fingertips.

"But, orders aside, it seems your proposal has value that must be taken seriously. Maybe we should erase the computer's data, but it's on *your* head."

If the alliance fell, Julian thought, this man wanted to pass the blame to someone else.

"There *is* another way. We could leave the computer's data as is and surrender to the Imperial Navy. By offering them this valuable data, maybe they'll treat you with leniency."

Julian himself had meant to be sarcastic, but Henslow went silent, and the boy was astonished to see a selfish expression come to the man's face.

"Understood," said Julian. "I'll take full responsibility. Allow me to erase the computer's memory."

There was some internal hesitation in his declaration, but if he didn't do this, the situation would stall. With Machungo's help, he erased the computer's memory and, when he returned half an hour later, was welcomed by an unexpected scene. The hall was completely empty, and only a single commissioner was left sitting on a sofa in blank amazement, deserted by his incompetent superiors. He knew this place hadn't originally been a hub of law and order, but such irresponsibility was beyond imagination. He understood that if the alliance government got wind of this, they would face serious consequences for abandoning their posts. Or maybe they'd given up on the future of the alliance itself. Julian's heart turned cold at the thought.

"You…you…I beg of you, take me to a safe place," said Henslow when he saw Julian.

In all honesty, Julian saw the man as a burden, but he couldn't very well leave him there. After telling the commissioner to change into more comfortable clothes and to ready some cash and a blaster, Julian made an automatic firing device using a charged particle rifle and set it up in a second-floor window. He found the commissioner, changed and ready, wandering aimlessly on the ground floor. When they left the building, they heard the wheels of mobile armored vehicles approaching.

"What do we do now? Is there *any* point to all this? If not, we're screwed."

They were out of enemy hands for the time being. As they half-ran through the back alleys under cover of night, Henslow reverted to his default arrogance. Having never known a day of hardship or adversity in his life, he seemed put off by the fact that a young man not yet thirty was now his protector. Even as he envied the shrewdness of his colleagues, Julian answered, having no other choice.

"We'll look for an independent merchant."

"And when we do, what then?"

"I plan on getting him to offer us a ship to escape Phezzan."

The commissioner shook his head.

"Hmm…But will it go as well as you seem to think?"

That's what Julian wanted to know even more. But they couldn't just stand there looking on while the world changed around them. He wanted to return to Yang. To the place where he belonged. He shot a contemptuous look at the commissioner. If only Yang were standing there instead of this man unworthy of respect. How much it would lift Julian's spirits…

Over the next four days, Julian took shelter in a secluded alleyway and continued his search for a way to escape Phezzan. One thing about Phezzan for which Julian was grateful was that almost anything could be bought for the right price.

The man introduced to Julian by Machungo had thinning hair and sagging skin, and gave the impression of someone tired in his middle age. But his eyes were unexpectedly vibrant.

"My name is Marinesk, acting captain of the independent merchant ship *Beryozka*."

The man told Julian he thought he could be of some use. Because he was originally an administrative officer, he had no confidence in getting the ship off the ground by his own devices, but he assured Julian he'd personally see to it that an expert was hired.

"Truth is, we're not total strangers, you and I, although there are two degrees of separation between us."

"Two degrees?"

"My captain, Boris Konev, and the ensign's guardian, Admiral Yang. When the two of them were children, well, they seemed to get along well enough to be called good friends."

Julian's eyes brightened, but he was discouraged to hear that the once-friendly captain was now in the alliance capital of Heinessen.

"But I do know another highly skilled pilot. You can count on me. To a Phezzanese, a contract is always sacred."

It would, he added, require money.

"Whatever you pay, I trust it will be commensurate with the courage and skill required for this mission. I don't think this is too much to ask."

"Neither do I. I assure you, it will be enough. Can you find this person right away?"

Ignoring Henslow's protestations, Julian took five thousand marks from the commissioner's thick wallet and handed them to Marinesk as a down payment. After he left, Warrant Officer Machungo looked at his boy superior thoughtfully.

"Can we trust him?"

"I think so, but…"

He couldn't say he trusted him completely. But there was no other way, and in any case, he had to leave his life and destiny in somebody's hands. Julian wondered if this Konev, in addition to being Yang's childhood friend, wasn't the same ace pilot Ivan Konev, the so-called Cousin of Phezzan. He would never know for sure unless he met him.

"Ensign, seeing as we're trusting him, under the circumstances we should be prepared to kill him if he decides to betray us. What do you think?"

At this, Julian's elegant shoulders tilted at a slight angle. Sometimes, he felt like he was being compelled by some invisible other to carry out responsibilities and duties beyond his ken. Was this what they called reaping what you sowed? Was this the consequence for wanting to become a military man? Either way, Julian had to do whatever it took to get back to Yang, and he had his heart set on doing just that.

Mobile armored vehicles, equipped with double-barreled heat guns, roared down Main Street, beating the air with the sounds of their nuclear fusion turbines.

A man looking down at them from a third-floor window clicked his tongue in disgust, one of a group of independent merchants gathered in a room of a bar called Dracul. With half of the spaceports already blocked, most of them were out of work, and all they could do was congregate and distract themselves from their resentment by drinking.

"You say Phezzan had wind of this beforehand? I can't believe what I'm hearing! And yet they couldn't even forecast an imperial invasion?"

"And what have those jackasses down at the commissioner's office in Odin been doing all this time, sending all those useless reports about parties and the weather? I guess government officials are useless after all."

"Are you really so surprised? I don't know about other nations, but here on Phezzan we've got talentless morons running the show. It would be pointless to expect any beneficial reports from their end."

These insults lacked luster, and the ones spouting them knew better than most that trying to improve the present situation by cursing out other people was never going to turn back time. Dark clouds were hovering in the background of each of their hearts as they spoke of the day when they would no longer use the calendar they had always known.

"But where the hell do we go from here?"

"Where to go from here, you say? History will change. The Goldenbaum Dynasty, Phezzan, the Free Planets Alliance—all of it will disappear. Then that golden brat will become emperor of the entire universe."

"He's not satisfied with just bringing down the Goldenbaum Dynasty? It's pure greed, I tell you. There's nothing endearing about him."

"Endearing or not, can a moron ever succeed? In that respect, our nation's dignitaries are just as despicable."

Their banter inspired laughter, despite a certain ring of desperation.

"Remember, we're free citizens, not some idiots who proudly call ourselves the Free Planets Alliance, or whatever it might be. We're a free people. A benevolent emperor is the last thing we need."

As one of them launched into his speech, another pulled at his sleeve. Among the group was a senior member, an elderly merchant who was respected as the oldest among them. He opened his mouth.

"I wish I'd never lived so long. Then I'd never have to see the imperial fleet profaning our streets with their fancy military shoes."

The old merchant heaved a sigh, and the younger men around him were silent, devoid of consolation.

"Since this era held out for a hundred years, I only expected it would continue for a hundred more, but when you think about it, no such precedent exists. Even when I saw the Goldenbaum Dynasty, which lasted for five centuries, turned into a wretched version of its former self, I never once thought Phezzan would perish. How stupid of me."

At the word "perish," the silence deepened, broken by a lone voice.

"It's a frightening prospect, yes, but it may only be temporary. Phezzan will rise again. We'll rebuild our fortress of independent merchants for free citizens. As I was just saying, we don't need some emperor to order us around."

The man who said this was Kahle Wilock, more renowned as an astrogator than a merchant.

There was applause, and everyone turned around, their pessimism fading. A newcomer standing by the door clapped again.

"That was a great speech, Wilock."

Wilock smiled at his old friend.

"Why, if it isn't Marinesk of the *Beryozka*. And to what ulterior motive do I owe the pleasure of this rare appearance?"

"I've come with a job for you. That is, unless you'd prefer giving speeches to piloting a ship."

"Sure, count me in."

"I'm surprised. You accept without even asking the terms of the job?"

Marinesk smiled wryly at Wilock's blind determination.

"I'd accept a request from the devil himself just to get out of this rut. And I'll take you over the devil any day."

Wilock smiled boldly.

∨

On December 30, at 1650 Phezzan Standard Time, Reinhard von Lohengramm stepped foot on Phezzanese soil together with his closest aides.

Senior Admiral Mittermeier and Admiral Müller, accompanied by forty thousand guards, welcomed the imperial marshal. It was the moment when the day handed over its sovereignty to the night. It grew dark steadily, and beneath the sky, in which a bottomless blue was transitioning into a rose-colored band, the young blond figure looked like something out of a poem. Even those who despised him couldn't help but recognize his overwhelming magnificence. Until the day they died in battle or of old age, the soldiers watching Reinhard stand on the spaceport would boast to their wives, children, and grandchildren of the time they saw that golden-haired young man towering in the twilight. The soldiers arose in songlike jubilation, their fervor and power strengthening with every cheer.

"Long live the emperor! Long live the empire!"

Mittermeier leaned in toward the young marshal.

"They're calling you their emperor."

"They're eager."

Reinhard's officers caught his exact meaning. He wasn't denying being called emperor. As he waved to the soldiers, another round of cheers erupted into the evening sky.

"Long live the emperor! Long live the empire!"

Reinhard wouldn't be crowned emperor until the following year. But on Planet Phezzan, this day would be remembered as the first on which he came to be officially known among his soldiers as "our emperor Reinhard."

Reinhard set up a makeshift marshal's office in a commandeered high-class hotel. His first declaration was that the imperial occupation would in no way harm the many civil rights that the Phezzan people had always enjoyed. He further stated his hope to see the imperial mainland and the self-governing dominion of Phezzan in one airtight unification, and this was no lie. He simply failed to mention that this was one step toward his ultimate ambition of conquering the Free Planets Alliance and that everything would be carried out under his strict leadership.

Mittermeier offered his apologies to Reinhard for failing him on three counts: not being able to apprehend Landesherr Rubinsky, failing likewise with Commissioner Henslow of the alliance, and finally, not being able to extract any data of use from the commissioner's office computer. Reinhard shrugged his shoulders, his face calm.

"There's no such thing as total perfection. If you couldn't do it, then I doubt anyone else could. There's no need to apologize."

Reinhard hardly cared what became of someone like Commissioner Henslow. And for now, even Julian Mintz was far from his mind. While the incident involving the commissioner's office computer was indeed regrettable, they had managed to get all the data from the Navigation

Bureau, so it was far from an unrecoverable failure. What he could not shut his eyes to, however, were Rubinsky's unknown whereabouts.

"What do you think, Fräulein von Mariendorf, about the Black Fox's intentions?"

"At this point, I think he has accepted defeat and burrowed back into his hole. On the other hand, he probably foresees that Commissioner Boltec will never control Phezzan. He might very well believe his turn will come again when Boltec fails miserably. Whether it's Your Excellency or the people of Phezzan, it doesn't matter who he courts."

"So it's come to that, has it?"

Reinhard accepted Hilda's analysis. Rubinsky had spent time trying to bait Reinhard with the emperor's abduction and passage through the Phezzan Corridor, but it had worked utterly against him.

Reinhard detected something other than total victory lurking within his neural pathways. For the time being, it was a mere seed of suspicion, but if nourished with time, it could blossom into a flower of anxiety. Boltec and Rubinsky were hiding something. Whatever it was would become clear sooner or later.

After finishing dinner with his officers, Reinhard headed for the Navigation Bureau with his imperial guards in tow. When he was led to the computer room by Commodore Klapf, head of defense operations, Reinhard left even his personal guard Captain Kissling to wait outside and entered the room alone.

The empty computer room was so mechanical that the very air smelled of electricity. Reinhard walked silently between the machines and stopped before a display screen, looking up at its giant, shining blank surface.

"Yes, this is what I wanted."

His voice had the tone of someone dreaming. He put his hands on the console and without hesitation started booting up the computer.

His manipulations were more than deliberate, like those of a pianist inspired to play an impromptu. But what he played was, of course, not music. He brought up a star map on the screen—a galactic system of two hundred billion fixed stars. He enlarged it. The Free Planets Alliance territory appeared before him. The name of each fixed star system appeared, along with the routes connecting them: the alliance's capital planet of Heinessen; the Astarte Stellar Region, where he had once consigned an enemy fleet twice the size of his own to oblivion; the Dagon Stellar Region, where, 158 years ago, the Imperial Navy had suffered a crushing defeat; and countless other fixed star systems, stellar regions, and battlefields besides. He pined for the day when he would conquer them all.

Reinhard became a living sculpture before the screen. After a while, he took the silver pendant hanging from his neck in his palm and, opening it, stared at the small lock of red hair concealed inside.

"Let's go, Kircheis. The universe is ours."

Even after Siegfried's death, Reinhard spoke to his redheaded friend.

Reinhard brushed back his golden hair, lifted his shoulders proudly, and with a gait that no one could imitate, left the computer room.

SE 798, year 489 of the imperial calendar, had shrugged off the yoke of the past amid confusion and turmoil. Humanity was aware of what it should do and what kind of pedestal it would occupy in the grand museum of history. Could one count a few among the total of forty billion people?

Cries of "Long live Emperor Reinhard!" now overwhelmed the entire universe. Only time flowed impartially for those who heard them as good omens or evil ones.

SE 799, IC 490, was knocking at their door…

ABOUT THE AUTHOR

Yoshiki Tanaka was born in 1952 in Kumamoto Prefecture and completed a doctorate in literature at Gakushuin University. Tanaka won the Gen'eijo (a mystery magazine) New Writer Award with his debut story "Midori no Sogen ni..." (On the green field...) in 1978, then started his career as a science fiction and fantasy writer. Legend of the Galactic Heroes, which translates the European wars of the nineteenth century to an interstellar setting, won the Seiun Award for best science fiction novel in 1987. Tanaka's other works include the fantasy series The Heroic Legend of Arslan and many other science fiction, fantasy, historical, and mystery novels and stories.

HAIKASORU

THE FUTURE IS JAPANESE

TRAVEL SPACE AND TIME WITH HAIKASORU!

USURPER OF THE SUN—HOUSUKE NOJIRI

Aki Shiraishi is a high school student working in the astronomy club and one of the few witnesses to an amazing event—someone is building a tower on the planet Mercury. Soon, the Builders have constructed a ring around the sun, threatening the ecology of Earth with an immense shadow. Aki is inspired to pursue a career in science, and the truth. She must determine the purpose of the ring and the plans of its creators, as the survival of both species—humanity and the alien Builders—hangs in the balance.

THE OUROBOROS WAVE—JYOUJI HAYASHI

Ninety years from now, a satellite detects a nearby black hole scientists dub Kali for the Hindu goddess of destruction. Humanity embarks on a generations-long project to tap the energy of the black hole and establish colonies on planets across the solar system. Earth and Mars and the moons Europa (Jupiter) and Titania (Uranus) develop radically different societies, with only Kali, that swirling vortex of destruction and creation, and the hated but crucial Artificial Accretion Disk Development association (AADD) in common.

TEN BILLION DAYS AND ONE HUNDRED BILLION NIGHTS—RYU MITSUSE

Ten billion days—that is how long it will take the philosopher Plato to determine the true systems of the world. One hundred billion nights—that is how far into the future Jesus of Nazareth, Siddhartha, and the demigod Asura will travel to witness the end of all worlds. Named the greatest Japanese science fiction novel of all time, *Ten Billion Days and One Hundred Billion Nights* is an epic eons in the making. Originally published in 1967, the novel was revised by the author in later years and republished in 1973.

WWW.HAIKASORU.COM